CW00872096

THE GIRL IN THE WOODS

WADE DALTON AND SAM CATES MYSTERIES
BOOK 1

JIM RILEY

To the Most Beautiful
You always were and always will be

1 HOW CAN HEAVEN AND HELL BE SO CLOSE TO EACH OTHER?

A GRAY SQUIRREL HERALDED THE DAWN OF A GLORIOUS day with incessant chatter. It could not have been more wrong.

The hunter strained to get an unobstructed view of his prey.

One more step! C'mon! Just one more step!

The hunter's pounding heart shattered any hope of keeping the cross-hairs steady on his target. The onerous task stood in stark contrast with the natural beauty of his surroundings. Sweat poured from his forehead despite the chill in the air. His finger gently squeezed the trigger slowly and carefully, preventing him from jerking the rifle. The explosion of the cartridge startled him.

The crash of the body and subsequent thrashing disturbed the serenity of the forest as the prey fell immediately to the ground. The hunter tip-toed over to the fallen figure in the leaves, knowing he had made a perfect shot that would cause the termination of life. He stopped about two feet from her with a self-satisfied smile of a job well done. He did not want her to suffer an agonizing death.

The hunter had watched the morning sunrise over the horizon on this crisp November morning in the National Forest in south Mississippi a few hours earlier. He realized this was one of the purest and most fulfilling pleasures in life. The bright orb glistened off of the dew-laden leaves in the early fall as the woods came to life. It wasn't long before the squirrels were busily gathering up the fallen white oak acorns, scurrying across the forest floor for these prized possessions. The hunter had learned what the animals instinctively knew; the white oak acorns were larger and much sweeter than the acorns from the other oak trees, such as the live oak, red oak or pin oak. In the rites as old as nature itself, mating time abounded in the animal kingdom, and the males of the species chasing the females. The old male squirrels were hard pressed to keep up with their younger counterparts as the young females made life difficult for all of them by performing the most acrobatic of leaps from tree to tree seemingly effortlessly. A grin crossed the hunter's lips.

If only I had those kinds of hops. I'd be the best basketball player ever!

A tom turkey gobbled on the other side of the creek bed, probably spotting an owl or maybe just showing off for one of the many hens in the area even though the primary mating season in spring had long since been over. The hunter imagined the strutting bird spreading his enormous tail feathers and fluffing up his body until he presented an image twice as big as normal. The purr from a hen affirmed nature once again would provide the resources for the future of the species when the two of them would get together. The old Tom wouldn't stop with just one hen, however. His drive, embedded in him by nature itself, would force him to mate with as many hens as he could in the short breeding seasons available to them.

The hunter smiled at the simplicity of the wild.

Why did humans make it so difficult to perform the same tasks of life; gathering enough to eat, finding a place to sleep and perpetuating the species?

He knew the basics of life were not enough to satisfy the human spirit. More impressive tools and toys drove mankind throughout their lives only to leave them behind. In fact, that is precisely why he was out in the woods on this gorgeous morning. The complexity of the human spirit drove mortal men to do more than just survive.

He watched the little whitetail doe stop at the creek for her first drink of the morning or more than likely her last drink of the night since she normally would have fed all night and now was seeking a thicket to lie down for the day. To the hunter, the symmetry and grace of the whitetail deer set them apart from the rest of the entire animal kingdom and made them one of the most sought after game animals in the world. While he spent only a modest amount on the sport, he knew of the billions of dollars spent each year by the hunting industry in the pursuit the elusive whitetail deer, only for most hunters holding a deer tag to come up empty-handed. When the little doe turned sideways to feed her way back up the oak flat on the other side of the creek bed, the hunter slowly raised his rifle and focused the telescope right behind her front shoulder. He knew the heart and lungs were the vital organs to pierce and by doing so would limit the distance the doe could run after being hit. Looking through his scope, he could discern the intricate details of the deer's body and marveled that nature could manufacture such a graceful creature right here in south Mississippi.

Bang! You're dead! But not this morning!

He lowered his rifle, knowing before he had taken aim this was not the prey he was after this morning. The little doe slowly meandered right and left up the other side of the creek, munching on the few white oak acorns the squirrels had not already stashed in their winter dens. The doe was old enough to know that the first hard frost would turn the sweetest of the acorns bitter to the taste, and she would then feed in the open food plots the hunters had constructed around the edges of the forest. A much more dangerous prospect than reaping the nutritious bounty provided by nature. She had been fortunate so far because most of the hunters in this area did not readily discriminate between harvesting the bucks and the does. This hunter, as most other hunters in the South, loved venison. For most of them, the tender sweet tasting flavor of the does was preferable to the testosterone-laden meat of the old bucks.

The hunter leaned back against the enormous beech tree, dressed in blending camouflaged hunting clothes. The old beech tree was hollow, which made it available as home to a whole nest of cat squirrels with their cotton-white underbellies and the equally white flashes on their long tails that flashed as they quickly maneuvered through the forest tops.

A squirrel came out of the hollow tree and descended directly down the immense trunk above the hunter's head. When the squirrel reached a spot three feet above the hunter, it stopped and tried to figure out what this big blob was at the foot of his tree. He wildly chattered in the unique high-pitched voice of his kind, setting off alarms throughout the immediate vicinity. As he raced back up the beech tree, the woods became alive with birds chirping and squirrels chattering. Each knew a danger lurked, though none knew what the danger was or how close it was. The hunter chuckled as he witnessed the effectiveness of nature's Neighborhood Watch program.

It doesn't require meetings with a quorum of members of the community once a month to set up the rules and assign the tasks. There is no budget and no disagreements on scheduling.

The hunter didn't budge and waited for the forest to settle down. After only a few minutes, life returned to normal, and he slowly turned his head from side to side, waiting for the singular prey that would fulfill his plans. A big Whitetail buck stepped into the small opening around the beech tree, hastily gobbling down acorns and beech nuts as he fidgeted down the same path that hundreds of his ancestors had in previous decades. The hunter had once heard a whitetail buck described as a mere bundle of nerves wrapped in skin. He believed it because he knew they had to be afraid of everything that moved just to stay alive. The quick jerks of the buck's head verified its concern that the forest was full of predators dependent on the death of the whitetail deer to sustain their own species. The whitetail had to be smarter or faster than the best of these predators just to survive. This deer was a mature buck, estimated by the hunter to be three and one-half years old and weighing well over two hundred pounds. His rack, riding tall on his head, sported four tips on each side, making him an eight pointer in the local vernacular. Sweat broke out on the hunter's forehead, for this magnificent animal was truly a prized trophy, especially for hunters limited to pursuing their game on public land.

The hunter again slowly raised his rifle and focused on the hairs right behind the front shoulder.

Bang! You're dead! But not this morning!

The temptation to squeeze the trigger was overwhelming, but the hunter knew this big buck, as beautiful as he was, did not fill the requirements of today's hunt. He reluctantly lowered his rifle and watched in genuine admiration as the buck vanished as quickly as he had appeared. The hunter had deep doubts as the white flickers of the buck's tail became indistinguishable among the brambles and the briars surrounding the small opening in the woods. He stared in the direction the buck had disappeared for several minutes after all traces of the deer were absent.

Still very early in the morning, the hunter determined to be patient in his quest for the day's perfect trophy. As the morning passed, the sun warmed the forest floor and an overwhelming dreariness overcame the hunter, unaccustomed to getting up so early in his everyday routine. As he leaned against the big beech tree, his eyelids became heavy and had trouble staying open. He nodded off despite his best efforts to stay alert. Before long, he was fast asleep dreaming about all the good things in his life.

A snapped branch brought him wide awake in an instant; his bleary eyes struggling to focus on the source of the sound. Another branch broke, and he knew the intended prey wasn't far away. He brought the rifle to his shoulder and slowly turned in direction of the sound. As soon as the figure filled the scope, his heart rate jumped and his breathing became erratic. Although he could only see the outline of his intended target, he knew he could not afford to pass up this opportunity. He took a deep breath and slowly exhaled; his aim through the scope becoming much steadier as the air escaped his lungs.

One more step. C'mon! Just one more step!

The explosion from the rifle barrel violated the serenity of the morning.

The hunter's shaky knees threatened to give as he stood over his prey. The body of nineteen-year-old Rachel Chastain twitched uncontrollably at his feet, her big hazel eyes searching out his.

She mouthed the question, "Why?" as her very lifeblood oozed from the exit wound into the moist dirt beneath her.

He did not answer, but knelt down beside her and stroked her long brown hair as the final seconds of her being slowly faded into the black oblivion of the afterlife. Those bright hazel eyes that had brought delight and joy to so many during her short time in this world clouded over and closed for the last time.

How can heaven and hell be so close to each other?

2 LIFE IS BUT A VAPOR

Sam Cates, the petite Sheriff of Evergreen County, drove her patrol car amid the growing number of hunters alongside the gravel road in the National Forest. She strode to the pickup truck containing the small body of Rachel Chastain in its bed. The men, almost all of them wearing camouflage with orange hats or vests, parted ways for the petite sheriff as she neared, allowing her immediate access without having to shove her way to get near. Sam instantly recognized Rachel even in this cold, lifeless form. Rachel was a little younger than Sam's sister, Connie, and attended the same small Baptist church in Evergreen. She saw Luke, Rachel's father, being consoled by some of his fellow hunters at the other end of the procession of trucks. He could not look at the body of his precious daughter lying in the pickup like a sack of potatoes as he sobbed uncontrollably.

Sam looked at Pete Jenkins standing beside the truck.

"I don't know how Luke can cope with this. Knowing someone shot your daughter, and she is lying unceremoniously in the back of a pickup truck in the middle of the National Forest is something no parent should have to endure."

Pete only nodded.

Sam reminded herself to go to him and express her sorrow after she questioned the hunters out of his earshot. Sam's stomach roiled and nausea swept through her body from being so close to someone she had known who had been so vibrantly living just a few short hours ago.

How fleeting is life? Had she heard this at one of the many sermons she and Rachel had listened to together, or was it something she had read in the Bible in one of the many Sunday School studies her Dad had forced her to attend?

She could not remember, and it really mattered little. The internal turmoil did not help her outward disposition, and she was brusque when questioning the other hunters.

"How long ago did you find her?"

Sam stared at Rachel's body while asking the question.

"About thirty minutes ago, Sam," Pete answered after spitting a wad of chewing tobacco in the ditch.

"Was she dead when you found her, Pete?"

"Yes, Ma'am. Shot deader than a door-nail.

Pete shoved another wad of tobacco in his mouth without thinking. The tobacco seemed to calm his nerves.

Sam glanced up to make sure Luke was still too far away to hear the conversation.

"So why did you move her?"

Nobody said anything.

Sam glared at the men standing around the truck.

"You may have messed up the crime scene and destroyed valuable evidence."

Sam slammed her fist against the truck bed.

Pete shuffled his feet nervously. He stammered, but had to shift the tobacco in his mouth.

"We didn't want to—the flies and the ants would have got on her and then Luke might have found her covered up with insects, Sam."

Sam could understand the well-meaning but misdirected intentions of the men who found her.

"Who found her?"

Pete stammered, stuttered, and kicked the dirt with his boot. He had always found Sam to be so easy to talk to in the past, but the thick tension in the air made it almost impossible.

"I did, Sam. Least-ways me and Bob did."

His chin jutted out toward the hapless man standing next to him, as if this revelation would spread the blame a little for moving the body.

Just as Sam examined the body a little closer, a green Ford truck with the caricature of a huge whitetail on its frame pulled up and Wade Dalton jumped out and raced to Sam's side. Wade was an ex-FBI agent and was now operating a commercial hunting ranch in Evergreen. He was Sam's fiancé and her confidant when she most needed one. He had worked with her on the only other murder case she had ever investigated in Evergreen without her dad's help, one of victims in that case also being a young girl.

And Sam desperately needed help.

3 EVEN THE LOWEST MEASURE OF COMMON SENSE IS LOST ON MOST PEOPLE IN A TIME OF CRISIS

"Are you doing okay, Sam?" Wade hugged her. "Where can I help?"

She looked at him with wide eyes. "I can't believe this is happening again in Evergreen. Thanks for coming."

"You know you can always call me, Sam."

He released his hug.

Sam nodded her head and almost imperceptibly stepped even closer to Wade, seeking his protection once more.

"I don't think we'll find much evidence here."

Sam pointed towards a thick stand of trees.

"They found Rachel shot in the woods and carried her out to the road."

Wade shook his head. "They really didn't do that, did they?"

"I'm afraid so." She stared at Rachel's body.

"They don't get it, do they?" Wade rubbed his temples.

He understood that the local hunters knew little of the disciplines of detective work or modern forensics and did what their instincts drove them to do. He looked around at the couple of dozen hunters and guessed about half of them had already visited the crime scene looking for clues leading them to the identity of the shooter.

Wade immediately took control from Sam of this tragic situation, even though he was no longer officially in law enforcement.

He was careful to keep his voice low enough so Luke could not hear.

"All right, guys. Can you guys move in here a little closer so you can hear me? Not you guys with Luke, but the rest. Thanks. Now, how many of you have gone back there in the woods to where they found the body?"

Four hands went in the air, but the rustling of the small crowd told Wade that some of them were probably not being forthright.

"Okay, here's how it'll be. I'm going there to rope off the area. We're gonna bring in a team of detectives and take a mold of every boot print back there. If your boot print shows up and you tell me you haven't been back to the scene of the shooting, then I'll consider you a suspect in the shooting. Do you understand?"

The crowd of men murmured, looking around at each other. Most reluctantly nodded.

"Now, how many of you have been back in those woods?"

Almost every hand went in the air. Wade groaned. The chance of finding the boot print of the shooter just went from difficult to almost impossible.

"How many of you urinated, uh, took a piss back there?"

Two hands inched toward the sky.

"Okay, all of you that went into the woods; take off your boots and put them in the back of my truck. You'll be able to pick them up in a few days at the Sheriff's office. Anybody that took a piss close to the body needs to let me or Sam know. We'll need samples of your DNA."

Wade watched as the men undid shoe strings and laces and ambled to Wade's truck and tossed their boots in the bed.

"Hold on, guys. How am I supposed to know which boots belong to whom? Take a piece of masking tape from the cab of my truck, write your name on it, and attach it to your boots. Pete, you make sure everybody puts their name on their own boots."

Wade shook his head again as the grumbling men retrieved their boots from the bed of his truck and began the search for the masking tape. He moved back beside Sam.

"Even the lowest measure of common sense is lost on most people in a time of crisis."

Sam looked at the crowd of hunters and nodded.

Wade looked in the truck bed.

"We might as well send her to the morgue in the back of the truck instead of waiting on the ambulance to get out here. Baking out here in the sun won't do her or her father any good. We'll get what evidence we can off the body back at the morgue."

Sam nodded. "I'll get Pete to take her in and let Luke ride with them."

Sam squirmed through the hunters to reach Luke and explained what they had decided and expressed her condolences. She put her hand on his shoulder and gave him a brief hug, feeling inadequate trying to console a father who had just lost a daughter in such a violent manner.

As Pete's truck pulled out with the body, the other trucks lined up behind him in a processional that mirrored a funeral. The events of the morning deeply affected all the men, some more than others. The most macho of these strong-willed hunters cried. With the trucks gone, Sam and Wade stood by themselves in the middle of the gravel road, each lost in private thoughts.

Finally, Wade broke the silence.

"Did they find anything at all traipsing around in the woods?"

Sam pulled out a small clear evidence bag containing some long strands of brown hair mixed with several pieces of pocket lint.

"One guy found these next to the body, but I think almost every one of them had to look. So they passed them around, and then Joe put 'em in his pocket to save for me."

Wade's gaze shifted down to the ground, and he shook his head in wonder.

"I think those guys should get together and collaborate on a book together: *How to Screw up a Crime Scene in Ten Easy Steps!*"

Sam grinned, and a little of the pent-up tension left her body. She had not realized just how tight her muscle tissues had become since getting the unexpected and unwanted phone call an hour ago. But now, Wade was here to help her.

"Or '*Crime Scenes for Dummies*'. That should be a best seller in New York," she responded.

"Let's go see where she was shot. Maybe, just maybe, they left something of value behind."

4 WHY WOULD HE INTENTIONALLY LEAVE INCRIMINATING EVIDENCE BEHIND?

It wasn't hard to find the spot where the men found Rachel lying on the forest floor. The hunters trampled a trail leading to the body in their quest to exchange opinions about who did it and how it had happened.

When he spotted the small circle of dried blood, Wade stopped and pointed for Sam to see. He put his finger to his lips, indicating his need for silence. For a reason he had never fully understood, when he talked it dulled his other senses, and he wanted all of his other senses to be on full alert at the crime scene. He motioned for Sam to sit down and he eased up to the blood on his hands and knees and cringed when he saw the number of fresh boot prints in the soft soil. When he reached the spot where Rachel fell, he tried to figure out the line of the direction of the blood splatter. The iron-like odor filled Wade's nostrils and confirmed the time-line of the heinous event. Wade grimaced when he saw the hunters had overturned most of the leaves. It made it almost impossible to correctly interpret the line of the spray. After circling the scene several times, he laid flat down on his belly and closed his eyes. He conjured an image of Rachel lying on the forest floor. The ex-agent opened his eyes, his body still prostrate on the bed of leaves just outside the ring of dried blood. Wade positioned his body up with the most probable line of splatter and looked up to see where the shooter might have been. His line of sight directed him to a huge beech tree one hundred and fifty yards across the creek.

Wade quietly inched his way across the creek bed and up the other side, keeping his gaze peeled on the ground, hoping to spot something of value. Finally, he found what he was looking for.

"Sam, can you come over here?" he asked only loud enough for her to hear.

When Sam closed behind him, he pointed at a small bare spot on the ground. Almost in the middle of the spot was a perfect depression outlining a boot print.

"Do you think that is his boot print, I mean the shooter's?"

She looked quizzical with her eyebrows arched at the bare spot.

"Without a doubt the shooter left this print," he answered, still staring at the imprint on the ground.

"How do you know?"

Sam put her hands to her temples, showing she was not as sure.

"Those guys that came in here after her death were mostly curious and wanted to see where she was shot. After seeing the blood, probably ninety percent of them just turned around and walked back to the road."

Sam thought about the logic behind Wade's reasoning and nodded.

"That makes sense. They wanted to tell everyone in

town they'd been to the actual scene of the crime and had seen her blood on the leaves. But for most of them, that would have been enough, and they had no desire to stick around a dead body."

"That's the way I've got it figured. The other ten percent probably didn't find much and stayed on the other side of the creek. It's a natural barrier and they wouldn't cross it without a reason. The way the leaves got trampled, I don't think any of them figured out the shot came from the base of the big beech up there."

"Gee, you learned something at the Academy. Maybe our kids won't have to get ALL of their smarts from their mama. They might even get into that little junior college in Baton Rouge."

Wade smiled and for a fleeting moment wondered how their future kids, if they had any, would turn out. He laughed.

"We'll probably have girls who look like me and boys that look like you. If the girls turn out favoring my looks, they'll get a lot of ribbing from the other girls."

He hit the side of his head with his hand.

"Why am I even thinking of kids at a time like this?"

"Seeing Rachel in the back of that truck reminded me just how quick life passes us by."

"Maybe if we have kids, they'll go to that little junior college that has put a whipping on those two Mississippi powerhouses in football for the last decade, if I recall correctly."

Sam was not giving up that easily.

"That's because we focus on academics, not on recruiting the best freaks of nature money can buy like you guys."

"I hit a nerve. Anyway, can we get back to this minor problem at hand?"

He did not want to get into an argument with Sam.

"Sure," she smiled. "I wouldn't want to derail the great train of thought from the Bayou Detective."

She smiled and laid her hand on his shoulder, looking back down at the boot print in the middle of the bare spot.

"Anyway, Sheriff." he said sarcastically. "My guess is the shooter planned for us to find this print. I believe he might have deliberately left it here for us to find."

"What makes you say that?" Sam lifted her hand from his shoulder and had a puzzled look on her face.

"First, there is no natural reason for a bare spot to be right here. No animal makes a perfectly concentric circular pattern when scraping for acorns. Even a whitetail's mating scrape is more oblong than it is circular."

Sam nodded, having seen plenty of whitetail scrapes at the Evergreen Plantation, Wade's exotic farm. Bucks scraped leaves and twigs away with their front hooves, and then urinated in the fresh dirt, indicating to the does in the area that he was ready to service them.

"Then, do you see there are no human scrape marks where someone inadvertently brushed aside the leaves and the twigs with his boots?"

Sam nodded, even though she had not quite caught up with his logic yet.

"Okay," Wade continued. "That means, in all likelihood, he carefully removed the leaves and debris with his hands to clear this spot out. Then he left the boot print right in the middle of it so we would be sure to see it."

Sam shook her head.

"That makes no sense, Wade. Why would he

intentionally leave incriminating evidence behind? Won't that make it easier for us to identify him?"

"Normally it would. Do you remember what Gus told us when we found those panties on Dixon's farm when we were trying to figure out who took Michelle?"

Sam thought back to everything the old grizzled Deputy told them during that murder investigation, but she couldn't recall anything that would relate to a boot print in the middle of the National Forest. And besides, most of what Gus ever said was not repeatable by a respectable young lady, anyway.

"No, I don't."

Wade remembered.

"He told us something your Dad had taught him. He said, '*If it swims like a duck, walks like a duck and quacks like a duck, then it's probably a decoy.* That's what we have here. I believe we have a decoy."

"Wait a minute," she protested. "You just said this is the shooter's boot print, and he left it here on purpose."

"That's why it's hard to teach a woman anything. You guys don't listen."

Sam jabbed her hand into Wade's shoulder.

"Now hold on Wade Dalton! I may be rattled finding one of my sister's best friends shot to death in the middle of the woods, but I distinctly heard you say this was the shooter's boot print. I haven't gone daffy yet."

Sam trembled, her nerves again on edge and her temper on the verge of eruption.

Wade put his arms around Sam to comfort her. "I wasn't trying to be cute. I'm just sorting it out in my mind and sometimes I say things before I completely get them straight myself. What you heard me say was the shooter deliberately left this boot print here for us to find. Let me show you what I mean."

Wade picked up a long slender stick and pointed toward the center of the boot print.

"Do you see how the heel and the middle of the boot print are deeper than the front and the edges along the sides in the middle?"

Sam nodded as the meaning slowly came to her.

Wade continued pointing with the stick.

"What that means to me is he put his hand in a boot that wasn't the same size or brand as his and pressed the print into the ground with his hand. That caused the deeper impression in the middle of the print instead of on the toes or the heel."

Sam understood.

"So we don't know if his real boot print is larger, smaller or the same size as this one. We only know this is not his boot print."

"That's about the gist of it, Sam. I would eliminate the possibility of this print being the same size as his. I don't think he would have gone to this much trouble to plant a print like his, but we can't be sure. This is a smart guy."

"That narrows down the list of suspects," she said sarcastically. "This clown could wear larger boots, smaller boots, boots the same size, tennis shoes or his Sunday-go-to-meeting loafers for all we know. Heck, he could be barefoot and we wouldn't know it."

"You're, Sam. But we have learned a lot about this guy because of the print, however."

"And what would that be?" Sam was now skeptical this single circle of dirt could reveal much else of consequence.

"He's cold and calculating. He planned this shooting well in advance and has good organizational skills. He is familiar with law enforcement policies and he knows even if we're skeptical of the authenticity of the boot print, we'll make a mold of it and his defense lawyer, if it gets that far, will use this as evidence pointing towards his innocence."

Sam didn't want Wade to know just how amazed she was that he gleaned all this from a single boot print.

"Anything else, Agent Dalton?"

Wade ignored the sarcasm and continued.

"According to the generic profile, he's probably white, over twenty-five, well-educated and a little shy. He feels comfortable in the woods and believes he is smarter than we are."

Sam nodded. "I would agree with him on the last point, at least for me anyhow."

She had now given up pretending she was not impressed with Wade's analysis of the scene. There is no way she would have had any idea what this one boot print could divulge.

"Anything else?"

Wade nodded. "My guess is that he wouldn't have left everything to the chance we find this single print and assume it was his. So I'm guessing we'll find something up by the beech tree, something like a discarded cigarette butt or a candy wrapper."

"I'll take a stab."

Sam turned attention to the base of the tree.

"The DNA on the candy wrapper or the cigarette butt doesn't' belong to the shooter. He picked them up off the street just to plant them here."

"That's what I'm thinking, Sam, but I'm not sure. See, it's easy when you think like him. The one thing in our favor is he underestimates us. He believes we're dumb and he can lead us wherever he wants us to go. That will work to our advantage if we use it right."

Wade rose and walked up to the beech tree, not wasting much time in between the bare spot and the tree. By now, he was fairly certain they would only find the evidence the shooter wanted them to find and the next logical spot to find that evidence was beside the tree. Sure enough, when they got to the tree they found what he'd left behind.

"Peanut shells," Sam exclaimed. "It'll be almost impossible to get DNA from those. Why would he leave those if he wants us to get DNA from the wrong person?"

"Precisely because of what you just said. He knows how difficult it'll be to get DNA from these hulls. But he also knows we'll spend the time, energy, and money to do it and eventually we'll come up with at least one sample if not more of somebody's DNA. The time, energy and money we spend on the DNA analysis will be that much that we can't spend on looking for him. My guess is only one or two of these belonged to someone else. The rest of them he cracked using gloves and mixed them in so we wouldn't find anybody's DNA on most, no matter how sophisticated the tests."

Sam's respect for Wade just reached a new high.

"You know, our kids might get into Mississippi State."

Wade just grinned, soaking up the admiration from the one person in the world that really mattered to him.

"Only the girls. The boys are going to LSU. You would have figured it out, given a little time. I just beat you to the punch."

Sam didn't want to tell him she could have spent years looking at the same evidence and would have not come up with the same conclusions he did in the last thirty minutes. Just then, something popped into her mind.

"Wade, what was Rachel doing out here, anyway?"

Wade's eyebrows furrowed as he wasn't sure where this was leading.

"I assumed she was hunting. Doesn't everyone around here hunt on a Saturday morning hunt during deer season?"

"Oh, I agree, she was hunting." Sam paused for effect. "Then where's her gun?"

"Damn," was all Wade could say, his gaze turned toward the sky.

5   I'D BET OUR MAYOR HAS SOMETHING UP HIS SLEEVE

"There you are."

Wade grinned at the sisters.

He met Sam and Connie in the parking lot of the church the following morning just before services began. Several of the church members loitered in small groups around the lot, most of them talking about the events of the day before.

"You guys look nice."

Wade gazed appreciatively at the two sisters, each very distinct in her own way. In his opinion, both would draw the overt attention of most men. He tried to be cheerful despite the pall hanging over the community because of the murder.

"Good morning, Wade."

Sam gave him a quick kiss.

They hugged when an impeccably dressed man in his mid-thirties approached.

"We've got company."

Sam's stiffening body indicated to Wade she was not happy to see the man approach.

"Good morning, Mayor. You know Connie. Let me introduce you to Wade Dalton, my fiancé. Wade, this is Ed Moore, our Mayor."

Sam forced a grin.

"Thank you, Sam. Good to see you, Connie. And Wade, I've heard so many good things about you. It's good to finally meet you."

The mayor shook hands with Wade and kissed both ladies on the cheeks.

"Ed, what brings you here? Aren't you a member of First Methodist?"

"I'm still a Methodist. I wanted to see you this morning and ask if you had some time this morning. We need to discuss the—er, events that happened yesterday."

"I'd be glad to Ed, but I've already promised Wade and Connie I would attend services with them."

"Why don't we have lunch after the services?" the mayor asked.

Glancing at Wade and Connie, he added, "Wade, I wanted to talk to you about the events of yesterday also and I would never miss a chance to have lunch with you, Miss Connie."

The Mayor gave Connie a long look from head to toe, even though his gaze didn't spend much time on her head or her toes.

"Miss Connie, I'd love for you to join us for lunch."

Wade wondered how politicians became so glib. Was it something they were born with, or did they learn to lie at an early age? They never seem to be at a loss for words and can turn any conversation to what they want to talk about, which is usually themselves.

"Okay, Ed. Where would you like to meet us?" Sam said with a hesitant voice.

"How about the Gulf Club?" Ed smiled. "We can have a little more privacy there."

"That sounds good. I haven't been there in a long time. We'll see you right after the services, Ed."

After Ed hurried back to his vehicle, Sam whispered to Wade, "You'll love the food if you can stand the company. It's kind of highfalutin' for Evergreen."

"I don't usually do *highfalutin*, but I'll make an exception for you," Wade responded.

Sam watched the mayor retreat.

"I don't either, but I'd bet our mayor has something up his sleeve."

6 STILL OTHERS THINK IT'S AN ABANDONED GARAGE IN DETROIT

THE TRIO SETTLED IN A PEW NEAR THE BACK OF THE sanctuary and sang with the rest of the congregation. They enjoyed the special song a mother and daughter duet sang right after the offertory. As Wade learned from his previous visits to the church, the Pastor had a unique custom, asking if anyone had questions they wanted to discuss before he began his sermon.

One young lady raised her hand.

The Pastor nodded to her, and she asked, "Brother Jeff, where is Purgatory and who's there?"

"Miss Elaine, that is an excellent question. Some folks believe it's where the soul resides until the coming of the Lord. When He comes back at the Rapture, the souls will rise to meet Him. Others think this is where the Old Testament followers of God went after their deaths and doesn't apply to people who died after Pilate crucified Christ. Some in another denomination think it's a place we go where our imperfections are perfected after death through the prayers of the living and we go to Heaven if the live faithful say enough prayers on our behalf."

He paused for a second or two.

"Still others think it's an abandoned garage in Detroit. They think it's kind of like the teenage boy's appreciation for a girl's mind. It really doesn't exist, although it's talked about a lot. The Bible is not clear on this subject, so the best answer is I don't know."

"Thanks, Brother Jeff. I was just wondering." Elaine nodded at the pastor.

Another young man stood up.

"Pastor, I guess you heard about Rachel, my friend who got killed up by Beaver Creek. Why would God let someone kill her when, according to what everybody is saying, she was just walking through the woods? I mean, she wasn't doing anything wrong."

Tears streamed down the young man's face.

"Amen," an elderly lady shouted.

"Yes, Yes." One of the older ladies added.

Many of the members attending that morning nodded and started dabbing their eyes with tissues.

"Joe, we don't know why some things happen to good people. But we know two things: one is that God gives us over to our own wills, and some folks are not bound by His will. Number two is that the Bible states that everything, whether we understand the circumstances, works together for the good of those that love Christ. So, we can take comfort in that while we mourn her death, something good will eventually come out of it."

"What good can come out of it, Pastor?"

"Knowing that answer is just a tad above my pay grade, Joe. Hopefully, God will reveal that in the not too distant future. In the meantime, we can concentrate on the good times we had with Rachel and what she meant to all of us that knew her. She was a special young lady."

Wade's mind could not focus on the rest of the sermon.

What if it had been Sam or Connie hunting there yesterday? How could the murder of an innocent young lady be justified by some greater good?

This was a tenet of the Baptist doctrine he had heard in the past, but in this case, he had some difficulty accepting it.

After the services, the Pastor greeted the entire congregation as they left. When Sam, Connie and Wade shook the ex-agent's hand.

"Have you guys set a date for the wedding yet?"

"Not yet, Brother Jeff. We want you to conduct the services. We just haven't set a date."

"Just let me know, Sam. It'd be an honor to be the Pastor who married you guys."

"Thanks, we'll give you as much notice as possible."

"I would appreciate a long notice, Sam. You know how my schedule is these days. Do you have any idea who might be responsible for what happened to Rachel? She was just a child."

"Not yet, Brother Jeff. We picked up some evidence and have some ideas, but nothing concrete."

"I see. We'll be praying for justice, and that God's power and wisdom will guide you, Sam." He clasped her hands in his.

"Thanks, we can use it."

She reached on her toes and kissed the Reverend on his cheek.

Wade had forgotten Sam had told him Rachel was a member of the church and the Pastor knew her personally. That made him wonder even more how the Pastor could think something good would come out of this murder. It seemed like a foreign concept to him.

7 IF HEAVEN IS THIS GOOD, I CAN'T WAIT TO GET THERE

ARRIVING AT THE GULF CLUB, WADE WAS LESS THAN impressed by the drab exterior. Not that it was run down or need of any repair. It was just the building would have fit in at any office complex in Evergreen, very plain and mundane, without the flair Wade was expecting for what was supposedly an exclusive hang-out for the upper-class and elite of the town.

When they entered the small door and arrived at the end of the little hallway leading to the dining area, Wade's impression transformed. His jaw dropped when he saw the adorned marble floors swirling with intricate patterns Wade could only imagine belonged in the mansions of the despots ruling the Middle East oil-enriched nations. The granite waterfall to the left and a huge saltwater aquarium on his right added to the posh amenities. Wade noticed the chandeliers were pure crystal, emitting an intermittent glow that reinforced an aura of pure luxury.

"You can close your mouth now, Agent Dalton." Sam whispered in his ear. "You're starting to drool."

The exotic Philippine hostess dressed in a full-length

form-fitting silk dress ushered them to their table. Watching her from behind as she gracefully floated along, Wade understood completely why the Mayor enjoyed eating here. Sam's elbow poking his ribs brought him back to reality, and he politely seated himself between the two sisters, only to find himself immediately rise again when the mayor stood to greet Sam and Connie.

"Oops. Sorry." His face reddened a bit. Embarrassed, he held the chair out for Sam and then eased himself back into his own chair, looking around to absorb the sheer elegance of his surroundings.

"I hope you find this acceptable, Wade. We think of the Club as our little oasis in the midst of the turmoil of the outside world."

"Oh, I'm sure it will be fine, Mayor."

"Please, call me Ed. You're almost part of the family now. I've known Sam's father since I was born, and I've known both girls since they were nothing more than trouble with pony tails and freckles."

Ed and the two sisters made small talk, catching up on family and acquaintances.

"When will we get some menus?" Wade whispered to Sam, his stomach growling.

Sam nodded in the direction over his shoulder. As if on cue, another exotic young lady arrived at the table without menus, but carrying a tray of bowls. She sat the bowls down in front of each of the diners. Wade smelled the distinct aroma of Cajun seasoned crawfish. The sweet odor of buttered crab meat permeated his nostrils.

After only a few bites, Wade was truly impressed.

"This isn't like anything I've ever tasted. It isn't a gumbo, and it isn't chowder, but somewhere in between. To put it simply, it's great!"

He took another huge spoonful.

The sweetness of the crab and the tangy taste of the boiled crawfish mixed with a dab of mayonnaise, ketchup, lemon juice, soy sauce and local hot sauce made it seafood perfection in a bowl, continuously tingling Wade's sense of smell and his taste buds.

Wade was the first to empty his bowl, but Connie was not far behind him.

"That was good!" She exclaimed.

Immediately the next course appeared in the hands of the exotic waitress. It consisted of red watermelon balls, yellow watermelon balls, small strips of kiwi, slices of fresh pineapple, and green melon topped with huge shrimp. On top of the crustaceans, a dash of home-made whipped cream mixed with a glaze of strawberry syrup.

"This is fantastic!"

Wade made no attempt to hide his impression of the Gulf Club's cuisine. He thought this might be the dessert for the light seafood lunch, but he was mistaken.

As soon as they inhaled the fruit combinations, the young waitress seemed to appear out of nowhere with a salad comprised of fresh spinach leaves, tiny cherry tomatoes, black olives, Cajun pickles and fresh-baked French bread bits topped with crumbled bleu cheese dressing, fried oysters and bits of fried bacon. Even with the oysters and bacon, this course was less alluring than the first two. Wade wasn't nearly as hungry as he had been minutes before, but the food was so good, he could not stop eating.

Just when he didn't think he could eat another bite, the sensuous young lady brought out the entrée; a surf and turf special with grilled Bison tenderloin steaks that melted in his mouth and Bluefin Tuna roasted to medium rare perfection on a cedar plank. Both were seasoned with a variety of ground peppers and topped with charbroiled oysters. The side dish of Andouille sausage and chicken jambalaya with Cajun spice was over-the-top wonderful.

If Heaven is this good, I can't wait to get there. But I can't eat another bite without exploding.

There had to be dessert and Wade was not disappointed with the huge wedge of Mississippi Mud Pie, which had three layers of various shades of chocolates and probably more calories than Evergreen County had residents. A taste of sorbet followed to cleanse the palette.

Wade leaned back in his chair, wondering why the button on his pants hadn't popped off yet.

How can a restaurant of this quality exist in a small town like Evergreen and I've never heard of it?

Then he remembered Sam told him it was an exclusive club where few local residents visited. As he sipped from his cup of Community Coffee, he asked the question on his mind.

"How can you guys afford to come to a place like this on a regular basis?"

Ed laughed.

"Actually, I probably couldn't, but it is a perk that comes with the office. The gracious tax payers of Evergreen are paying for your meals today."

"Are you kidding me?" Wade gasped. "Do you mean you write this off on a city account?"

"Now Wade, don't get in a huff. Most of the public government managers have a membership here. I know the School Superintendent has one, each of the City Councilmen have one, the Fire Marshall has one and I believe the County Librarian has one. I think everyone has one except the Sheriff's office. Sam, your dad refused to take a membership."

"That sounds like Dad, although he never told me about it." Sam said without smiling.

"Now that you're acting Sheriff, I guess it's up to you if you want one or not." Ed lifted his cup of coffee.

"I'll pass, Ed. The Evergreen Café is about as upscale as the Sheriff's office can afford. And Ed, I know you didn't invite us here to discuss the menu. What's on your mind?"

"You're direct just like your dad, Sam. I like that. I've, uh—run into a bit of a situation."

He pulled out a brown letter-sized envelope and handed it to Sam.

Sam pulled out some photographs. They did not portray the flora and fauna of Evergreen.

8   I WOULDN'T STEAL A DIME

THE PETITE SHERIFF LOOKED AT PICTURES OF ED AND Rachel in compromising situations. Sam glanced at a few and handed them to Wade.

Wade shuffled through the photographs.

He asked, "Are you being blackmailed?"

Ed replied, "Not yet. I only found them on my doorstep this morning beside the paper. I came straight to you, Sam, and I have told no one else—including my wife."

"Do you know who took the pictures, Ed?"

She looked intently in his eyes.

"Nope, but there had to be hidden cameras in the hotel rooms over the last couple of years. There are some from different times when we were together in different cities, so I don't know who put the cameras there or what they're after now."

"How long has the affair been going on?"

Ed hesitated.

"Let's just say it has been going on since she turned eighteen."

Wade almost spit out his coffee.

"Tell the truth." He glared at the mayor. "You can't admit having an affair with Rachel when she was less than eighteen years old. There are laws in Mississippi for anyone having sex with a child under eighteen years of age. The courts have ruled that children don't have the right to consent to sexual liaisons. You would be admitting to a felony if she was sixteen or seventeen when the affair started."

Ed looked down at the table. He didn't say a word.

"Is, or was the affair still going on, Ed?" Sam broke the silence.

"I wouldn't call it an affair, Sam. Once a month, we would get together. A lot of times, we came here because this place isn't on the regular beat for most of the town folks. Afterward, we'd go to a hotel in Biloxi or Gulfport and I didn't think anyone would know. It's not like I ever told her I would leave my wife and kids or anything like that. It was just a mutual relationship, kinda like I would get an itch and she would scratch it."

"What did she get for scratching your itch, Ed?"

The judgment in Sam's voice was unmistakable.

Ed lowered his face and cupped his chin with his hands.

"Sam, I know what I did was wrong. If I could start over, I'd never get involved with a teenager again. But when I heard about her murder yesterday, I was actually a little relieved. I know that sounds terrible, but I wanted to stop this relationship for so long, but I just couldn't force myself to do it. I thought it was finally over yesterday. Then I found the pictures on my front porch this morning. To answer your question, she was on the city payroll as a consultant, making five thousand dollars a month."

Ed's voice softened and his gaze stayed on the empty coffee cup in front of him.

"What were her duties as a consultant, other than to scratch your itch?"

Sam's voice became a little louder.

Ed grimaced at the obvious sarcasm in Sam's tone.

"She helped us apply for grants and low-interest loans from the state and federal government. She was good at it, too."

"Do you mean she did the work?"

Sam arched her eyebrows.

"We've been able to get over one hundred and thirty-two million dollars in grants for everything from bridge inspections to more computers for the classrooms in the local schools. She had a real knack for knowing just what to put on the applications to get us approved. I don't think we've ever gotten over twenty million dollars in any year in the past."

"Did she also keep track of how the money was disbursed?"

"No, that fell under different venues under my direction. That's one reason I'm so popular, I guess you could say. I get to say how to spend the money we get from these programs."

"So if I'm getting all of this straight, she would apply for any grant or loan she could find available, get it approved and have the feds or the state send the money into the Evergreen general fund designated for some program you and she dreamed up. Then you got to spend the money and say it was for the designated program. Undoubtedly, she would then help you document those expenditures."

Ed hesitated and inhaled a big gulp of air.

"You have it about right, Sam."

"How much have you stolen from these grants, Ed?"

Sam continued to glare at the man.

"Sam, you know me. I wouldn't steal a dime."

Ed stiffened defiantly in his chair.

Sam just stared at him coldly, saying nothing.

Ed sagged conspicuously and continued, "There might have been a questionable expenditure or two, but we spent every cent within the broad guidelines."

"Did she ever question you?"

"Let's just say she had some concerns recently. But as long as she got her five thousand per month, she was satisfied."

Ed could no longer sit erect and slumped in his chair.

"What were her concerns, Ed?"

"She just wanted to make sure that no one could blame her if funds were misappropriated."

Sam glanced at Wade before turning back to the mayor.

"In other words, Ed, she didn't want to take the heat for stealing from the grants and loans when you misappropriated them."

"That's a harsh way of saying it, Sam. I guess, looking back on it, that would kind of sum it up."

Ed's posture sagged a little more.

Sam nodded, "You know this makes you a prime suspect in her murder."

"I know how it looks. That's why I wanted to meet with you three. You guys solved the murder of that little girl outside of Evergreen. Wade and Connie, I know ya'll don't work for the Sheriff's office, but I'd like to hire you to help Sam find out who did this."

Wade answered, "No thanks, Ed. I don't need your

money, and for a Mayor to be screwing a teenage employee just doesn't sit well with me. I'll help Sam in any way she wants, but it won't be because of any obligation to you."

Connie had been quiet up to this point.

"Ed, I always thought well of you, but right now I have no admiration for you at all. The only reason you called us is because you don't know who has the pictures and you want to find out before they go public with them or blackmail you with them."

Ed nodded, knowing that even he could not hoodwink his way out of this predicament.

"What's going to happen now, Sam?"

This meeting had not gone the way Ed had planned.

"I'm gonna sit on the pictures, at least for now until I see how they fit in this overall mess. But I have to tell you, Ed. If I need them later, I'll use them, no matter who sees them. Do you understand that?"

"The only request that I have is to let me know a little in advance so I can talk to my wife."

Ed's voice had a plaintive ring to it.

"If I can give you some notice, Ed, I will. But I can't promise anything. Where were you yesterday when the shooting took place?"

"I know this will sound suspicious, but I was hunting on my uncle's land about two miles from where they found Rachel. I was alone and knew nothing about the shooting until I got a call on my cell from Pete. I went directly to the morgue to see some men there and then went to the Evergreen Café to lend my support.

Wade was almost sneering.

Typical politician. Never let a crisis go to waste if you can use it for your own gain.

"You're right, Ed. That sounds suspicious," Sam responded.

The three of them rose and abruptly strode out of the restaurant, leaving Ed alone with his thoughts. Ed continued to sit in his chair and asked the exotic waitress to bring him something to drink a lot stronger than coffee.

9   A TEENAGE GIRL LOOKS LIKE CANDY AND SMELLS LIKE A FRESH-BAKED PIE

"What do you guys think?"

Wade opened the conversation as they drove back to the church to pick up Sam's patrol car.

"I think his story stinks more than a pig in slop." Connie offered.

"He's lower than a snake's belly in a wagon rut. How could he take advantage of Rachel like that?" Sam was visibly upset.

"At five grand per month, are you sure it wasn't the other way around?" Wade asked.

"So you think she was blackmailing him? That doesn't sound like the Rachel I knew."

Connie leaned forward from the back seat.

Wade knew what he thought, but wanted Sam to give her opinion first. She was more than willing.

"I think he took advantage of her when she was underage. I don't know how old she was, but I don't believe she was eighteen when they started this thing. He probably wined and dined her in a way no boy her age could or would, so the lifestyle attracted her more than Ed."

"I agree with you, Sam. It probably started out with some flirting which led to the wining and dining. Before long, she found herself in bed with Ed. I'll bet he made her some outlandish promises he had no intentions of keeping, but he didn't want to give up sex with the teenager when he could have her any time he wanted. At some point, she would have realized the promises would never come true and decided there were other ways she could make this arrangement pay off for her."

"So you think she placed the cameras in the hotel rooms and used the photographs to blackmail him?"

"I don't know. I don't see how anyone else would have put the cameras in a hotel room when Ed didn't know which room they would get."

"Why would Ed give us the pictures and admit to a crime when we might never have seen them?"

Wade took a little time before replying.

"I think he panicked. He is worried they might become public unless we get to the bottom of this. I'd like to think somewhere inside that political body of his, there's a real human being who regrets having an affair with a teenager and he wanted to tell someone. Her murder gave him an excuse to get it off his chest."

Sam shook her head, "He just admitted to malfeasance in office. That means he must resign as mayor of Evergreen."

"Sam, if you were in his shoes, would you rather get charged with malfeasance or murder?"

"I see what you're saying, but the door's still open to charge him with both."

"That's the confusing part I'm still trying to get sorted out in my mind. He didn't stop an investigation, but started one on himself by giving us the pic's. He's as dumb as we think or he's more brilliant than any of us can imagine and I don't know which it is."

"I think he's a dumb ass who doesn't know 'Come here' from 'Sic em'. I mean, how brilliant is it to start a relationship with a teenager when you're thirty-something and a mayor?"

Connie's shrillness indicated a growing disdain for Ed.

Wade laughed, "Connie, to a 'thirty something', a teenage girl looks like candy and smells like a fresh-baked pie with that wonderful aroma tempting you to take a bite."

"Most people are smart enough to know what is underneath the crust on the pie before they bite into it. He isn't."

"I don't know, Connie. When all the blood rushes from a man's brain to other parts of his body when he gets aroused, sometimes logic and long-term consequences go out the door and don't return for a long, long time."

"If you guys kept that little thing in your britches, you'd be a lot better off."

"That's a lot easier said than done, Connie." Wade paused. "A lot easier said than done."

Little did Wade know just how true he would find these words in the near future.

10 WHAT WOULD SAM THINK IF SHE COULD SEE ME NOW?

WADE'S TRUCK EASED DOWN THE GRAVEL ROAD LEADING to Evergreen Plantation. He marveled at how much tension left his body as the big electric gate closed behind him and he could see the cedar lodge directly ahead. He loved this place that he won as part of his settlement for leaving the Agency under some very unusual circumstances. The rolling hills and numerous lakes and ponds provided the perfect backdrop for the gigantic whitetail deer and beautiful exotic animals including North American elk, axis deer, blackbuck antelope, North American bison, European red stag, fallow deer and Pere David deer that originated in China. All of them called the Evergreen Plantation home. He did not know how many of each species were on the ranch and would never know. It was impossible to find them or determine the exact number, no matter how many times he sat in a stand or at the edge of a field.

A single hunter called Wade Saturday afternoon and booked for Sunday after his meal at the Gulf Club. Wade was still building up his customer base and finding it difficult because of the activities that had taken place on the ranch under the previous owner. No politician wanted his or her name associated with the ranch, and even some locals shied away given the publicity resulting from those activities. So he was gladly accepting reservations and even anticipating a single hunter on a Sunday afternoon. Since it was only one hunter, Wade told his cook and the two guides to take the day off. He felt like he could handle anything a single hunter needed.

He was washing down one of the all-terrain vehicles when the white minivan pulled up next to the lodge. As he walked up to meet the hunter, he saw not one, but three people get out and walk toward the lodge. Not sure if this was the hunter or more likely some locals out for a Sunday afternoon drive, he approached the gentleman.

"Good afternoon. I'm Wade. May I help you?"

The affable middle-aged man stuck his hand out.

"Hey Wade, I'm Bruce Thomas. I talked to you on the phone yesterday afternoon. I hope you don't mind, but my daughters decided they wanted to hunt with you today. This is Mandy, and this is Mindy. They're twins, and this is their birthday present. They turn nineteen tomorrow."

Wade glanced at the two slim teenagers. "No problem finding them a place to sleep tonight, Bruce, but I let my guides off today and I'm the only one left to sit with one of them at a time in a stand."

Bruce grinned. "That's okay. I don't mind sitting with one of them if you will sit with the other one. Just don't let her shoot something too expensive."

Wade nodded. "No problem. You give me the budget and we'll keep her under that. Follow me and I'll show you to your rooms."

Wade felt an odd attraction to the girls who looked identical to him. They had long rusty-blonde hair with lean bodies that had not yet filled out completely and intriguing hazel-green eyes that captivated him. It had always amazed him at how many types of females attracted men and the way men found some defined feature in a woman more alluring than the others. Some men liked the big busty frames and others soaked up the petite girly frames. But no matter where on the scale most men were, more than one type of female attracted them.

When Euripides said, "Variety is the spice of life" or something to that effect, he wasn't kidding.

Wade showed them to their rooms and finished getting the ATV ready, letting the back seat down so the four of them could ride together to the hunting stands. When they came out, one twin sat in front with Wade, and the other sister sat in the back seat with Bruce.

Bruce leaned over from the back seat. "I'd like to keep the tab under five thousand for each of them, Wade. Can we get a good animal for that?"

Wade nodded without turning around.

"What kind are you looking for? We've got something for everyone and for that price you can get a good Axis, Fallow or Blackbuck to hang on the wall."

"It doesn't matter to me. If she sees something she likes and we can keep it within our budget price, let her go for it."

Bruce sat back in his seat beside the other twin.

"I don't doubt we'll find one she'll like. I'm gonna take her to one of my favorite stands in a white oak bottom. It almost never fails us."

Wade pulled up to a stand on the edge of a vast field planted with winter peas and turnip greens. He motioned for the two in the back seat to get out. Before they left the ATV, Bruce leaned forward and whispered, "Mindy, you pay attention to Wade and do what he tells you to do."

At least Wade now knew which sister he had with him. As soon as the Mule was out of sight of the stand, Mindy squeezed next to Wade in the front seat with her hip wedged next to his. He wasn't sure if she was afraid of the woods or if this was only an inadvertent movement, but either way, the feeling of her hip rubbing against his with every bump aroused his hormones in anticipation of the next couple of hours together.

He parked in a clump of bushes and they eased the rest of the way to the stand on foot, being careful to make no undue noise. Climbing the ladder, Wade found his face only inches from Mindy's posterior when she suddenly stopped. He looked up only to find her gazing down at him, smiling.

"Enjoying the view from down there?" She asked softly.

"It sure beats some I've had lately," he replied, quickly averting his gaze toward the ground.

As they settled into their chairs in the stand, Mindy stood up and moved her chair right next to Wade's.

"Just in case we need to talk, I don't want the deer to hear us," she said.

Wade nodded, but he did not feel as comfortable with the situation of being alone in the stand with an almost nineteen-year-old girl that was not unattractive. A bead of sweat formed on his forehead.

As the afternoon sun heated the stand and the surrounding woods, there was very little life in the food plot of winter oats and brassicas. Wade was intently searching for any sign of movement in the wood line when he felt Mindy's head on his shoulder; her steady breath and tightly closed eyes sure signs she had dozed off. Her head slipped on his shoulder and he reached down and put his arm around her to keep her head from falling hard on the corner of his chair. As his hand went around her waist, she pinched it with what seemed to be a subconscious movement of her arm and kept his hand pinned against her body. Over the next thirty minutes, Mindy twisted and turned in her sleep until Wade's hand was directly beneath her small breasts. With one last wiggle, Mindy's body slipped down only an inch, but it was enough to make Wade's hand cup one of her breasts, almost as if he had placed it there on purpose.

As her chest rose and fell with each deep breath, Wade could feel the firmness of her breast and her hand moved to cover the outside of his. If he wasn't so sure she was asleep, he would have abruptly moved his hand, but all indications were that all of this was happening while she was in dreamland. Her hand tightened and he could feel his hand now squeezing her breast in rhythmic motion. Mindy muttered in her sleep and was calling out a name, but Wade couldn't understand it. Wade could feel the testosterone tension building as the rhythm became more and more rapid. The pulsating titillation forced alluring images in his mind.

Suddenly, Mindy sat up.

"Did I miss anything?" she asked.

With the distraction inside the stand, Wade had not watched the food plot, which was now full of animals. He put a finger from his free hand to her lips and pointed outside toward the trophy whitetails and exotics that were now only steps from them. He removed his arm from her around her. Mindy looked out the small window of the stand and whistled under her breath at the number and the size of the animals within a few hundred feet.

"Which one should I shoot?" she asked.

"Which one do you like?"

She slowly surveyed the ever-growing herd of deer and

elk steadily devouring the winter oats and pointed to a majestic Axis buck.

"He's cute. Can we afford him?"

"Yes. Is your gun loaded and ready to go?"

She nodded and slowly raised her rifle and rested it on the window of the stand. She tried to hold the scope steady on her target, but the end of her gun was waving like a baton.

"Can you hold me?" Her hazel-green eyes pleaded with him.

He put his arm around her waist and tried to hold her steady.

"A little tighter, please," she whispered.

He raised his arm slightly until it was right beneath her breasts and hugged a little tighter.

"That's it." She said.

Before he could reply, the gun erupted and Wade saw animals running everywhere from the plot. He realized that he had just committed a cardinal sin of guiding when he wasn't watching the intended target as the hunter fired.

What do I do now? This could be a real mess trying to figure out where the Axis buck went if there isn't a good blood trail.

To his amazement, the buck lay dead right where Mindy shot it. Mindy pivoted and kissed him directly on his lips.

"Thank you so much!" She paused before continuing. "For everything."

She glanced down at his arm still around her waist. In the excitement of seeing the buck in the middle of the plot, he'd forgotten to release his hold on her. As he got untangled, she spun and ended up on his lap in his chair with both arms around him. He could feel the firmness of both breasts through her thin shirt.

"Wade, that's the first animal I've ever killed. Can you just hold me for a little while?" He held her tightly and gently rocked back and forth. That is when an image of Sam appeared in his mind.

Is this how it started out, with Ed and Rachel, holding and comforting each other? Where would it go from here? Am I willing to give up a lifetime dream with Sam for a few moments of pleasure with Mindy? What would Sam think if she could see me now?

An icy chill went down his spine as he imagined Sam watching him and Mindy in the stand, and all the sensuous thoughts that had flooded his mind evaporated in an instant. His resolve stiffened as he realized he would find no one like Sam again in his lifetime, and he was not willing to risk that relationship for a cheap thrill with Mindy or anyone else. He gently pushed her back and stood up.

"Let's go look at your trophy," he said with a stern tone.

Mindy harvested a magnificent trophy with thirty-seven inch main beams and heavy mass throughout its antlers.

"Of all the exotic animals on the Plantation, the Axis deer is the most regal." Wade looked down at the trophy. "It carries itself upright in a fashion that mirrors royalty."

Wade ran his hand over the exquisite fur and looked up at the twin.

"An Axis deer never loses its spots, and its brown and white coat is cherished across the world as a fine treasure. In the distant past, royalty in the nation of India trained the bucks to pull carriages, further associating them with the upper echelon of society."

"That's great!" She giggled. "I just think he's cute."

So much for revealing historical facts to a teenager.

Wade retrieved the ATV and loaded Mindy's trophy in the small rear bed. The efficiency of the utility vehicle constantly amazed him, and he wondered how he could manage a place like the Plantation without one. The ATV combined as a work vehicle, an invaluable transportation for the hunters and the game in the fall and as a fun ride for adults and kids in the summer. They had come with the Plantation when he got it so he didn't know how much they cost, but whatever it was, they were worth every penny.

Just as he finished loading the Axis deer in the Mule, they heard a shot in the direction of the stand where he had dropped off Bruce and Mandy.

"That would be Mandy. I hope she is as good of a shot as you are." Wade said, gazing in the direction of the sound.

"She probably didn't get the kind of help that I did," Mindy grinned.

Wade looked away, not wanting to say what was on his mind.

Instead, he said, "I bet she got enough help to get what she was aiming for. Seems to me you and your sister get what you're after most of the time."

"That's true, Wade. We do!"

Mindy batted her long eyelashes.

Darkness settled across the landscape in southern Mississippi by the time Wade and Mindy arrived at the other food plot. Pulling up to the base of the ladder, Wade startled when the door flew open and Mandy raced down the steps, followed in a more composed manner by Bruce.

"Mindy, I got the prettiest animal I've ever seen. I'm not sure what it is, but it's absolutely gorgeous!"

Both girls hugged each other. Wade's mind started racing.

I forgot to show Bruce the various animal mounts in the

lodge and explain what type of exotic each was and how much each of them cost. Now, Mandy has shot something neither she nor Bruce know the identity of or how much I have to charge them for it.

But Mandy's feet were barely touching the ground as she sprinted across the plot, motioning for Mindy to follow her. Wade and Bruce followed the girls, not talking to each other, but enjoying the pure elation of the sisters. Wade had often wondered about the bond between twins, and now he witnessed it firsthand. Watching the sisters sprinting across the field together, he could not imagine a more pure relationship than two people that shared the same genes.

When he arrived at the fallen animal, Wade smiled and chuckled out loud. Lying on the ground was an Axis buck identical to the one in the back of the ATV. He should have known.

They are twins, after all.

11   WHAT IS HE HIDING?

Wade hauled the animals and hunters back to the lodge and dropped the hunters off while he went to the skinning shed to take care of the animals. He found a pleasant surprise when he returned to the lodge. The twins were already preparing the evening meal. He found them in the kitchen busily heating some red stag steaks and pork ribs.

"I hope you don't mind," one twin said. Wade still wasn't sure whether it was Mandy or Mindy speaking.

"Not at all. Did you find everything okay?"

"We did. We're warming up leftovers we found in the fridge. Some of them looked like they might have been in there for a few days, so we wanted to use them before they spoiled."

The youngster continued to prepare the steaks.

"Great, are you guys available full-time?"

Wade marveled at how at-ease the girls were in a strange kitchen.

"Nope, we've already got jobs down at City Hall." One of the strawberry-blondes replied.

Wade's ears perked up when he heard this.

"Did you guys know Rachel, the young lady that was killed yesterday?"

"We went to school with her and saw her down at City Hall now and then. She was working on some project or something for the city, but I'm not sure what. You might ask Dad. He'd probably know what she was working on. Have you figured out who shot her yet?"

"Not yet. Did you say your father works at City Hall also?"

"He's the City Manager. He does all the work, and the Mayor gets all the credit. At least, that's the way it seems to us."

This was the other twin, but still Wade didn't know which one.

"It's a shame what happened to Rachel. I hope the sheriff finds out who's responsible and real quick. I know a lot of hunters afraid to go out in the woods after that happened."

Wade wanted to reassure them they were safe going out in the forest, but he could not. He did not know if there was some clown that was indiscriminately shooting hunters, if Rachel was the only target of someone with a reason or if someone just liked shooting young women. He didn't want to share his suspicions about the mayor with the young ladies.

Bruce joined them in the kitchen and the men sipped on some coffee while the girls finished preparing the meal. Bruce seemed like a nice guy.

I wonder how nice he would be if he had seen me fondling Mindy in the stand that afternoon. I imagine his disposition might be altogether different if he knew.

Wade took a sip of coffee.

"Your daughters tell me you're the City Manager. Does that mean you run the city?"

Bruce laughed, almost spilled his cup.

"It depends on what you mean by running the city. If you mean getting blamed every time the mayor says or does something stupid, then I guess you could say so."

"I had the pleasure of meeting the mayor today. He's quite a character."

Bruce laughed again.

"That's one way to put it. I hope he didn't hit you up for a contribution to his re-election campaign."

Wade shook his head. "I'm helping Sheriff Cates in the murder investigation of Rachel Chastain. I understand, again from your daughters, that you knew Rachel from the office."

Bruce's demeanor changed almost imperceptibly, but Wade was watching closely as he answered.

"She was in and out of my office a good bit. I believe she was working on a project for the mayor."

"Do you know what kind of project she was working on?"

Bruce glanced at his daughters and motioned for Wade to follow him into the large den. After settling into one of the large rockers, he looked back at Wade.

"What did Ed tell you she was working on?"

Bruce's entire demeanor changed.

Wade was intentionally vague in his response.

"He said she was helping on some paperwork in the office, but he wasn't very specific."

"That sounds like Ed. He can talk for hours and hours and say nothing. He makes everyone think he just told them exactly what they wanted to hear and that he's on their side of every issue. I don't know how he does it."

Wade nodded, but remained quiet.

Bruce continued, "I don't know everything she was working on, but I know she was working on a large project with Ed to bring a big facility to Evergreen."

"What kind of facility?"

"I'm not sure, but there were several local bigwigs involved, and they were really excited about it. When I say excited, I mean some of them were real excited that we may get it."

Bruce held his arms widespread toward the ceiling before dropping them quickly.

"And some opposed it."

At that point, one sister stuck her head out of the kitchen.

"Dinner is on. We don't deliver, so come and get it if you want some."

Wade smiled and didn't realize how intently he had been listening during his brief discussion with Bruce.

Why hadn't Ed mentioned this enormous project if it was so important? What is he hiding?

The dinner was tasteful and yet uneventful. The girls did a good job grabbing leftovers out of the fridge and adding a few spices and condiments to turn them into an enjoyable meal. They even volunteered to clean the kitchen when the meal was over. Wade felt totally at ease with the whole family. Little did he know the chaos the twins could cause.

12 WE MAINLY RAISE A LOT OF HAVOC

Bruce got a shower and changed into more comfortable clothes. While he was out, Wade steered the conversation back to Rachel without being overly obvious. He looked at one twin.

"What do you guys do down at city hall?"

"Don't tell Dad, but we don't do much. We mainly raise a lot of havoc."

Wade had a questioning look with his eyebrows arched, so the sister continued her answer.

"Most of the time, we dress exactly the same so nobody can tell us apart. Then one of us will take off for the afternoon and they won't realize it, because they see the one that's left there."

The other sister piped up.

"We've been doing it since they hired us. I don't think Dad knows we're doing it."

They both giggled in unison.

"We do look different, though. You're a detective Ranger or something like that. Can you figure out which one sat with you this afternoon and I mean real close to you?"

Even their voices sounded the same.

Wade turned a little red as he stared at the sisters, trying to see some discernible difference. They both had rust-blonde shoulder length hair, both weighed within a pound of each other, both were exactly the same height and each had the same mannerisms as the other. He motioned them to turn their backs to him, but he still did not see a difference. As they turned back to him he saw the distinguishing feature. One of them had a small freckle that was barely noticeable on the lobe of her left ear.

He felt sure he would have seen it in the stand as close as he had been to Mindy's ear. He looked at the one with the small freckle.

"Mandy, you guys sure make it tough for a fellow to know which one is which."

The sisters looked at each other with surprise.

"How did you know?"

"Because I'm a detective Ranger, remember?"

"Wow, we're gonna have to be careful around you. You just might get us in trouble."

"Now why would I want to get you guys in trouble?" Wade grinned.

Mindy smiled. "A girl sometimes might not have be as asleep as she might have seemed, even a blonde, Detective Ranger."

Wade stammered.

"What—?"

Just then, Bruce came back into the room.

"I hope I'm not interrupting anything important."

"No, Dad. Detective Ranger Wade was just telling us

about the different animals on the place and how dangerous some of them are."

Mandy was smiling now. Both of the girls giggled as though they had the key to a big secret.

What are these girls up to? Did they deliberately set me up? But what would they gain with an accusation when it would be my word against theirs? Even then, Mindy was of age, and I'm not married. So what does it matter? Besides, I didn't intentionally fondle Mindy. Or did I?

As all of this went through Wade's mind, he barely kept up with the conversation around him. Finally, he regained his focus on the father of these two mischievous young ladies.

Bruce was talking straight to him.

"This place is fantastic, Wade. Why don't more people in Evergreen know about it?"

"I believe the focus of their marketing was on out-of-town guests before, Bruce. I think it primarily catered to state and federal politicians, if I recall correctly."

"Well, it is just plain magnificent. We saw Buffalo, Axis, and Fallow. At least I think that's what they were and some animals I've never seen before. We even saw a huge white Elk. I've never even seen one of those on TV before."

"Are you sure it was a white Elk, Bruce? I haven't seen him before, and I've been here several months. I thought I'd seen every animal back there."

"I know an elk when I see one, Son. The European elk or stag has that little crown at the top of his antlers, but the elk just has straight antlers. No Sirree, this was a North American elk; only he was white. And it wasn't an albino either. He didn't have pink eyes like albino animals have. He was a White Elk. Didn't we see him, Mandy?"

"We sure did, Dad. In fact, I took a picture of him with my cell phone."

She pulled out her phone and showed it to Wade. Sure enough, standing in the middle of the plot was a beautiful White Elk, with six long tines on each antler. Wade whistled out loud at the picture of the magnificent animal.

And to think he's been back there in the hunting area all of this time and nobody has seen him. I wonder what other animals I have back there that nobody has seen yet.

"That's amazing, Bruce. I truly had no idea he was back there."

"What would you charge a hunter to take his, Wade?" Bruce took the cell phone from Mandy.

"I don't know, Bruce. Are you interested?"

"Absolutely! I'd be the talk of the town." He continued to stare at the picture.

Wade thought about it for a few seconds. "Make me an offer, Bruce."

"How about thirty thousand Wade? That wouldn't be bad for an animal you didn't even know you had."

"I just don't know, Bruce." Wade wasn't trying to negotiate, but he truly didn't know the worth of a White Elk.

Bruce mistook his hesitance for negotiations.

"All right, fifty thousand, and that's my last offer."

Wade laughed.

"You got him if you see him again, Bruce."

Fifty thousand dollars for one animal was more than Wade could imagine just a few short months ago. Now it was a reality. The men shook on their deal.

"I'll take you and the girls out to the same stand tomorrow, Bruce. Hopefully, the activity of this afternoon didn't scare him too much."

"Great! But the girls told me they wanted to stay here and help you with breakfast. I think they kind of like you. You better be careful, Wade. They have a tendency to gang up on people." Bruce chuckled.

Wade grimaced, having already had a little experience with the rust-blonde twins. He wasn't sure he wanted any more intimate experiences with them.

13 WE FIGURED IF ANY MAN COULD TURN DOWN A FREEBIE, THEN WE COULD TRUST HIM

IN THE PREDAWN HAZE BEFORE THE SUN CAME UP Monday morning, Wade took Bruce to the stand where he'd seen the White Elk. He could sense many animals in the food plot, but could not see them as Bruce slowly climbed the ladder to the stand. Wishing him luck, he headed back to greet the sisters, halfway hoping they would be late risers.

When he entered the lodge, he knew they were already up when he smelled the distinct aroma of bacon sizzling on the flat grill in the kitchen. One twin emerged from the kitchen, and it took Wade a little while to discern which one it was.

"Good morning, Mindy. How are you today?"

"Good morning, Wade. I'm still not sure how you can tell us apart since we didn't tell you what was different about us. Maybe there's more different about us than we thought."

"That might be, Mindy." Wade smiled as he poured a cup of coffee. "Why are you guys up so early?"

"We wanted to talk to you. And the only time to talk with you alone is when Dad is on a deer stand."

Wade was curious now.

Will I find out the devious plan the two sisters had plotted for me?

He decided the less he said, the better off he might be at this point.

Mandy entered the room carrying homemade biscuits and bacon on a tray with some jelly and butter. This was simple, but very appetizing; arousing a hunger in Wade that he did not realize was there. They settled down to enjoy the breakfast.

"First, I want to apologize for yesterday." Mindy was the first to break the silence. "We had to test you to see if we could trust you. I intentionally put you in a position to take advantage of me and you didn't. I appreciate that."

"So you weren't asleep after all!" Wade blurted, taken aback. "But why would you put yourself in that position without knowing me from Adam? There is no telling what might have happened yesterday if it were someone else in the stand other than me. I mean, you two are attractive young ladies and you just can't be putting yourselves in situations like that."

"Normally, we wouldn't," Mandy replied. "But we know about you and Sam. You know, the relationship you guys have and everything. And we've heard about your background with the FBI, so we wanted to see if you would help us. But first, we had to make sure we could trust you."

Mindy picked up the explanation from there.

"We figured if any man could turn down a freebie, then we could trust him. Believe me; you weren't going to get any further than you did even if you'd wanted to. But we were pleased you didn't."

Wade was still not seeing the logic behind the actions.

"Let's be clear. I didn't stop because I wasn't enjoying it

and didn't want to continue. It's just that I have too much to give up with Sam, and I won't risk my relationship with her for anyone or anything."

"We'd heard that, Wade," Mindy was still talking for the two of them. "But we had to find out for ourselves before we put our trust in you. We've also got too much to lose right now for us to depend on the wrong person."

"Okay, I can't say that I approve of the way you girls did it, but I'm glad to know what you were up to and I appreciate you telling me. Now that we're all on the same sheet of music, what's so important that you would put yourselves in danger?"

"It's about what's going on at work," Mindy sighed.

"At City Hall," Mandy clarified.

14 WHERE WOULD RACHEL GET THE MONEY?

WADE SETTLED BACK IN HIS CHAIR, QUIZZICALLY scratching his chin; not sure what the sisters were involved in and not sure he wanted to get involved. He really didn't want to get mixed up in the local politics, but was mildly curious until he heard Mindy whisper, "We think Rachel might've been killed because of what's going on at City Hall."

That got Wade's attention, and he sat straight up in his chair.

"What do you mean? I had the impression from what you said earlier that you didn't know her very well."

Mandy answered, "We were close to the same age. In fact, I think she was only six months older than we are. So now and then, we would take our breaks together or go get some lunch together."

Mindy, leaning forward, couldn't wait to get involved.

"Most of the time, she went to lunch with the mayor or one of the other guys in the office. From what she said, most of the time the guys wanted more than fries on the side for lunch, if you know what I mean."

Wade wanted as much information as he could get without making the sisters too uncomfortable.

"If you mean the guys wanted sex, then I know what you mean. Did Rachel give them what they wanted?"

"That's exactly what we mean and from what she told us, her knees were complete strangers to each other. They never got close together long enough to see what the other one looked like. She was more than willing to provide them with what they wanted if she got some favors in return."

"What favors?"

"It started out with some fancy restaurants and weekend getaways, but there was something bigger than all of that put together. She was in way over her head and she knew it, but didn't know how to get out of it. Someone else figured out how to get her out of it."

"Who was she going to lunch with?"

Both sisters hesitated before Mandy finally spoke up.

"She started with the mayor, but before long there was a city councilman, the District Attorney, the Purchasing Manager and a couple of prominent businessmen in town. Just about anyone that is important has been to lunch with Rachel."

Wade hesitated before asking, "Does that include your father?"

The girls looked at each other before nodding. Mandy verbalized what each was thinking.

"He started seeing her about six months ago. Then, it's like he changed right before our eyes."

Tears ran down Mandy's cheeks.

"He took long lunch breaks, then stayed over nights with her and then left with her for weekends. At first, we thought it was just a mid-life crisis thing that you men go through, but it is, or was something much more serious."

"What does your mother say about all of this?"

Wade lowered his voice, but didn't know why.

"We don't really have one. She left us when we were eight years old, saying she wanted to discover herself and we were in her way. She left with a musician that came through town and we haven't seen her or heard from her since."

"What makes you think it is more than a mid-life crisis? I mean, Rachel was an attractive young lady and your dad may have been stricken with her looks and was just taking advantage of the situation."

"That's what we thought at first. Then a few weeks ago, suddenly, money came in that we've never had before. How can a City Manager pay for two Axis deer and fifty thousand for a White Elk on his salary? The City has significant benefits, but the pay isn't that great."

"What makes you think Rachel is the source of the money?"

"That's what we're not sure about. But everyone close to her is suddenly spending money on new cars or exotic vacations. The only common denominator seems to be Rachel."

"Where would Rachel get the money?"

Wade alternated his gaze to each of the twins.

"We don't know that either. That's why we want you to help. We know Dad is up to his neck in this mess, but we don't know what 'this' is, if you know what I mean." Mindy answered.

"Let's make sure we're together. Your Dad, the mayor and several other prominent politicians and local businessmen are, or were all sleeping with Rachel." He paused. "Rachel operated some scheme that brought in a ton of money, which she distributed at least some to these men. And because of her involvement in this scheme, one or more of the men might have murdered her. Am I correct so far?"

It was Mindy's turn to cry.

"Yes, that's what we think, Wade. Dad is a real good man and has always been known for his honesty and integrity. Now, he's going in circles and can't decide on anything. It's like he has changed into a person we don't know most of the time."

She dabbed at the tears.

"Then for a few minutes he'll change back into Dad. Can you help us?"

She quit trying to hold back the tears. Streaks ran down both cheeks. Mandy joined her emotional twin.

"I'll try. But I'm still not sure there is a tie between what Rachel was doing and her death."

Mandy looked at Mindy and they nodded toward each other as if to give joint approval to an unspoken proposition.

"We weren't sure either until we found something at the office yesterday afternoon when we went by work before going out. We had to get a package Mindy left there Friday. That's when we found it."

Wade wasn't sure what "it" was. He was on the edge of his seat, waiting for one of them to tell him. Instead, Mindy rose and went to the bedroom the girls had shared the night before. When she returned, she was holding a manila envelope. When Wade opened the envelope, his jaw dropped noticeably, and he stared blankly at Mindy and Mandy.

It was Rachel's hunting license.

15 HOW DID A NINETEEN-YEAR-OLD GET INTO THE MIDDLE OF A MESS LIKE THIS?

Looking at the license closer, Wade could see the faint blood stains on the edges of the document in his hand. He had no doubt that someone took the license from Rachel's dead body after he shot her in the national forest. How it ended up at City Hall sometime Saturday afternoon was the mystery.

"How did—? Where did you find it? I mean, where in City Hall did you find it?"

Wade had trouble vocalizing his thoughts.

Mindy spoke up this time.

"It wasn't hard to spot. It was lying on the receptionist's desk when we went in. Dad's name was on the envelope, so we picked it up and took it home. We looked inside and never showed it to Dad. We don't want a lot of people snooping around City Hall and finding out about Dad's relationship with Rachel."

Mandy took it from there.

"Then we thought about you and Sam. If we took it to Sam, she pretty much works for the Mayor, so you can see the conflict of interest there. We figured if we brought it to you, it could be unofficial evidence until you guys need it. Does that make any sense at all?"

Wade nodded.

"I can see your logic, even if some of it is a bit flawed. I can't sit on evidence any more than Sam can. But we don't have to show the public or the Mayor all the evidence we've found."

Both sisters smiled.

"See, I told you he could help," said Mindy. "So what can we do?"

"Go back and keep your ears open at the office. You're probably right that someone there has a hand in this and eventually, some word will leak out. When you hear it, let me know."

"Okay, we'll fix Dad some breakfast while you pick him up."

Wade's mind wondered as he made the drive in the Mule to pick up Bruce.

How many people at City Hall were involved with Rachel? What kind of project was she involved in that would generate the kind of money that would drive someone to murder? How did a nineteen-year-old get into the middle of a mess like this?

16 THIS MAY BE HAZARDOUS TO YOUR HEALTH

When Wade arrived at the stand, Bruce was sound asleep. Wade climbed the stairs to the stand and knocked on the door to wake him.

"Did you see the white elk?" He asked when Bruce appeared in the doorway.

"No," Bruce replied. "He might have come in late and I dozed off. Just couldn't keep my eyes open. Must have been that big meal last night. I'm not used to eating that much. You know, trying to keep trim for the job and all."

Wade meandered back to the ATV while Bruce gathered his hunting gear. He wished he had sat in the stand with Bruce, but was glad he had the private time with the twins, especially after learning they recovered the hunting license.

Soon after Bruce finished his breakfast, Wade took Rachel's hunting license still in the manila envelope to the Sheriff's office to meet with Sam. Entering the office, Wanda greeted him. She took over from the previous receptionist that had been a mole with the same federal agency where Wade worked. Wanda was efficient in her job and she did not disappoint this morning.

"Good morning, Wade," she greeted him. "I've set up interviews with some hunters who were in the woods with Miss Rachel Saturday. The first one starts right after lunch for you and Sam. I ordered Chinese for you guys; hope you don't mind."

"No, that's great with me. Is Sam in?"

"She is expecting you."

When he entered Sam's office, her unblemished beauty once again took him back. Every time he saw her, he found the petite Sheriff to be more attractive than the time before. Normally, the more he was around an attractive female, the more flaws he would find. Being with the twins for the last two days, he considered them attractive, yet flawed.

They can't hold a candle to Sam. They just aren't in the same league.

He gave her a big bear hug and gently kissed her. She said nothing at first, but then returned the kiss with one much deeper and longer.

"Did you bring me a present?" she asked, nodding toward the brown envelope he was still holding in his hand.

"In a way, yes. But I'm not sure how much you'll like how I got it."

Wade took a seat in the wooden chair.

"Before you start, let me get Gus in here. There's no need to repeat telling me what you found."

When Gus came in, he looked like he hadn't been to bed all weekend. Not that that was unusual for Gus. Every time Wade saw him, the old deputy looked like he had been wrestling with a bear.

"Rough weekend, Gus?" Wade asked, chuckling.

"Man, I ran into this young filly Friday night and she was something else."

Gus was looking straight at Wade and ignoring the glare of disapproving eyes from Sam.

"She should have been wearing one of those labels the government makes us put on everything now. You know the one that says, *'This may be hazardous to your health'*. Hell, she was more than hazardous. She did things I didn't know were possible anymore."

"Gus, you should be more careful at your age. One of these young ladies may be more than you can handle some day." Wade chuckled.

"Hah! That'll be the day. Besides, I've figured out the problem."

Wade had to ask.

"And that would be?"

"It's not the ladies or the drinking that gets me feeling like this."

"It's not?"

"Nope, it's the sleep. You see, I didn't go to sleep since I met her and started drinking Friday night. I didn't quit until this morning after midnight, and I felt fine the whole time. Then I go to sleep for a few hours this morning and I feel like sh—, I mean, I feel like dirt." He glanced at Sam, knowing she didn't like for him to curse in the office.

"So I've decided just to give up sleeping since it makes me feel so bad. Besides, that'll give me more time for drinking."

Wade nodded.

"Now that sounds like a plan, Gus. Not a very good one, but a plan nonetheless."

Gus leaned back in his chair and closed his eyes.

"Go ahead, Son. I'm all ears."

Wade recounted to Sam and Gus his conversations with the twins and how they found the license at City Hall. Sam listened intently as Wade told everything he had learned about Rachel from Bruce, Mandy, and Mindy. Gus grunted now and then just to let them know he hadn't fallen asleep. When Wade finished, he leaned back in his chair, waiting for a reaction from Sam or Gus.

"So the twins think Rachel was sleeping with the mayor, the city manager, the purchasing manager, a councilman and at least two prominent businessmen in town to promote some scheme that made everyone involved a lot of money. And they think one of them shot her and brought her hunting license to City Hall to put the blame on Bruce or to confuse us. Is that pretty much the summary?" Sam asked.

"That's the abridged version, for sure. Have you told Gus about our meeting with Ed yesterday?"

"No, not yet. Gus, are you in condition to understand anything I tell you this morning?"

"Young lady, I may not be as young as I used to be, but I can hold my liquor."

As soon as he finished the sentence, Gus dozed off and snored.

"Can you help me move him to one of the empty cells to sleep it off?"

Wade was more than happy to oblige.

"You know there could be some dire consequences if anyone finds out Gus is intoxicated while working in your office?"

After they had half carried and half dragged Gus to the cell, they returned to Sam's office. Wanda brought in the Chinese food as they were settling down.

"So, Sheriff. What's the plan?" Wade dished out some Kung Pao shrimp and handed it to Sam.

"I don't like it when you call me '*Sheriff*'. You know that."

"Sorry, Sam. Where do we go from here?"

He spooned some Twice-cooked Pork for himself.

"First, I've got to get Gus into some counseling. Since he lost his brother, he's been going through some self-destructive episodes. I don't want to wait before it's too late."

"Won't that look bad on his record?"

Wade took an egg roll.

"Yeah, but what choice do I have? Either he gets counseling, and it looks bad or he continues doing what he's doing and eventually kills himself or someone else."

"You're right as usual, Sam. I just hate to see him throw his career away."

Sam thought for a few minutes and then smiled.

"There may be another way."

Then she picked up the phone and hit one of her speed dials. After just a few seconds, she said, "Hey, Brother Jeff. This is Sam Cates. I need an enormous favor from you."

Wade then realized that Sam was calling on the Pastor from the local Baptist church to counsel with Gus. There would be no official record of the counseling, and Brother Jeff probably had more experience counseling people with drinking problems than most professional psychologists. Wade's admiration for Sam once again reached extra levels if that was possible.

"Now we can start interviewing the hunters that were out there Saturday morning. Surely, at least one of them saw or heard something that will help us."

17 I JUST HOPE THE TWINS CAN KEEP A SECRET

Sᴀᴍ ᴄᴏᴜʟᴅ ɴᴏᴛ ʜᴀᴠᴇ ʙᴇᴇɴ ᴍᴏʀᴇ ᴡʀᴏɴɢ. Aғᴛᴇʀ interviewing a dozen men who were hunting in the National Forest with Rachel, Wade and Sam had no more useful information than they had when they begun. None of the hunters were sure they heard the exact shot that had killed Rachel. Evidently, she had wandered from where she had told her father, Luke, that she would be and the consensus among the hunters was that this was an accidental shooting. They believed someone had mistaken her for a deer, shot her and not wanting to admit such an egregious error, had fled telling no one. Each of them voiced suspicion of the other hunters.

Obviously, Wade did not believe this was an accidental shooting. The evidence pointed to someone with meticulous prior planning and execution, not of someone that got caught in a happenstance situation and panicked. The hunting license showing up at City Hall was odd and did not fit into any viable theory Wade and Sam could conjecture.

"If one of the City Hall gang, for lack of a better term, did this, why would he want to bring attention to City Hall?" Sam finally asked as the evening sun set.

"I've been trying to figure that out myself, Sam. It really wouldn't make much sense." Wade paused. "Unless, by leading us to City Hall, he thought he would lead us away from City Hall."

Sam looked totally confused.

Wade leaned back in the conference room chair.

"This guy knows how smart you are and how much you learned from your dad. He may believe that you're too smart to follow planted evidence and will go in a different direction from where that planted evidence would take you. If the evidence points at City Hall, but you're sure someone planted it, you would normally focus on other areas and not City Hall. Am I correct?"

"That logic would make this guy a genius."

She paused and ran her hands through her long blonde hair.

"And if that's the case, how are we going to catch him?"

"Because one day our kids will ask us about this case and we'll be able to say we worked together and the two of us combined were smarter than he was. That is, unless their Mama sends them to Bama. Then they'll be asking if they can dress the boy dolls and the girl dolls the same."

Wade smiled, knowing the long-term rivalry between the major state universities in Mississippi and University of Alabama was a sore spot for most of the residents in Mississippi since the Tide of Alabama began dominating in the almost sacred sport of football.

Sam was getting a little testy.

"If I ever send one of my kids to Bama, it will be to

educate them on the choices we make in life and the long-term consequences we must pay for poor choices like getting a degree from Bama."

"Do what?" Wade put his hands on the conference table.

"That will tell them you can't go into the Battle of Life unarmed. Like getting a degree from Bama."

Wade laughed, for even he had not realized how deeply rooted the feelings were between the states. He also knew he had to calm the waters right now.

"Speaking of kids, when do we talk with Brother Jeff and get this process started?"

"Oh Wade." Sam pushed her chair back and rose. "Let's find out who murdered Rachel before we plan a wedding. I can't do both at the same time."

But at least now she smiled.

"I agree," he knew he had dodged another bullet. "Why don't we start with your distinguished mayor in the morning and then work our way through the rest of them?"

"That works for me." she said, exiting the room.

"What do we do with the license?"

Wade followed her into her office.

The petite Sheriff plopped into her comfortable chair behind her desk.

"The only people that know where it is are you, me and the twins. Gus won't remember anything about it. I think we should keep it that way, at least for the time being. While you might be right about why it was left there, I see no advantage in letting everyone know we have it."

"I agree. I just hope the twins can keep a secret. That seems hard to do in this town."

"Well, when we talk to the mayor in the morning, we

can ask him how he thinks the esteemed staff at City Hall fits into all of this."

"Do you mean other than poking fun at the attractive intern?"

18 HE WILL EVENTUALLY COME OUT AND THE PLAN WILL COME TOGETHER

The hunter stalked the next prey on his list, knowing this time it would be much more difficult to be successful. He watched his target for several weeks, going to and fro, from home to work and then to play. The prey did not change his schedule because of the incident in the National Forest the prior Saturday. The schedule was fairly predictable, except for the play after hours. Sometimes, the intended victim wouldn't play at all and go straight home after work. Sometimes the prey would stay out overnight, fulfilling his wants and desires.

The hunter wore many disguises to keep from being recognized by the hunted and the people that surrounded his intended target. Sometimes the predator dressed up as a construction worker replete with a hard hat and overalls complemented by a rough costume beard and mustache. He filled the overalls with padding, making the hunter appear much heavier than his actual weight. He dressed as an overage flower child a couple of times, complete with the tie-dye shirt and a long scraggly grayish beard. A few times, he used a brunette way to appear as a middle-aged woman with padding in the right places under the dress. He even used butt pads to make his posterior appear more feminine. When dressing as a woman, he was careful to apply enough facial powder to cover the hair growth on his face. There wasn't much he could do for his Adam's apple other than wear a scarf to cover it up.

A few days of surveillance after the incident in the National Forest, the hunter was ready to make his move. The prey partook in the activities of *The Golden Cup Club* in Evergreen, the most prestigious of all the strip clubs in the county. The predator never followed the intended victim inside the club and often wondered how he spent its time within the walls of this establishment. However, he spent his time, he usually reached the stage of inebriation before he emerged.

The parking lot was fairly dim and there weren't as many customers on a late cloudy night when the prey would usually call it quits. It was because of these factors, the inebriation, the dim parking lot and the lack of bystanders that made the hunter pick this locale as the best place to take his victim.

The hunter had his own schedule to deal with, but assumed correctly that he could leave the premises with the prey inside *The Golden Cup Club* and return several hours later without fear of losing track of it. He left the club at six pm and did not return until after eleven. Sure enough, the prey was still at the club.

The wait is worth it. He will eventually come out and the plan will come together.

As the prey exited the building and approached its car, the hunter eased up behind it and quickly placed a cloth saturated with chloroform over the prey's mouth and nose. He knew chloroform was riskier than ether, but this was of little consequence with the results he had in mind. He had a very special night in mind for this prey and needed to complete this phase of the plan uninterrupted.

19 THEY ARE A SEDUCTIVE LITTLE PAIR, AREN'T THEY?

"I wish he would hurry. The funeral starts in two hours and the way Ed likes to talk, he couldn't order a hamburger in less than an hour."

Sam paced back and forth in the conference room at the Sheriff's office. Ed Moore, the mayor of Evergreen, had not yet shown up for the interview he had agreed to when Sam called him the night before.

"Do you think he skipped town on us?"

Wade didn't know what to think.

"I only met the Mayor Sunday. I wasn't overly impressed with his character. I think Ed believes he can talk his way out of any situation he gets into, so I don't think he's the kinda guy that would leave town."

Sam quit pacing and rested her hands on the back of a chair.

"I tried to call him on his office phone and his assistant said she hasn't seen him this morning. Then I tried his cell, and he has it turned off. It seems to me he's avoiding us after agreeing last night to meet with us."

"Don't you think he will be at the funeral? I mean,

Rachel worked at City Hall and I can't imagine that he wouldn't show up at the funeral." Wade was trying, with little success, to get Sam to calm down.

"He has to show up eventually. He is the mayor."

Sam looked at him and smiled.

"You're right, Wade. Ed won't ever miss a public appearance at a high profile funeral or wedding any more than he would miss his own birthday party. And I assure you he will never miss a gathering where his favorite subject gets attention, that being himself."

Sam paused before continuing, "Do you think whoever murdered Rachel will be at her funeral, assuming that it isn't Ed?"

Wade rose from his chair.

"I think it's likely that he will. When we get there, I'd appreciate it if you would introduce me to all the players from City Hall. I'd like to watch them during the funeral just to get their reactions to what the preacher says about her."

"The twins mentioned some prominent businessmen. They didn't throw out any names, did they?"

Sam asked as they were walking out of the conference room.

"I forgot to ask." Wade admitted, somewhat embarrassed.

"Now which twin would have distracted you enough to make you forget such an obvious question? Was it Mandy?"

Sam enjoyed this moment. She seldom saw Wade caught in an awkward moment.

"Or was it Mindy? Maybe both of them, huh?"

Wade fumbled for a response.

Sam laughed. "And what were they doing that was such a distraction? They are a seductive little pair, aren't they?"

The phrase, *'seductive little pair'*, made Wade flash back to his time in the stand with Mindy where that phrase took on a whole different meaning. But he didn't want to share those thoughts with Sam at this moment.

He took a step toward Sam. "Look, Sam. You know there isn't a woman alive that could make me forget what I have with you."

Sam walked over next to him and put her arms around him. He bent down and began kissing her, first on her forehead and then moved to her lips, softly caressing her body with his powerful hands.

"Hey, kids. I'm not interrupting anything, am I?"

They had not noticed Connie in the doorway.

"I just wanted to see if you guys wanted to ride to the funeral with me. But if you're too busy, I can hang a '*Do Not Disturb*' sign on the door and tell you about it when I get back."

The beautiful blonde laughed at her sister's discomfort.

"We'll ride with you, Little Sis. I need to get out of this uniform into a dress. Why don't ya'll wait up front for me?"

Before they left her office, Sam whispered to Wade, "I noticed you said nothing about twins not making you forget me."

And with that, she hurried to to the dressing room, leaving Wade behind wondering just how much her woman's intuition was telling her.

20 WHAT DID SHE SAY TO HIM?

THE TWO SISTERS SAT IN THE FRONT SEAT WHILE WADE sat in the back on the way to the funeral, sorting out everything he knew so far. There were a lot of facts that made sense and converged into a cohesive theory in the case, but there were just as many that didn't fit and led him in a different direction. He was so engrossed in his thoughts he didn't realize they reached First Baptist of Evergreen.

Wade, Sam and Connie milled around outside the church until it was almost time to start the service, hoping to catch the mayor to find out why he had not shown up for the scheduled interview. Sam was getting angrier by the moment, pacing up and down on the concrete walk in front in of the church building. She hardly noticed Brother Jeff when he came to the top of the stairs and motioned for everyone outside to enter so the service could get underway.

Wade did not know Rachel and wondered what kind of person she really was. The pastor was making her sound like Mother Teresa, although at least three people that worked closely with her had told Wade about a lifestyle she led that contradicted almost everything the Pastor was saying. He didn't know if she would go to heaven or go to hell and figured that was between her and the Lord.

What would people say and think about me at my funeral, especially if I died at a young age like Rachel did? How long would it take Sam to find someone else? Would that new someone be like me or completely different?

With these thoughts drifting through his mind, Wade hardly noticed that the Pastor finished the service until Sam poked him in the side with her elbow. Sam and Connie's eyes were tearing as they rose to join the line that passed by the casket one last time. They greeted Rachel's parents standing at the end of the casket.

Luke and Carla Chastain looked like they had not slept since the tragedy happened three days earlier. Luke had large dark bags under each eye from crying and the stress he'd been under. Carla was more in a comatose stupor and looked like she had been taking a sedative to calm her nerves. He could not blame her if she had. In his mind, no parent should ever have to see their child buried. Even Wade felt a tear in the corner of his eye as he looked down on Rachel.

The funeral parlor had done a magnificent job making her look as natural as ever, and Wade almost expected her to rise out of the coffin. Looking at the peaceful girl laying in the coffin, he could not imagine what her last thoughts were as the bullet pierced her lungs and she fell to the ground.

Had she lived long enough for her killer to come stand over her? If so, what did he say to her? What did she say to him? Did she know him and did she know why he had shot her?

He realized that Sam had gotten several feet in front of him and he was holding up the line of people that wanted to pay their final respects to Rachel. He quickly took two long steps and closed the gap between them in time to hear her tell Luke, "We'll keep you informed, and we'll catch the bastard that did this!"

Wade knew Sam didn't curse, and for her to use that language in church made him a little uneasy. He had been in law enforcement in the not too distant past, and he knew any officer had to keep his emotions separate from the investigation. That would not be so in this case with Sam.

The quaint graveyard was next to the church. As people filed out of the church, they gathered in small groups waiting for the family to lead the short procession from the church to the grave site under the green tent just inside the fence.

Sam whispered to Wade, "Let's just wait here and we'll leave when they get inside the graveyard."

Wade nodded and turned his attention back to the church just as two pairs of arms circled his waist. He instinctively jumped a little before looking down on two strawberry blonde heads that could only belong to the twins, Mindy and Mandy. Somewhat embarrassed from his reaction and somewhat from his instant recall of the events that took place in the hunting stand, he fumbled for the right words to say.

"Sam, this is—I mean these are—"

He gave up trying to get the words from his brain to his mouth.

Sam laughed at him.

"It's okay, Wade. Connie and I know Mindy and Mandy."

"What are you two doing here?" he asked and then turned even redder as the answer was obvious to everyone but him.

"We worked with Rachel," Mindy said. "You know,

down at City Hall. Do you remember our conversation yesterday at all?"

Mandy jumped in, "Maybe you had your mind on other things and wasn't listening to us."

Wade was squirming because they still had their arms around him and Sam was just standing there next to him smiling, doing nothing to ease his discomfort.

"Oh, yes. I remember the conversation." He finally managed. "You caught me a little by surprise."

Mindy pressed on, "Sam, how do you keep someone that looks like him under control? You never know what temptations he might run into on the big ol' ranch of his."

Sam remained calm.

"I don't worry about it, girls. It really doesn't matter where he builds up his appetite as long as he eats at home, if you know what I mean?"

Mandy replied for both twins, "Oh yea, we know! We might just try to build up his appetite the next time we go to the ranch."

The girls gave him one last hug before catching up with Bruce as he followed the crowd to the graveyard. Wade shook his head as he looked down at Sam.

"Seductive little pair, wouldn't you say?" She said as she walked off.

21 WHERE IN THE WORLD WAS SHE KEEPING THAT GUN?

Six young men, about the same age as Rachel, carried the casket to the grave. Wade watched it exit the church and progress toward the site. Luke and Carla followed closely behind the exquisite box holding the earthly remains of their daughter as if not to lose touch with her in these final moments. The entire congregation that attended the funeral waited patiently by the fence as the young men stepped in unison as Brother Jeff led the short procession the few yards from the fence to the hole in the ground. The Pastor stepped aside to let the men under the tent and three of them went on one side of the grave and the other three went on the other side.

Wade wasn't paying much attention to the processional, still trying to sort out the interaction of Sam and the Thomas twins when he heard a loud bang. He looked up to see the casket laying cross-ways atop the opening of the grave, three of the pall bearers sprinting back toward the church, the other three and Brother Jeff staring stupefied into the grave. Carla Chastain took a step forward and put a hand on the casket before peering into the hole. She let out a little whimper and fainted, crumpling next to the chairs lined up by the graveside.

Luke rushed to his wife's side and knelt down beside her before looking to see what had caused this reaction. When he looked, he took three quick steps to the end of the tent on the opposite side of the fence and started throwing up. Two of the ladies in the processional quickly took his place beside Carla, careful not to look into the grave.

Wade surprised himself at how quickly he instinctively grabbed his .357 revolver as he raced toward the grave, not knowing what to expect when he got there. The .38 caliber revolver in Sam's hand equally surprised him as she stayed step for step in getting through the crowd to the grave.

Where in the world was she keeping that gun? I am going to have to be real careful around Sam in the future if she can hide a revolver like that. At least she didn't pull it out on the Thomas twins.

When they reached the side of the grave, Sam and Wade sneaked a peek into the darkness of the earth and quietly put away their weapons. Wade noticed Sam discreetly lift her skirt and place her gun in a concealed holster between her legs.

So that's where it was! Next time, I'll have to check there.

Lying inside the grave was the answer to the question they'd asked all morning; Mayor Ed Moore was prone on the bottom of the hole with a gaping bullet hole squarely in his forehead. He had no shirt on and there were cuts and slices over his entire torso. Most of them were only a little more than skin deep, but a couple were much deeper. Part of the mayor's intestines was protruding from one of the deeper gashes, creating a grotesque picture that greeted those unsuspecting souls that previously looked into the grave.

Sam cringed and whispered to Wade. "Ugh, he looks like a slaughtered pig."

"Brother Jeff, will you get everyone back into the church until we can get someone down here to remove the body?"

Wade took control, though it was technically Sam's job. Wade noticed for the first time that a newspaper photographer was there; Evidently taking photographs for the story that would run in the Evergreen Weekly about the murder and the funeral. Wade grabbed him and pulled him close so he could hear.

"Take a picture of everyone at this funeral. Hell, take two pictures of everyone here just to make sure you don't miss anyone. Do you understand me?"

The photographer nodded and quickly started aiming and clicking as he scrambled back to the church with the rest of the congregation. Women were crying and men were shaking their heads as word spread through them about a body beneath the casket. Shock and bewilderment were clear on each face in the crowd. Only Connie stood by Wade and Sam at the grave site when the doors to the church closed.

"Wow, I need to sit down for a minute," Connie exhaled for the first time, letting out some built-up tension.

She and Sam sat down in the front row of the seats under the grave side tent that the church reserved for Rachel's family. They said nothing for a long time, each trying to sort out thoughts before sharing them with each other.

After what seemed like an eternity, but was in reality only a few minutes, Wade spoke softly, "It appears someone believed the mayor either killed Rachel or knew too much about who did. The killer tortured him for one of those reasons and then killed Ed. At least, that is what the blood pattern suggests from what I can see."

"Show me so I can understand what you're seeing." Sam rose and edged closer to the grave, careful not to get so close that she might accidentally fall in.

Wade pointed toward the Mayor's body.

"You see the dried bloodstains from the cuts are almost all draining down onto his pants."

Sam nodded.

"That tells me he was standing up when someone made those gashes. There are a bunch of them, over forty I've counted so far. But none of them are life threatening; the culmination of them might have led to him losing enough blood to kill him, but that was obviously not the intention. The cuts are too shallow and meant to cause pain and terror or to get him to talk about something. A few of them are deeper, and I suspect not intended to be so. They probably are a result of Ed squirming and reacting. And the blade went deeper than it was meant. But the bottom line is that his pants are soaked in blood, even though there doesn't appear to be any cuts below his waist."

Sam nodded again.

"You see the tiny pool of blood underneath his head from the bullet wound? That tells me that his heart probably wasn't pumping, and he wasn't moving much before the killer shot him. There is very little blood around the wound in his head and the little that is there drained sideways and not down his face. So he was lying just like he is now when shot in the head."

Sam had a tear form in the corner of her eye.

"Poor Ed. I was ready to cut his nuts off with a butter knife myself three days ago, and now I feel sorry for him.

He was a poor excuse for a man, but even he didn't deserve this. Why would someone do this to him?"

"The obvious answers are that someone was trying to get him to talk about something he didn't want to talk about or they were out for revenge for something he did. I'm not sure we'll know which one of those is correct until we find out who did it."

Connie was still in a state of bewilderment. "How are you going to find out who did it if you don't know why they did it?"

Wade shook his head. "I wish I had the answers, Connie. But anything I told you would be pure speculation."

Connie blurted out, "Sam, someone needs to tell his wife and kids before they hear it from somebody in the congregation."

"I'll get a deputy to go by his house. I don't remember seeing them at the funeral."

"She's here, Sam. But I don't think the kids are."

Connie didn't want to be the one that broke the news to Ed's wife that the body in the grave was her husband's.

Sam looked at Wade, "I've got to go tell her. I'll be back."

As she three slow steps toward the church, Wade caught up with her and put his arms around her.

"Let's do this together," he breathed.

They clung tight together as they got Ed's wife off by herself and told her the bad news. Wade left her in the care of Sam and one of the deacon's wives, wailing and sobbing uncontrollably. There was no comfort in a time like this.

After the coroner removed the body from the grave and the detectives removed the crime scene tape, the burial service resumed without incident. Wade looked over the crowd standing by the site and didn't notice anyone that really stood out as odd or nervous. However, after the service ended, Wade noticed Bruce Thomas and four other men gathered away from anyone else, having a somewhat animated discussion. He wished he had a microphone planted to listen to that.

Then he noticed the twins had discreetly slipped next to the group, acting disinterested in anything the men were discussing. However, Wade noticed the girls were not speaking much, which was highly unusual for them and knew they were eavesdropping on their father and his companions. Gazing at the intensity on the girls' faces, he surmised that they were catching the entire conversation almost word for word.

"Quite a seductive little pair, aren't they?" Sam startled Wade as she took his arm at the elbow. "Or maybe you were just admiring their minds the way you were looking at them. I guess my high school anatomy teacher forgot to tell me where the mind is located on teenage girls."

Sam walked away before Wade could formulate a response.

Connie was standing a few feet from him, grinning,

"Caught you, didn't she?"

She turned and followed her sister.

22 A SINGLE TEAR ROLLED DOWN BRUCE'S CHEEK

"Something about this situation stinks more than the portable toilets at a baked bean contest."

Gus circled the conference room table as he, Wade and Sam tried to piece together the facts of a case that seemingly had no consistent core except for City Hall.

"I agree with you, Gus."

Wade sat next to Sam, still trying to overcome the comments she made at the graveside.

"Let's try to put together a plan and see what we come up with."

Sam tried to get the two men to agree on a direction to take in the investigation.

Gus stated. "We need to go down to City Hall and start interviewing everyone there."

Wade didn't agree.

"We need to start with the Thomas twins and find out what they overheard at the funeral services."

Sam looked across the table at Wade.

"Are you sure that's why you want to talk to them again?"

Finally, they compromised and asked Bruce Thomas to come by for a visit. He seemed more than happy to oblige and showed up within thirty minutes of the request. After Wanda showed him into the conference room, the four of them exchanged pleasantries and then got down to the subject utmost on all their minds.

"Bruce, we want to start with the Rachel Chastain case and then get into what happened with the mayor, if that's all right with you?" Sam stated.

Bruce nodded.

Wade broke in. "We're only looking for information. Relax and tell us what you know. If you can't answer a question because of confidentiality with the city, we understand."

Sam frowned at Wade and then turned her attention to Bruce.

"You hold the position of City Manager. How does that differ from the Mayor's position at City Hall?"

Bruce's voice was anything but steady.

"As I was telling Wade out at the Plantation, Ed was the public figure for the city, always in the news or in the public supporting new businesses or a policy change or something like that. But he did very little in running the city, you know, the administrative side of things. That's where I come in; I take care of running the office, coordinating all the various departments, implementing whatever policy changes that occur and managing the city behind the scenes. Ed was more of the macro-manager and I am more of the micro-manager."

"Was there ever any friction between you and Ed?" Sam asked.

"Anytime there are millions of dollars spent and hundreds of people employed, there will be friction. When you throw in the various egos involved with public office, the chances of friction are multiplied exponentially."

Bruce looked Sam directly in her eyes when answering.

Sam glanced down at her notepad on the table.

"Before we go too far down that road, let's get back to Rachel. Were you aware she worked at City Hall?"

"Yes, part of my job is knowing everyone that works down there, which department they work in and what their job responsibilities are. I knew the City employed Rachel."

Sam decided not to tell him about their conversation with the mayor.

"When you say employed by the City, do you mean she was an employee or was she a contractor? We have received some information that she was on a contract basis with the City."

"You may be right, Sam. I'm not sure of the specific arrangements that Rachel had with the City. She was one of the few employees, or contractors if you will, that I had no input when she was hired."

This was the first sign Wade saw that indicated some hedging in the answers being given by Bruce.

He interjected. "Wouldn't you, in the four days since her death, want to have made sure what kind of employment arrangement Rachel had with the City even if you didn't know before?"

Bruce's eyes widened. "I—I assumed Ed knew. I wasn't privy to the terms of her employment."

"Who made those arrangements?"

Sam sat on the edge of her seat now, fully engaged in the interview process.

Bruce squirmed in his seat.

"I believe Rachel and the Mayor negotiated the terms of her employment directly. As far as I know, there was nobody else involved in her hire. You might check with the Human Resources Manager if she was an employee or the Purchasing Manager if she was a Contractor. If you like, I can follow up on that for you."

Sam scribbled a note on her pad.

"Please do. That might clear up some things for us. Do you know who Rachel worked for at City Hall?"

Bruce again paused, a sign indicating a desire to be less than forthcoming in his answer.

"It was my understanding that she worked directly for Ed, but had access to all the departments while she was working on a project."

"What was the nature of the project she was working on?" Sam asked.

"I can't say, Sam. She was working closely with Ed and a few other managers in the office, but I can't say exactly which projects she was helping with."

Wade noticed the precise terminology in the answer.

"You can't or won't name the projects she was working on, Bruce? You are going to great lengths to find a way not to answer the question directly, so let me put it another way. Do you know the focus of the projects Rachel was working on and have an obligation not to reveal that information?"

"That would be an accurate statement, Wade." Beads of sweat formed on Bruce's forehead.

"What kind of obligation could prevent you from helping to solve this young lady's murder? Seems to me if you're much of a man, you'd want to help find out who did this." Gus was much more direct and much less polite than his fellow mates.

Bruce wiped his forehead. "I'm still employed by the City and there are certain issues we are prevented from speaking about. I don't believe this project had anything at all to do with Rachel's murder. I will do everything possible to help you find out what happened to Rachel because I want to know myself."

A single tear rolled down Bruce's cheek.

Sam took back the lead in the interrogation.

"You really cared for her, didn't you Bruce? You were a lot closer to Rachel than you were leading us to believe, weren't you?"

More tears followed the first.

"Yes, she was the sweetest young ladies one would ever hope to meet."

"Tell us about how you got to know Rachel."

Bruce grabbed a napkin and dabbed at the corners of his eyes.

"It was two or three years ago. One day this vivacious young lady with a great big smile and nice little figure popped into my office and said she was there to help me and the mayor. I knew she was about the same age as my twins, but she had it all together; I mean, she was so sure of herself and where she was going. Her confidence and energy level just made me feel so happy to be in the same room as her."

He closed his eyes as if to soak up those moments of the past.

"One day she came in and said that my lunch date had canceled on me at the last minute. One of her duties at the time was to keep up with my appointments. She told me she had made reservations in the steak house inside the hotel next door and it was probably too late to cancel them, so I invited her to join me. The City keeps a suite of rooms at the hotel for guests coming into town, and one of her other duties was to keep up with how many of those suites were being used. You might have guessed by now that there was a suite available and we ended up in it. To this day, I don't know if I seduced her or if she seduced me, but I know in the law's eyes it really doesn't matter because she was underage, anyway."

Having just admitted to a felony, Bruce looked up to see if anyone at the table were reaching for their handcuffs. When he saw they weren't, he continued.

"She was one of the best things to ever come into my life. When I got up in the morning, she was my first thought and when I went to bed at night, she was my last thought. Before she came along, life was such a drudgery. I have two teenage daughters that I don't understand and they don't understand me. My wife left me, and working for the City is hardly a reason to stand on the street corner and celebrate. With Rachel, I had a reason to live. We were always discreet. You know, we didn't make our relationship obvious at work. We didn't text each other or email each other or even call each other very much. When we went to the hotel, we did so separately. We left the office and came back at different times. I don't think anyone at the office ever suspected anything. How did you guys know?"

Wade answered, "The possibility of a relationship between you and Rachel came up during our investigation, Bruce. We just wanted to confirm it. Was she seeing anyone else while you two were—uh, dating?"

"Heavens, No! I would have known if there had been anyone else and I assure you there was nobody else. The only thing that has interfered with us lately was her workload. Ed had really turned a lot of stuff with the project over to her, and that kept her so busy it cut into our time together. She barely had time to talk to me, much less meet me at the hotel."

"How close were Ed and Rachel, Bruce? I mean, aside from the work."

"Their relationship was all work related. Ed, for all of his faults, never strayed from his loyalty to his wife and family. He was very particular that way. He did Rachel some favors at work, but only because she deserved them."

"Did you do her any favors at work, Bruce?"

Bruce couldn't pick lift his gaze from the table and face them.

"I wasn't exactly truthful about knowing her work status. I guess you already know that, though."

The three of them did not know, but had guessed that Bruce was not telling the entire truth when he had said he wasn't sure about her contract status. They weren't prepared for what he told them next, however.

"Ed hired Rachel on a contract basis for two thousand a month as a student intern. Over time, he raised that figure to five thousand a month because she was so good at what she did and always received the very best performance appraisals. I added some incentive clauses to the contract that she could easily meet; Attending a safety meeting once a quarter, volunteering at one of Ed's outreach meetings and things like that. Incentives in our contracts are not that uncommon, and it was within my prerogative to amend her contract. With the incentives, she was making over ten thousand per month."

Wade realized that Bruce was being truthful when he said he had no idea about Rachel's relationship with Ed or any of the other politicians and businessmen. He wondered how she could manipulate so many men with none knowing about each other.

"Bruce, you said Ed had increased the workload on Rachel. Do you know what this extra work was and who else participated?"

"Yes, I know about some aspects of the project, but I

don't know the entire scope of the project. I, along with several others, have signed a non-disclosure agreement and short of receiving a subpoena can't say anything about it. And I don't think you will get a subpoena for requiring us to reveal this project. It goes way above Evergreen."

"Okay, how about the other part of the question? Who else was Rachel working closely on the project?"

"There is the purchasing manager, Frank Davis; there are the two city councilmen working on the Project, Bill Brogan and Ray Patrick; there is the District Attorney, John Grimes and Ed, who is not with us anymore."

"Did any of these guys have any relationship with Rachel outside of the project?"

"Goodness, no! She wasn't that type of girl."

Sam stifled her first response.

"Okay, Bruce. We're just about done talking about Rachel, but I have to ask you a couple more questions."

Bruce again looked down and nodded.

"Do Mindy and Mandy know about your relationship with Rachel?"

"No way! We were discreet. And besides, my twins are just kids playing in the grown-up world down at City Hall. They aren't old enough to know about the adult things that go on down there."

Wade marveled at the blinders a man could put on when it came to his kids and his partner in a relationship. To Bruce, Mindy and Mandy, although almost the same age as Rachel were still just kids unable to comprehend a love relationship while he had elevated his opinion of Rachel to being a superior lady-in-waiting, capable of doing no wrong.

How devastated would Bruce be if he ever found out he was being used by Rachel along with a lot of others down at City Hall?

Sam glanced down at her pad.

"One last question about Rachel. Where were you Saturday morning when she was shot?"

Bruce turned almost ashen.

"I could never hurt Rachel. I just couldn't. She meant everything to me."

"Okay, just tell us where you were last Saturday morning."

Bruce again looked at Sam directly.

"I was at home by myself. The girls spent the night with some friends, and I was catching up on some chores around the house. The girls got back around two in the afternoon and told me about Rachel. I'm not sure where they heard it from, but it doesn't take long for news like that to get around Evergreen. After that, I was too numb to go much of anywhere. It took everything I had within me to bring the girls out to the Plantation Sunday and I only did it because they begged me to. It's funny. I didn't even know they knew about the Plantation before Saturday night."

So the girls were telling the truth, at least about the trip to the Plantation. They set it up just to get to Wade and get him involved with the investigation to protect Bruce. It looked like Bruce needed all the protection he could get. Wade believed Bruce, but didn't know if that was because of Bruce's sincerity or because of the influence on him by the twins.

Sam folded the pad.

"Okay, Bruce. Do you need to take a break before we talk about Ed?"

"Please. You know, I guess that I'm filling in for Ed temporarily until the Council can meet and appoint a stand-in until they can hold a special election. I need to call in and see how everything is going down there this morning."

Sam led Bruce to an empty office down the hall and closed the door so he could have a little privacy while discussing city business. She returned to the conference room to find Wade and Gus in a deep philosophical discussion.

23 WHY DO I FEEL SO GUILTY EVERY TIME SOMEBODY MENTIONS THE TWINS?

"But how could a nineteen-year-old girl control so many adult men? I could understand if these guys were just coming into puberty, but these were grown men, for heaven's sake." Wade was shaking his head.

"It's called young boobs and a firm butt, Son; All wrapped up in a little package every one of those guys wanted to open all for themselves. Just like Santa Claus. You never want to stop believing."

"But she was nineteen! Most of these guys were more than twice her age."

Gus nodded.

"Which made it even more fun for them to be the one that opened that package and imagining that Santa picked it out especially for them. Each of them wanted to believe they were the only one with that chance. Hell, you own the laboratory out at the Plantation for this behavior. Grown men aren't that much different from animals."

Wade's thoughts immediately went to the twins, and he was afraid Gus had somehow found out more than he should before he gave Gus a puzzled look.

"Son, when one of your does or red hinds goes in heat in your big pen, what happens?"

"If she's in the hunting area where all the bucks and stags are, a bunch of the bucks or stags will chase her around two or three days, fight like the dickens with each other and then one of them will breed her."

"Some of them fights are doggone violent, too." Gus said, cleaning up his language now that Sam was back in the room. "I've seen them break off horns, gore each other and even kill each other for the right to breed that little doe or hind. They will ignore everything their basic survival instincts tell them to do just for the chance to poke fun at the little lady."

"But they only get to breed for about three months out of the year. These men could do it anytime they want."

Gus shook his head.

"Son, you're mighty young. When you double your current age how many chances do you think you'll have to poke fun at an attractive nineteen-year-old gal, particularly one with a little class?"

"Not too many, I reckon." Then Wade noticed the look on Sam's face. "I mean, not that I would want to, anyway. I'll be perfectly satisfied with what I have at home, I'm sure."

Gus guffawed.

"When a man quits looking at attractive young ladies, one of two things have happened; He's gone blind or he's dead. I guess there's a third thing, but I don't think you're that kind of fellow." With that, he showed Wade a limp wrist. "And even those guys look at pretty gals because they're jealous."

Sam opted in, "Gus, I've already told him it doesn't matter if his hair grows all day wherever he goes. He's going to have to come to the barbershop at home to get it trimmed. Otherwise, the barber will trim more than he wants."

They all laughed, momentarily forgetting the serious business that brought them together in the conference room. When Bruce came back in, the mood in the room immediately sobered as though three kids were playing and their parent had come in.

"Is everything okay down at City Hall, Bruce?" Sam asked.

"As well as could be expected, what with us losing Rachel and Ed within a few days of each other. A lot of employees are in shock, and there's not much work being done. But talking with Human Resources and a Counselor, they say it's better to give them a little time to talk with each other and let them get their emotions under control before trying to get in a normal routine again. They need an adjustment period, I guess."

"That makes sense to me. We're still in a little shock down here and we didn't' work with them every day."

"How about you, Bruce? Do you feel like moving on and talking about Ed or do you need some time?"

"I'm okay. I'd rather finish up and then I'm going home to see my twins. I somehow seem to have not paid a lot of attention to them in the last few months. I need to make sure they're okay."

Wade could feel the steady stare of Sam's gaze on him and was careful not to look until he was sure she had looked away.

Why do I feel so guilty every time somebody mentions the twins? Gee whiz, I've only known them for three days!

"All right, let's talk about Ed. Do you know anyone that wanted him dead?"

"In the position Ed was in, he made a lot of friends and

a lot more enemies, but it was all business type relationships, both the friends and the enemies. I don't think Ed was the guy who anyone considered a dear friend or a devoted enemy, just someone either on their side or the other side of issues."

"Do you know if he was seeing anyone else or had a relationship outside of his marriage?"

Bruce held his hand up.

"Didn't we already cover this? Besides, I think I would have known if he had. There was a rumor at one time he had a girlfriend over in Biloxi because he went over there a lot on weekends, but he told me he went there to get away for a couple of days now and then, and there wasn't any more to it than that. Even though Ed didn't like to show it, the pressures of being the mayor would sometimes get to him."

"Were there any other issues that Ed, as part of his job, would have led to someone killing him?"

Bruce shook his head. "Sam, you've lived here all of your life. This isn't Chicago or New York. We don't have a mob here waiting to get even with the Mayor for some business deal."

Sam wrote more notes.

"How about the unions? Isn't he in negotiations with the public employees union now trying to redo their contract?"

"I guess that technically you could say he was, but he really wasn't that involved. With the extra money the city has through some federal grants and loans after the hurricane, we're in the black and he balanced the budget, as least for the time being. I'm the one negotiating with the union and we are making excellent progress. We, I mean the administration, realize the union employees don't want to give up everything they've earned over the last couple of decades and they realize the city can't keep up payments on unrealistic pension plans. So we should reach a compromise fairly soon."

"How about this big project? Is it serious enough to get him killed?"

Bruce looked up at the ceiling a long time before replying.

"I sure hope not. If it is, then a lot of us are in danger."

"What do you mean, Bruce?"

"I was just thinking out loud more than anything else. You know I can't say anything about the project, but I don't think there is enough information that has gone out on it to put anyone in danger. None of us but Ed and Rachel knew the entire scope of the project."

"Okay, did Ed treat everyone the same at work or did he have some that he really liked and others that he didn't like?"

"He was fairly consistent. He liked to be around the high energy people like most of us do. You know, Sam; People like you that have a lot of confidence without being conceited. That's the people he enjoyed. He would slough off the whiners and complainers to a department manager or to me."

"Can you name a few of these high energy people?"

"Sure, Rachel was probably his favorite, but she was the favorite of a lot of managers at City Hall. Another was the purchasing manager, Frank Davis. He has a boatload of energy and never stops. He's always positive no matter the circumstances and expects the best out of everyone around him."

"How about on the other end? Who did the mayor not care to be around?"

"I'm not sure I should answer that. These walls have a way of being real thin, and if I would give you an opinion like that, it might somehow get out and cause a lot of grief down at the Hall."

Sam nodded. She wanted to contradict what Bruce was saying, but he was probably right. There are no real secrets in Evergreen.

They were wrapping up the interview when Sam, after giving Wade a curious glance, asked one final question.

"Bruce, do you know the name of the friends that Mandy and Mindy spent Friday night with?"

Bruce looked down at his shoes and then shook his head. He then hurried out of the conference room, obviously not as at ease as he had been when he entered earlier that morning.

After they were sure he could no longer hear them, Sam closed the door to the conference room.

"Well, gentlemen. What have we learned?"

Gus snorted.

"We learned those portable toilets have turned over and sh—well, the contents are all running down the hill toward the parade."

"That's one way of putting it, Gus. But we confirmed there is some mega-project in the works, or at least being considered by a few of our elected officials and a few of the prominent businessmen. Did you notice how nicely he avoided talking about the businessmen? We still don't know their identity or what this project is about."

Wade spoke up next.

"I learned that I've been underestimating Rachel. She evidently was quite a remarkable young lady, able to use and manipulate a lot of smart men at the same time."

Gus couldn't resist.

"If you mean she led some horny men in their late thirties, forties and fifties around by their peckers, then I guess I would agree to that."

Wade shook his head.

"But it was much more than them chasing—a young girl. She balanced a half dozen relationships within a tight circle of intelligent men and used those relationships to get to some end. We need to find out where she wanted them all to end up at, and then maybe we'll know how it all ties together."

"So, assuming the two murders are connected, we have a half dozen or more suspects; Bruce, the purchasing manager, the District Attorney, a city councilman and at least two of our esteemed citizens."

Sam paused for effect and then looked at Wade.

"And we can't forget the twins, either."

24 IT MUST BE A WOMAN THING

"Wonderful, isn't it?"

Sam and Wade sat on the back porch of the Lodge, watching the sun set in the western sky. From this view, they could see the largest pastures where animals of all kinds gathered right before dusk. A majestic Elk and a spring-legged Black-buck Antelope emerging from the wood lines pranced in the cool autumn air. It was the highlight of the afternoon. But as they sat in adjoining rockers holding hands, their thoughts and focus were on the two murders that had rocked the tranquility of Evergreen.

Sam broke the silence.

"Who do you think killed Rachel and Ed?"

Wade kept staring out toward the pasture as he took his time answering.

"I honestly don't know. I think we have to look closer at this super-secret project, whatever it is. That's the common factor for all the suspects we have right now. But who knows how many others were involved and if the project even had anything to do with it?"

"I know, but I talked with Judge Wilson this afternoon

and he said there is no way that any of the local judges will ever give us a subpoena to get the paperwork on that project. So at least one judge knows about it and he isn't budging."

"What could be so important that two people would get murdered over it and a judge wouldn't give the Sheriff a subpoena?"

"I have no idea and I'm not sure I want to know."

Suddenly, the tension in Sam's grip rose dramatically. Although she remained facing forward, her eyes strained to see in the lodge behind her.

Wade whispered, "I know. I heard it too."

His muscles tightened. He furtively looked around without being too obvious for a weapon. Both he and Sam left their revolvers in the den while they enjoyed a cup of Community coffee on the back porch. The closest item of any use was a sidewalk broom four feet from the rockers. They both heard the footsteps approaching nearer and nearer. As the back door eased open, Wade leaped out of the rocker and grabbed the broom and flipped it so that the business end of the handle could fend off the intruder.

Mindy burst into laughter.

"Relax, Detective Ranger. It's just us. And you've already swept us off our feet, so there's no use for that."

Mandy and Mindy stood in the doorway, or inside the doorway since they took a couple steps backward when Wade suddenly turned on them.

"Sorry, girls. I didn't know who you might be. We weren't expecting any company tonight."

"That's okay. We're not really company, anyway. We're just the twins and nobody pays any attention to us."

Sam wasn't yet sure what to make of this intrusion.

"I wouldn't be so sure of that. I think some people pay a lot of attention to you two."

Mandy looked at Mindy and sighed.

"That's one reason we wanted to come by and talk to you two tonight, Sam."

Wade felt the tension in his body building rapidly. He didn't know what the twins might say or how Sam might react to them. The chances of the twins saying something Sam would like to hear weren't much better than a worm in a fish tank.

I'm the worm in this fish tank.

Mindy continued for the twins.

"Sam, we want to apologize to you and Wade for our behavior at the funeral. There was no call for it and we're sorry. Wade was nothing but a gentleman when we came to the lodge Sunday and we should not have led you to believe anything else. We could tell by your reaction after the funeral we had gone too far kidding around with him and we don't want to be responsible for trouble between you two."

Wade could physically see a ton of tension flowing out of Sam's petite body. His own body reaction mirrored Sam's. Thinking of all the things the twins might have said, this was better than any he imagined.

It's a good thing the fish weren't biting today.

Sam smiled. "I appreciate that. Sometimes, even though we trust each other completely, I can tell if Wade is attracted to someone and—let's just say he is attracted to the two of you. It's not so much that I resent that attraction. It's that I know it's there and I can't control it."

Mindy moved a little closer to Sam.

"Believe me, Sam. You have it under control. There are a

lot of men attracted to us. We're not conceited and we don't believe we're overly attractive even, but some men live in a fantasy world and getting to two twins at the same time would top their dream world off. That's been the way it's been for us all of our lives and probably will be for the rest of our lives unless we move thousands of miles from each other."

Mandy added, "Down at work, there's not any guys that wouldn't do us at the same time if we gave them the chance. But we know Wade is not of that ilk. He is in love with you and I don't think, in fact, I know he won't do anything to hurt you. We were wrong to give you the impression that he would."

"I don't know what to say. I didn't know my feelings were that easy to read, but I really appreciate this."

Sam stepped forward and gave both of the twins a big hug. All three young ladies were crying, although Wade did not understand why.

It must be a Woman thing.

Sam motioned for Wade to join them in a hug, and as he did he felt a hand slip down to his butt and it gave him a tight little squeeze. He stepped back and Mindy winked at him.

They are a seductive little pair, aren't they?

Mindy looked back at Sam as though nothing had happened, but she had a coy smile.

After giving the girls a few minutes of chatting and bonding with each other, Wade asked, "I couldn't help but notice after the funeral. You two were close enough to that group of men that included your Dad so you could overhear them. Do you mind sharing what you heard?"

Mandy put her hand to her mouth.

"Oh, my goodness! Sam was right. You are watching us. Mindy, we'd better wear tent dresses for now on!"

Wade turned red, and all three girls laughed.

"We're just kidding, Wade. We saw you watching the men and then we moved closer to them to hear what they were saying. But we didn't hear much. When we got close and quit talking to each other, they noticed we were there and started talking about the service. I know they were talking about something else before, but they were careful when we got close enough to hear them."

"No problem. We'll find out soon enough what they were talking about. I've never seen a secret that could be kept quiet if enough people know about it." After a slight pause, he added, "Especially in Evergreen."

Mandy stood right in front of Wade.

"What did Dad tell you this morning? Did he tell you he was sleeping with Rachel?"

"Mandy, you know we can't reveal what people tell us confidentially, particularly as part of an ongoing investigation."

Mandy turned away.

"He was sleeping with her whether he admitted it. And a bunch of those other guys were sleeping with her too. She was playing these old geezers like a fiddle, and they didn't have a clue."

"How do you know that, Mandy?"

"Not much is going on at City Hall other than people standing around talking about Rachel's murder. And now, they'll be talking about the mayor's murder. So we've had time to do some digging on our own. And guess what we found."

Wade sat back down in the rocking chair.

"I'm not guessing. With you two, it could be anything."

Mandy ignored the sarcasm from Wade.

"We found three different contracts for her *'services'*

from three different departments, all in effect at the same time. And we found where Dad altered one to give her a lot more money."

They confirmed what Bruce told them that morning. Only now it seemed a couple of the other Department Managers felt the need to compensate Rachel over and above the normal compensation rate.

Just how much money was Rachel making down at City Hall? Wasn't she aware that at some point, somebody had to find out about her compensation?

"Who signed off on the contracts?"

"Mayor Moore signed the first one and then Dad added a bunch of incentives so it doubled to ten thousand dollars a month. The Purchasing Manager, Frank Davis, did the second one, but it was only for three thousand a month, so he was getting the best bargain, so to speak. Then the District Attorney, John Grimes, had one on file up to Monday, but it disappeared. Unfortunately for him, we know where all the files are backed up electronically and he forgot to delete the backup file. He was getting hosed for seven thousand per month. So we know that Rachel was making at least twenty thousand per month off those guys. Not bad for someone our age."

"Outstanding work, girls. You didn't make copies of these contracts, did you?"

"Of course not. That would have been illegal." Mindy said as she pulled a sheaf of papers out of the vanilla folder lying on the table behind her. "But, here's some paper we found in the trash and we thought you might enjoy reading it."

Wade knew that Sam could not use these stolen contracts in any prosecution of anyone since they obtained them outside of the prescribed procedures. He also knew they would be of great use when interrogating both the Purchasing Manager and the District Attorney. Just the knowledge that she had them would give Sam a powerful edge, especially with the District Attorney since he had already taken steps to cover up his contract with Rachel.

Sam glanced at the paperwork and nodded.

"Thanks, girls. But I don't want you two getting in over your heads down there at the Hall. It looks like two people have lost their lives over something going on and we don't need any more casualties. You have to promise me you'll quit digging and be more careful."

The twins nodded in unison and shrugged their shoulders.

Mandy asked the next tough question, "Who killed the Mayor and Rachel?"

Sam answered, "Honestly, we don't know. We have the same list of suspects that you two have, but we have nothing on any of them that would narrow that list down to any above the others. We even had you two on the list of suspects since you guys were the ones that discovered the hunting license at City Hall."

The girls looked at each other with their mouths gaping open.

"We hadn't thought of that. Do you really think we could kill Rachel and the mayor? Sam, you don't know us very well, do you?"

"Not really. You're closer to Connie's age than mine. But I've seen so many people recently that could do things I never dreamed they could or would do. I'm not sure who is or isn't capable of anything."

"Sam, we like to play games with people's minds. You know, like we did with you and Wade to make you jealous and get him in trouble. But we can't even think in terms of murder."

Wade could see why Bruce made the distinction between Rachel and his twin daughters. Rachel was a young woman making her own decisions in a grown-up world. Some of these decisions were not wise and probably resulted in her death, but she was making them on her own. The twins were still playing teenager games with people and were not yet engaged in the adult environment. They didn't realize the serious consequences of their actions on those around them.

25 SO, AS MUCH AS I HATE TO ADMIT IT, YOU ARE RIGHT AGAIN

Frank Davis, the Purchasing Manager, sat across the conference room table from Wade and Sam. So far, the meeting was not going well.

"So Frank, you're saying you didn't even know Rachel Chastain or what she did at City Hall?"

Sam breathed out in exasperation. She rose from her chair and paced back and forth.

"That's not what I said, Sam. Please don't put words in my mouth that I didn't say."

She quit pacing and stared at the large man in the chair.

"So what are you saying, Frank?"

"Like I told you before. I may have seen Miss Chastain at City Hall, but I don't distinctly remember her working there."

Frank fidgeted in the chair.

Sam leaned over the table.

"But she had a contract with your department, Frank. How could she have a contract agreement with your department and you not know about it?"

"I just told you, Sam. I don't recall a contract between

the City Purchasing Department and Miss Chastain."

"And I guess you know nothing about a big project she was working on with you and your colleagues down at the Hall?"

"I work on a lot of projects for the city, Sheriff. Can you be more specific?"

Frank refused to look directly at Sam.

She ignored his question.

"And if an attractive young lady was in several meetings about this project with you and it was the most secret project you've worked on at City Hall in your entire career, you wouldn't recall the project or the girl? Is that what you expect me to believe?"

Frank wiped his brow.

"I can only tell you what I recall, Sam. You can't expect me to remember every attendee at every meeting for every project I've been a participant, can you?"

"Do you know what obstruction of an investigation is, Mr. Davis?"

Sam used his last name despite having known him for years.

"I have a general idea, Sheriff. But again, you're asking me to remember particular team members and details of every meeting I've ever been in."

Sweat continued to pour from the large man.

"Mr. Davis. I'm asking you to tell the truth; which I don't believe you're doing this morning."

"If you're advising me you're about to charge me with obstructing justice or lying to you, maybe I should get legal advice before proceeding."

He looked around the room for support.

"And I assume that legal advice would come from Mr. Grimes, the District Attorney."

Frank's confidence rose.

"In anticipation of this meeting, I consulted with John, uh—Mr. Grimes and he advised me that if the focus of the investigation centered on alleged municipal documentation or privileged negotiations or advice that I might have given the mayor, then it would be proper for him to provide counsel for me. I believe the questions you are asking me now would fall under those categories."

"Okay, Frank. If you don't recall meeting Rachel Chastain, why did you go to her funeral?"

Frank spoke as if he had rehearsed the lines.

"Obviously, I learned where she worked after her death and that she had some dealings with the City, through the mayor as I recall. I assumed many of the City employees must have worked with her at some point, and I was there to support them."

Wade shook his head.

"Did you and the DA go over every possible question we might ask and prepare a response to it?"

"I'm sorry, Mr. Dalton. I'm a little confused. What is your official capacity here?"

Wade glared at the city official.

"I'm assisting the Sheriff, Frank."

Frank's body posture exuded defiance.

"I take from that answer, Sir, that you have no official capacity in this meeting. Am I correct, Mr. Dalton?"

Wade shook his head again.

"You guys prepared for this interview, didn't you? Tell Mr. Grimes that I now understand the rules he wants to play by. Don't worry. I won't ask you any more questions. I have full confidence in Sam that she can get around your bogus answers without my help."

Frank Davis just smiled and did not respond. Wade was

getting a new respect for John Grimes, the District Attorney. He prepared Frank well for this interview, having him unable to recall anything about Rachel, the project, or the murders without denying his involvement with any of them.

Sam wasn't as sure of her abilities as Wade indicated, but pressed on anyway.

"Frank, are you willing to take a lie detector test?"

Frank again repeated rehearsed lines.

"I'm afraid not, Sheriff. I've been advised those tests are inherently unreliable and because of that can't be used in any legal proceeding. Knowing these facts, I believe it to be in my best interest to decline the invitation to take part in that exercise."

Sam plopped into a chair.

"Very well, Frank. How many people work in the Purchasing Department at City Hall?"

Frank beamed, assuming the more people that worked in his department, the more believable it would be that he was not that close to Rachel.

"I think there are a tad over fifty people in our department, Sheriff, give or take a few."

Sam stared across the table.

"So if I drag every single one of them down here and ask them what they know about your knowledge of Rachel, what do you think they will say?"

Frank swallowed hard. He and John had not anticipated this question, and he did not have a prepared response. Sweat dripped off his forehead and his lips got a little thinner.

He stammered and then said. "Sheriff, I would protest that action as being too much of an interruption to the ongoing business of the city."

Sam smiled. "And to whom would you protest, Mr. Davis?"

Not having a prepared line, Frank faltered.

"Either the acting Mayor or the City Council, Sam."

Frank was reeling now, off on an island by himself without the safeguard of his adviser.

Sam stiffened.

"We've already interviewed Bruce, and he gave us permission to talk to anyone at City Hall that we want. It is my understanding he's the acting Mayor and has that authority. To protest to the City Council, you would have to wait until their next scheduled meeting, which is three weeks away and those meetings are open to the public. You would have to explain to the citizens of Evergreen why you want to hide information from an ongoing investigation."

Frank slumped in his chair.

"I guess you're just gonna have to talk to them then. I'm through talking with you guys unless I have my attorney present."

"No, problem. You understand we'll be asking Mr. Grimes the same questions and he just might sacrifice your honor to save his. There might be a slight conflict of interest there, if you catch my drift."

Frank face reddened. He blustered, "He wouldn't do that to me!"

Sam continued to smile. "There are two people dead that were connected to this project that nobody wants to talk about. Do you believe somebody won't be thrown under the bus on this thing, no matter who pulled the trigger?"

Frank rose and walked unsteadily out of the room, leaving Wade and Sam alone with their thoughts. Wade was the first to speak.

"Gus was right. City Hall has turned into a cesspool

and now it's overflowing on the citizens."

Sam played with her hair. "The sad thing is the citizens accept it and think it's normal."

Wanda stuck her head inside the conference room.

"Mr. Grimes called and sends his regrets. He won't be available to interview with you, Sam."

"Thank you, Wanda." And then turning to Wade, "I suspect we won't ever get to interview Mr. Grimes unless his attorney allows him to testify at a trial. Which I doubt very much."

Wade looked at the ceiling.

"Sam, are we looking at this all wrong?"

"What do you mean?"

He turned his gaze to Sam.

"Does all the stuff with City Hall really tie into both murders? Are we looking for one or two killers?"

"I'm still not following you, Wade. Don't you think the same guy killed both Rachel and the Mayor?"

"I'm not so sure, Sam. Rachel's murder seemed so cold and calculated, planned out to the very last detail and neat if you can say a murder is neat. The mayor's murder looked more like either a murder of passion or one of torture; I'm not sure which. Regardless, it seems amateurish compared to Rachel's."

"The two have some differences, but Rachel and Ed were running in the same circle of friends and evidently close to the same project, whatever that was."

"We've got to find out about that project. But now, we're getting stonewalled by the people involved."

"Wade, I believe you may have an inside source that we can use."

Wade groaned, knowing where Sam was heading and not at all sure he wanted to go there with her.

"And that would be?"

Sam smiled, "You have a seductive little pair on your side, don't you?"

"Sam, they're just kids playing an adult game with adult players. I don't want to get them involved."

"Okay, but I just have a feeling that at some point, they're gonna get neck-deep in this thing, whether we like it."

Wade nodded in agreement, but hoped against hope that she was wrong. The twins had inextricably intertwined themselves in this whole thing, and they were going to be a factor in the outcome. But he didn't know at this point whether that was a good thing, a bad thing, or just an inevitable thing.

Wade tried to steer the conversation away from the twins.

"What I was trying to get to is that we may have a different situation than we thought. What if someone planned out the murder of Rachel and then someone else killed the mayor? Maybe Ed killed Rachel, someone found out he did it and whoever discovered that killed him. That would explain the different styles in the murders."

"But didn't you tell me out there in the woods that the guy that killed Rachel was smart, smarter than you and I combined? That doesn't sound like Ed."

"Actually, what I said was that he thought he was smarter than the two of us, which I believed then and still believe that he is underestimating us. However, I said he was intelligent and meticulous in his planning, which would eliminate Ed as a suspect. So, as much as I hate to admit it, you're right again."

"Don't worry," Sam said with a smile. "You'll get used to it."

26 THERE'S A LITTLE OVER THREE HUNDRED THOUSAND

THEY STOPPED BY THE EVERGREEN CAFÉ FOR A QUICK lunch. The café had once belonged to Gus's brother, Gabe, and now after his untimely death belonged to Gabe's daughter, April.

"April, it's so good to see you," Sam was back to her old self, which to Wade meant the world.

"Hey, Sam. Hey, Wade. Great to see you. I was beginning to think you didn't like my cooking anymore. I hardly ever see you guys. Is Uncle Gus causing trouble down at the shop?"

"He's like a two-month-old Boxer puppy, April. He just can't help but find trouble. And I think he enjoys it more than a puppy does."

April laughed, "That sounds like Uncle Gus. He may grow up one day, but that'd be a shame. Speaking of trouble, are you making any progress in the two killings?"

"Some. But we've hit a few roadblocks along the way."

"That's what I'm hearing here. Sounds like more than a few roadblocks from what I hear, though. I don't think you need to worry about turning down the invitation to the City Hall Christmas party this year."

By this time, Wade and Sam already sat at their table, but April continued to linger beside them. She was very hesitant before almost whispering, "Just remember; Not everybody plays by the same rules you do."

Then she abruptly left the table.

"I wonder what that was about."

Sam's voice was low.

Wade looked at the kitchen door.

"I don't know. Evidently we've upset somebody important, and I've heard there aren't any secrets in Evergreen."

"I've heard that, too."

Sam chuckled, then got more serious.

"She's heard something specific or she wouldn't have said anything."

Wade nodded. "That's what I'm thinking."

The two of them had a fairly subdued lunch of pork chops, fried cornbread and turnip greens with each of them lost in their own thoughts. April didn't come back by the table, and Sam didn't want to make too much of a scene at the restaurant.

"Remind me to get in touch with April later and find out what she knew that she wasn't telling."

They dropped in to see if Luke Chastain had recovered enough to talk with them. They arrived at the ranch style brick home on the outskirts of town and saw his pickup parked in the driveway.

Luke invited them in. Sam noticed he was much thinner than when she'd seen him the past Saturday on that gravel road in the National Forest. He looked as if he had not taken the death of his daughter well, and her death affected his health.

"Luke, are you up to taking a few questions? We'll be as brief as we can."

Sam tried to ease into the questions. Luke's wife, Carla, entered the room and sat beside her husband on the sofa. The dark rings around her eyes told Sam and Wade that she had not been sleeping well either.

"Yes, Sam. We need to find out what you know, who could have done this, and if it was an accident or on purpose."

"Fair enough. We'll tell you everything we know and you tell us everything you know and hopefully between us, we can get to the bottom of this."

Both Luke and Carla nodded.

"Do either of you know anyone that had ill feelings toward Rachel? I don't mean someone that may not have liked her, but someone that thought she had really done them wrong."

Luke looked over at Carla and began.

"Sam, I don't know how well you knew Rachel. I believe she was closer to your sister's age than yours. Anyway, Rachel has always been mature for her age. She was smarter and more aggressive than the other kids, and this set her apart from them. This has always rubbed people wrong a little, but over time she learned how to control her talents and make those around her more comfortable. But she was still different. There's no doubt about it."

After a brief pause, Luke looked at his wife before continuing.

"She volunteered down at the church. Helping the Music Minister get ready for rehearsals, working with the

Vacation Bible School and filling in for the Financial Secretary when she was out. I guess she could have done everything necessary at the church, but preach. And she probably could have done that too if she wanted to. At one time, we thought she might be a missionary or something like that because she spent all of her free time at the church. Then, she went to City Hall when she was only sixteen years old. She got in somehow as an intern and she loved it down there. She was born to be a politician, I think. When she would come home and tell us the stories about the mayor and the council, she'd have a grin from ear to ear. She was so happy down there and truly that was the first place that she fit in, you know. Sam, just like you were born to be in law enforcement, Rachel was born to be in politics."

Sam smiled, not knowing if she had just received a compliment or not.

"Luke, did you notice any changes in her attitude recently?"

"We thought she was just growing up, you know. She was a lot more serious than she had been. She was making a lot more money than most nineteen-year-old's and we figured she was taking her job a lot more seriously. We tried to get her interested in college, but she said she was doing okay where she was at and didn't think college was right for her right now. Her mama," nodding toward Carla, "has had joint custody of her banking account since she was fourteen. You know, the banks won't let a minor open an account by themselves, so Carla opened one with her. Anyway, after Saturday, Carla looked at her account and we were kinda surprised at how much money she's been able to save over the last couple of years. In fact, we're a little nervous about it."

Sam sat a little more erect in her chair.

"How much is in her account, Luke?"

Luke looked to Carla for affirmation before answering.

"There's a little over three hundred thousand in it. That seems awfully high to us, even for government work. We didn't have any idea she had that much money. I've worked all my life, and I haven't saved up that much."

Sam's eyes widened when she heard the figure.

"Yes, Luke. That's, how did you say it, awfully high even for government work. I work for the same government she did, and that's a lot of money to have saved up for the last couple of years."

"We spent none of it. We didn't know what to do with it and we wanted to talk to you first before we did anything. Can we turn it over to you?"

"No, Luke. You might want to get the advice of an attorney."

She glanced at Wade and thought for a second before continuing.

"And not one that is associated with City Hall, just in case there might be a conflict of interest there. My advice is to leave the money in the account until we get to the bottom of all of this, but I'd feel better if you had an attorney confirm my opinion. I don't know if she filed separate income taxes than you guys, but you will want to make sure taxes were paid on any income."

"Okay, Sam. We'll leave it there. There's one other thing that you need to know."

"What's that, Luke?"

Luke took a long look at Carla before answering. "We think Rachel may have had a boyfriend, possibly at City Hall. When Carla was going through her things, she found some birth control pills in her purse. We didn't know she was taking them, but Carla found them."

Luke dropped his gaze toward the floor and refused to look into Sam's face.

Sam was almost embarrassed for Luke and Carla. They were in the same little Baptist church, and the parents were afraid the news of Rachel's promiscuity would get out into the community. Sam wondered what they would think if they knew just how promiscuous Rachel had been with several of the dutiful servants of City Hall. But she kept that information to herself.

"Do you know who this boyfriend might be?"

"That's the frustrating part. We checked her email and cell phone and all that's in them are messages from the Managers and Supervisors. You know, business. We would have thought the kid, if he was that serious that Rachel would have slept with him, would at least have the courtesy to come by and meet us."

Wade almost shook his head, but restrained himself. Luke and Carla still kept the ideals of the past, while the world had moved on without them. They could not imagine that the reason the messages and phone calls came only from the Managers and Supervisors was that was who Rachel was having sex with, not somebody her own age that forgot to get her parents' permission first.

"Do you mind if we take the cell phone with us so we can find out if maybe she erased the texts from her boyfriend?"

"Texts? Me and Carla don't know nothing about no texts. Our phones don't do that."

"No problem. Hers might."

Wade knew all phones now had that capability, but didn't want the parents to find the text messages left on

Rachel's phone for the fear of what they might contain about their daughter.

Sam asked, "How did Rachel like to spend her weekends?"

Luke rubbed his temples.

"She worked a lot of weekends, especially lately. Some project she was working on took up a lot of her time. Most of the time she was at the Office, but sometimes she had to go to Biloxi for the project."

"Did she ever say what the nature of the project was?"

Luke shook his head.

"Just that it was a big project and that most of the people working on it were bigwigs."

Sam changed the subject.

"Who knew she was hunting in the National Forest last Saturday?"

"Just about everybody. We, meaning the folks we hunt with, talk all week about where we're going to hunt so we don't mess each other up by getting too close to one another. We don't want to have a bunch of us trying to hunt in the same place."

"That makes sense. Do you know who was supposed to hunt in the area where she was killed?"

"Normally, the mayor hunts in that area, but Saturday, he was hunting on some private land not too far from the Forest. At least, that's where he said he would be hunting. That's why Rachel was walking through that area to get back to the truck. Nobody was supposed to be there, and it was shorter going back to the road that way. We'd figured that out earlier in the week and I don't know who she might have told."

"Who in your group knew she would use that shortcut?"

Luke looked up before responding.

"I guess everybody did. We try to keep everyone up to speed on where we'll be so as not to get anybody accidentally shot, but—"

Carla cried softly, and Sam's face got a little puffy, but she held back the tears.

Luke continued, "I guess it didn't work this time. Wade, do you think this was an accident?"

"It's too early to tell, Luke. Do you remember seeing her rifle at the scene?"

"I haven't thought about it too much. I assumed one of the guys picked it up and would get it back to me whenever they got around to it. I don't remember seeing it in one of the trucks, but I doubt if I'd remember it if I did."

Wade went in a different direction with the questioning.

"Luke, you said Rachel was working on a big project. Do you know if the mayor supervised this project?"

"Rachel didn't say much about work other than she really enjoyed it."

"Do you know of anything else that would have connected the mayor to Rachel? The only reason I ask is that it's odd that someone dumped his body in Rachel's grave."

"You know, I've been thinking about that. The connection between the two of them. Obviously, the death of the mayor wasn't an accident. So if there is a connection, that means somebody deliberately murdered my little girl."

Carla couldn't take any more. She sobbed, her diaphragm expanding and contracting. Then she rose and went into the bedroom. Sam followed her while the men finished the conversation.

"That's kinda the way we have it sized up, Luke. We're

not sure there's a connection and nobody seems to know what the project they were working on was about."

Luke seemed deep in thought for a few seconds. Eventually, he looked at Wade.

"I hate to give out names without knowing if they're relevant. I don't want to get anyone in trouble if they had nothing to do with all of this."

Wade nodded.

"I understand. We're keeping this investigation real close, so we aren't giving out much information to anyone. So anything you tell us, we'll try to keep it between us."

Luke looked as he were torn between telling Wade and keeping some secret to himself. He took some time before speaking.

"I don't know the last names, but Rachel mentioned some people she was working with by their first names."

Here he paused, as if unsure whether to continue.

Wade nodded, but said nothing.

"She mentioned a fellow named 'Bruce' a lot, one named 'Frank' a good bit and 'John' and some others in passing. Another guy she just referred to as 'Bro', but she didn't mention him as much as the first three. It was as though he was an old boyfriend that she kept in touch with. She talked about Ed a good bit, but I believe she was referring to the mayor, but I could be wrong."

Wade was fairly certain that Bruce, Frank and John were the City Manager, the Purchasing Manager and the District Attorney and was also almost entirely certain that the 'Ed' Rachel mentioned was the mayor. He and Sam would have to look up the records at City Hall to see who 'Bro' might be. He could be one of the outside prominent citizens the group was working with.

The two men talked for another half hour without

coming to any conclusions, and Wade saw he would not glean much more useful information from Luke. He rose to leave and Luke walked to the bedroom door and knocked gently. Sam came out, but Carla remained inside the bedroom, not ready to face the world just yet without Rachel.

27 BE PERFECTLY STILL, SAM!

Inside the patrol car, Wade relayed their conversation to Sam, and she listened without saying much. She then told him that Carla hadn't revealed too much other than she could not find Rachel's phone the first day and then discovered it on the coffee table in the den the next day. She wasn't sure how she had missed it before, but in the haze of the aftermath of learning of the shooting, she guessed she had overlooked it.

They dropped by the Evergreen Café for some coffee and pie on the way back to the station. The reason wasn't because they were overly hungry, but they wanted to see if April would open up more without as many customers around in the mid-afternoon. When they got to the parking lot, they were relieved to see only a few cars next to the building. They entered and ordered two cups of Community Coffee and two slices of pecan pie.

Eventually, April stopped by their table and sat down in one of the empty chairs.

"How's the pie?" She asked cheerfully. "I made it myself this morning."

THE GIRL IN THE WOODS

"It's delicious, April. I believe you're a better cook than Gabe was." Sam wasn't stretching the truth on this. The food at the Evergreen Café was much better after Gabe's passing than it was when he was the main chef.

"Thanks, Sam. That means a lot to me. You know I couldn't have done it without you two and Uncle Gus."

"April, when we were here at lunch, you said something about everyone not playing by the same rules. We're wondering what you meant by that."

April looked around as though the entire room was full of people listening in while, in reality, they were virtually alone. She whispered, "The word is that you guys are getting into some business that you don't belong in, and some folks around here are upset about it."

Sam set her coffee cup on the table.

"What kind of business?"

"I don't know. But I know it has something to do with City Hall, and there's talk about getting you to back off. That's about all I know."

With that, April abruptly left the table and went back to the kitchen, leaving them in silence.

Sam finally smiled.

"I guess the good thing is that we won't have to order as many invitations for our wedding. Doesn't seem like we're going to be very popular around here for a while."

"We may have to elope if this keeps up." Wade was halfway serious. "I guess we'd better be careful until we get to the bottom of all of this."

Both Wade and Sam were consumed with the message they had received from April and weren't paying a lot of attention to their surroundings as they climbed back into the patrol car. This changed immediately as soon as their bodies hit the car seat. The unmistakable rattle of an

Eastern Diamondback rattlesnake filled the car with dread.

"Be perfectly still, Sam."

Wade froze, his eyes frantically searching for the source of the sound. They finally settled on the space between Sam's feet. On the floor under the brake pedal was a six-foot rattler with enough venom in his fangs to kill four adults the size of Wade. He knew if the reptile bit Sam, there would be very little chance of survival without immediate assistance.

Sam felt the snake crawl over her feet and then curl up right beside her left foot. Her nerves breaking, she whispered to Wade.

"Get out while he's over here."

Wade shook his head and almost imperceptibly reached for his cell phone. With only one finger moving, he dialed the Sheriff's office. Wanda answered the phone.

"Wanda, listen carefully. Get someone down to the Evergreen Café with a snake-bite kit and some rattlesnake antivenin. NOW!"

Wanda started to ask questions, but Wade hung up on her.

It wasn't long before the parking lot outside the café was full of cars with lights flashing and sirens wailing. The commotion made the snake nervous, its forked tongue flickering. Wade knew the snake had no ears and therefore couldn't hear anything, but the vibrations caused by the ruckus had the same effect and made the snake edgy. It curled up between Sam's legs and rattled, causing sweat to pour down Sam's face that she didn't dare wipe off.

One vehicle belonged to the City's Animal Control, and an Animal Control Agent brought out a long pole with a small clamp on the end. Wade had seen these used before, where the agent could grasp the snake right behind the head and control it without fear of being bitten.

"Okay, Sam. I'm going to get out and give them room to work without me being in the way. Are you okay with that?"

Sam barely nodded, the sweat now drenching her entire uniform. Wade felt an uncontrollable urge to make a lunge for the rattler and get it away from Sam, but knew in his soul that this situation was best left to those with experience in these situations. He eased the handle of the car door, supersensitive to every creak and squeak it made despite his best efforts. After what seemed like an eternity, the door was open and he barely moved, getting one foot and then the other outside the car onto the lot. He reached his hand out the door and was not totally surprised to see Gus there, holding it and helping him out of the car with the minimum of movement.

When he looked back at the car, his heart ached watching Sam sitting frozen with the big rattler still hissing between her legs. The Animal Control Agent eased up to the car and whispered to Sam.

"We've only got one chance at this, Sheriff. That bugger ain't gonna move on his own for a while and we need to get him before he gets you."

Sam barely nodded again, determined not to give the rattler a reason to strike.

The agent eased the pole into the open door side and advanced it ever so slowly toward the rattler. Even as he was advancing the pole, the agent calmly whispered to Sam.

"Sheriff, you just sit as tight as you can and leave it to us. Even if something goes wrong, just sit as tight as you can. We're gonna take care of you no matter what happens."

Even with his reassuring voice, Sam continued to pour sweat, even as she forced a smile to her lips to indicate she understood the agent. Wade strained to see the inside of the vehicle, unable to stand the tension overtaking him. Even when he had been shot at in previous cases, he had never been so nervous in his life, watching the most important person in his life in such peril. Goosebumps rose on each arm.

The end of the pole finally reached the snake's head. The clamp closed just behind his head, and the Agent quickly lifted the head above Sam's feet and yanked it toward him. He expertly twisted the pole so that the head was facing away from her legs as he dragged the snake out of the car. Everyone in the lot, and there were dozens of people by then, let out a gigantic sigh and clapped. Wade rushed around to the other side of the car, relief washing through his entire body.

"WOW! That was close!"

He heard Sam let out a huge breath and almost a giggle. That's when he heard the blood-curdling scream. He almost pulled the car door off its hinges and grabbed Sam and threw her out of the car. There had been a second snake under the seat the entire time and neither of them were aware of it.

The EMTs immediately grabbed Sam, cutting her uniform from below her knees to her ankle. They immediately applied a suction cup to the bite marks, sucking blood and poison from her body. They applied a tourniquet just above the bite and inserted a syringe of antivenin.

Wade knew he'd over-reacted, probably causing much more harm than good, and was now surprised to find his weapon drawn, aimed at the seat of the car. The second rattler had retreated under the seat. The old, wrinkled hand of Gus settled on the top of Wade's pistol, forcing it toward the ground.

"It's a little late for that, Son. They'll be able to reach in with that pole of theirs and get that bad boy now that Sam's out of the way and safe."

"Safe?"

That was the word that brought Wade back to this world. He turned and reached out to Sam, who was already on a stretcher with an IV in her arm that was feeding her more antibiotics directly into her veins.

"I'll be okay. Don't worry about me."

The EMT nudged Wade aside as he and his partner lifted the stretcher off the ground. He talked to Wade as he was working.

"We got most of the venom out and she's had a good dose of serum. But she's still gonna have some discomfort and swelling for the next couple of days. We normally wouldn't use the suction and the tourniquet, but it was only a second or two after she was bitten, so we thought that might be the best approach in this situation. She'll probably need to stay in the hospital for a day or two to make sure nothing gets to her heart."

Wade nodded, but the EMTs already had Sam loaded and were closing the door of the ambulance. Wade looked back and the Animal Control Agent was reaching the long pole underneath the car seat and was pulling out the other rattler that could have been a twin to the first one.

Wade's knees gave way and his exhausted body sank to the ground as tears flowed unashamedly down his cheeks. He was surprised when he felt the four arms surround his broad shoulders and give him tight hugs. He knew without looking up that the Thomas twins were there for him, their small breasts rubbing against his arms as he sat in the parking lot.

They are a seductive little pair, aren't they?

"Thanks, girls." Wade said, rising to his feet. "Why are you down here?"

"Are you kidding?" asked Mindy. "This is the biggest thing in Evergreen since Elvis died. I mean, how many other times are the Sheriff and her boyfriend trapped in a car with rattlesnakes? The whole town's talking about it."

Wade bent down and kissed Mindy on her forehead and turned to do the same with Mandy. To his surprise, Mandy reached up and kissed him on his lips.

"I'm not your sister."

Then Mindy reached around and kissed him on the lips.

"I'm not either," she said.

Wade looked around the parking lot. There were still cars parked all over the lot and lining the street for as far as he could see. He wondered how the image of the twins with their arms around him and kissing him would play publicly with the town folks. But his chief concern was for Sam.

Just then, someone shoved a microphone in his face. The female voice behind the microphone asked, "Mr. Dalton, I understand you and the Sheriff have a relationship."

Wade jerked back from the microphone.

"She's my fiancée, if that's what you mean by relationship."

"Who put the snakes in the police car? Can you tell us that?"

"I really don't know."

The FBI taught the former agent to keep his answers short and to the point.

"How is the Sheriff? Where was she bitten? Is she going to live?"

Wade tried to turn away from the reporter.

"I don't have all the answers, although I've been assured that she will recover."

The young lady stepped in front of him.

"If she is your fiancée, who were the two young ladies that were hugging you just then?"

"The Sheriff and I go to church with them and we were praying for her safety."

Wade hoped the Pastor and God would forgive him for this one little white lie.

"Now, I need to go to the hospital to check on Sam."

Wade moved away and then realized he didn't have his truck with him. He saw Gus in the crowd and went over to him.

"Can you give me a lift to the hospital?"

"You betcha, Pard! But I gotta stay and protect Sam's car until somebody can get here and check for fingerprints. You can borrow my patrol car as long as you promise not to leave any snakes in it."

Wade smiled. Even in times of distress, old Gus found something to laugh about.

Gus continued. "You didn't bother to get fingerprints off those snakes while you were spending all that time with them, did you?"

Wade shook his head.

"They weren't exactly in a cooperative mood, you could say."

"Sounds like most of my ex-wives. The only difference between them and the snakes is that them snakes only bite you once."

The crusty deputy handed over his keys to Wade.

Wade raced to Gus's patrol car and jumped in before anyone else could stop him and ask questions. He quickly sped out of the restaurant parking lot and toward the hospital. He hadn't gone far before he spotted the light blue sedan tailing the squad car. He didn't know if it was a coincidence that someone else decided to go to the hospital from the restaurant at the same time as him or if the car was following him. He decided to find out.

He turned right and then right again, directly away from the hospital on the next street. Sure enough, the blue sedan matched his turns. There was no doubt now that the car was following him. He quickly turned into a parking lot and made the full circle in the lot back to the only exit from the lot. The maneuver trapped the blue car behind him in the lot, but with the glare of the afternoon sun, he couldn't see who was in the front seat. Wade drew his pistol and yelled in his most commanding voice.

"Get out of the car slowly and I want to see some empty hands."

Both front doors of the blue sedan opened and the Thomas twins slowly emerged from the car. Mandy spoke first.

"You don't have to pull a gun on us to get a date. All you got to do is ask."

"What are you girls doing following me? Don't you know you might have been hurt?"

"We figure that we're the only ones you can trust." Mindy answered. "You don't have a lot of friends and you need one or two right now."

"Girls, this isn't a situation you need to be in. I don't know if you've noticed or not, but two people have been killed so far and Sam could have been killed this afternoon. You're only putting yourselves in danger by trying to follow me. I appreciate your kindness, but trying to keep up with you will just make my job harder to do."

"We won't get in your way, Wade. We'll make sure nothing happens to you. That's all."

Wade wasn't sure, but he believed this was Mindy speaking.

"Again, I really appreciate it, but I'd feel a lot more comfortable if I knew you girls were safe at home and not out chasing a murderer."

Mindy poked out her lips.

"We'll leave you alone for now, but call us if we can do anything to help you."

"I promise. If anything comes up, I'll call you."

28 SON, SOMEBODY'S GOTTA PAY FOR WHAT THEY DID TO SAM

H*E AWOKE WITH A START, FEELING FOUR ARMS AROUND* *him and small breasts rubbing his back and his chest.*

Seeing a Deputy standing outside of Sam's room at the hospital sent waves of relief through Wade's body. He stopped and talked with him briefly, reassured that someone would be inside or outside the room as long as Sam was there.

He stopped one step into the room, mildly surprised to find old Sheriff Cates sitting by his daughter's bed, but not at all surprised to find Connie there. Old Sam stood and shook his hand, and Connie gave him a huge long hug. Wade stepped by the bed and found Sam fast asleep from the sedatives administered by the hospital. Her swollen leg beneath her knee, bluish-purple with a tint of red. Wade hated to think about what may have been the results if the EMTs had not been on the scene and prepared to take action.

"Son, I'm glad you're okay. They tell me Sam will make a full recovery, but that it'll take a couple of days to a week for the swelling to go down."

The old Sheriff's words slurred, and he looked a lot older and more tired than Wade remembered.

"It's good to see you, Sheriff. You too, Connie. I just wish it was under different circumstances."

Wade had never spoken truer words. His heart was breaking, and he blamed himself for not making sure there was only one snake in the car. Every neophyte law enforcement official from any agency knows to make sure a scene is clear of danger instead of assuming an "All Clear". He had not done that and the consequences lay on the bed in front of him because of his carelessness. He wondered how much Old Sam blamed him for his oversight.

"Son, who did this?"

Old Sam was terse and wasn't in the mood for political correctness.

"I honestly don't know, Sheriff. What has Sam told you about the murder investigation so far?"

Wade knew that Sam would have conferred with her father, who had been the sheriff for over thirty years and had only recently stepped down. She got elected primarily on the name recognition that he had earned since they were both known as 'Sam', his for Samuel and hers for Samantha.

Old Sam told Wade that Sam had kept him fairly up to speed on the investigation, but he preferred that Wade go over the entire investigation. None of them were going anywhere soon.

Wade went through the entire investigation from the time he arrived on the gravel road in the National Forest until the night's unfortunate ending. He omitted the episodes with the Thomas twins, including the fact they found the license at City Hall. This was a fact that he and Sam had told no one so far.

Old Sam listened intently to Wade while staring at his

daughter lying on the hospital bed beside him. His gray stubble of a beard seemed to get shaggier and turn whiter as the facts emerged.

"Son, I know the evidence is leading you to City Hall and it would probably lead me there too. But I'll be amazed if someone down there is responsible for all of this."

Wade replied with respect.

"That's all I've got to go on, Sheriff. Everything pointing down there with this group of men and whatever project they've been working on."

"I'm not disagreeing with you. But when you've been around that rat's nest as long as I have, you'll find out there's nothing but cowards down there. Every one of them is a greedy pig looking out for themselves and nothing else. And I don't know a single one of them that could plan their own funeral, much less a major project. But I could be wrong. Maybe somebody down there finally grew a pair and learned something. I just don't know."

"I don't either, Sheriff. And that's the only place that has any information that we might uncover to get to the bottom of all of this."

Sheriff Cates rubbed his grizzled chin.

"Son, somebody's gotta pay for what they did to Sam, as well as the other girl and Ed. I don't care how long it takes; somebody's gotta pay for it."

"Sheriff, I'm gonna do everything in my power to make sure it happens. Which brings me to a favor I need to ask."

"What do you need?"

"So far I've been helping as Sam's unofficial assistant. Is there any way you can get me on in an official capacity?"

The old Sheriff smiled.

"Hold on just one second."

He picked up the cell phone and made a call, speaking

so quietly that Wade couldn't hear him. The phone call didn't last three minutes.

"Congratulations, Son. You are now a Special Investigator for Federal District Judge Ray Whittington. In that capacity you have the authority of the Federal Government behind you which will override any of this local BS that might try to stand in your way. Pick up your badge at the Federal Building tomorrow morning."

"Thanks, Sheriff. That'll help, particularly with the local DA. He doesn't want to cooperate very much."

"You're welcome. If there's anything else you need, let me know. I still have a little influence around here. Why don't you get some rest? Connie and I can handle sitting with her tonight. You need to be here when she's awake and can see you."

"Thanks, Sheriff. If she wakes up, please call me."

Wade stood up, hugged Connie, and shook hands with Sheriff Cates before leaving. He knew Sam was in excellent hands with these two watching over her.

29 SO MUCH FOR SECURITY

When he got back to the Plantation, he saw the blue sedan parked in front of his office.

How did the twins get past the gate? The yawn told him he was too tired to care. He found the twins in the kitchen fixing themselves a snack.

"How did you get the gate open?" He asked without hesitation.

"No problem. Mindy climbed over it and walked past the motion activator on the other side. It's really not that hard to figure out."

Somehow, Wade had never considered that possibility, but now it seemed obvious to him.

So much for security.

"Well, I'm too tired to care right now. You girls enjoy yourselves tonight and we'll talk in the morning."

"We got hungry with all the excitement. Hope you don't mind us making ourselves at home in your kitchen."

"With you two, I expect everything, anything and nothing. All at the same time."

"All right. Sweet dreams, Ranger."

Wade thought this was Mandy speaking, but in the early morning hours, he wasn't sure and it really didn't matter to him.

He went to his bedroom, got undressed and fell into bed without hesitation, almost instantly falling into a deep, peaceful sleep. He awoke with a start, feeling four arms around him and small breasts rubbing his back and his chest. Sure enough, Mindy and Mandy were in bed with him wearing only their panties and flimsy tee shirts. He jumped up with a jolt, trying to pull on his jeans and shirt at the same time.

"What the hell are ya'll doing in here?"

He was talking way too loud, but he had been caught unprepared for the morning surprise.

"Sleeping with you, Detective Ranger. Just sleeping, nothing else."

"Why—What—?"

Wade fumbled with his words in his confused state.

"We promised you last night that we would make sure nothing happened to you. How could we do that if we weren't with you?"

"But you aren't wearing any clothes."

"Yes, we are. We're wearing what we always wear to bed. That's the only way we've ever dressed to go to sleep. It's not like you've never seen a girl before, Detective Ranger."

Mindy pulled her clothes back on while Mandy took her time. Wade had trouble comprehending the unabashed nature of these twins. The inhibitions that had been ingrained in him as a child were completely missing in the girls. Maybe he was just getting older, but he doubted that most young girls acted like these two.

'A seductive little pair' was more apt than either Sam or

I could have imagined.

"Okay, girls. I appreciate you looking out for me, but I can't have you running around here half-naked. And I can't have you getting in my bed, with or without me. Do you understand that?"

"Yep, Ranger. We'll just have to figure out other ways to protect you." Mindy paused. "And Sam."

"Look, I'm perfectly capable of taking care of myself and Sam. I don't need you guys following me around."

"If that's true, how did you end up in a car full of snakes with her?"

Wade just shook his head, not knowing how to answer that question without looking foolish. Despite his admonishment, Wade had trouble not glancing at Mandy, who still had not put on a shirt.

Maybe I'm too old-fashioned.

"Look," Mandy said. "We're worried about you, but we're more worried about Dad. He's started drinking more since last Saturday, and now he's not sleeping at night. At the office, he's huddled up with John Grimes and Frank Davis all day. Nobody knows what they're talking about, but most people assume it has something to do with the murders. We need you to find out what is going on around here."

"Okay, I understand, but please keep your clothes on. I have enough distractions without having two attractive young ladies running around half-naked. Now, I have a few questions for you."

Mandy put a shirt on, and Mindy pulled on a pair of pants. The twins followed him to the kitchen. They sat down at the breakfast table and looked eagerly at Wade.

"When your father, John and Frank meet, does anyone else meet with them?"

Both girls shook their heads.

"Do you know if they have any frequent meetings with someone named 'Bro' at City Hall? I don't know his first or last name, only that Rachel referred to him as 'Bro'."

"There are a lot of guys that Dad calls '*Bro*' or '*Bubba*' down there, but usually because he can't remember their real first name. There's a couple we call 'Bro', but we may be the only ones that do."

Mandy's forehead creased, trying to recall anyone of significance.

"Wait, there's a City Councilman whose last name is Brogan. We don't know him very well, but most people down at the Hall call him 'Bro', I believe."

"Excellent, now we're making progress. What do you know about Mr. Brogan?"

"Not much. He drops by the Hall now and then. I've never seen him meet with Dad, but he may have. He mostly hangs around Frank Davis and talks about upcoming bids for city projects."

"Was he close to Rachel?"

"Not that I know of. Like I said; He doesn't come down there that often, and when he does, he doesn't stay too long. I never saw Rachel giving him any special treatment, if you know what I mean."

Mindy smiled as she said this.

"I know what you mean. Can you two find out what Frank Davis was working on with Mr. Brogan? I'll find out what I can through my sources. But don't arouse anyone's suspicions and stay out of other people's beds."

The girls giggled and finished their breakfast. Later, after they left to head back to town, Wade checked on the animals in the breeding pens, and then headed into town to check on Sam.

30 I SWEAR HE HAD MORE HANDS
THAN AN ALL-NIGHT POKER GAME

ENTERING THE HOSPITAL ROOM, HE COULD HEAR THE laughter coming from Sam and Connie. They became quiet as he entered the room, and he wondered what they were laughing about.

"Good morning, girls. How is my favorite girl feeling today?"

Connie jumped up and gave him a big hug.

"I'm feeling great. How about you?"

Wade turned a little red and looked at Sam.

"Don't look at me, Agent Dalton. You're the one that stepped into that one."

"Okay, how are my two most favorite girls, today?"

Sam giggled. "Do you mean us or the Thomas twins?"

Wade turned even more ashen as he wondered if Sam and Connie knew the Thomas twins had spent the night at the Plantation.

How am I going to explain this one?

Sam continued to giggle.

"Everyone told us how you were *'praying'* with them

right after the incident last night. We didn't know they knew how."

Thank goodness.

As difficult as that was to explain, it was better than explaining that he woke up in bed with both of the twins. That was a subject that he hoped he'd never have to discuss with these two sisters.

"Well, for your information, Sheriff; We were praying for you. But now that I can tell you don't appreciate that, I'll tell them not to do that anymore."

Wade figured a little lie couldn't hurt right now.

Sam and Connie grinned at Wade's discomfort.

"Look, the swelling in my leg has gone down. It's still red and blue and purple, but at least it's almost normal size."

"Great! Any lingering effects?"

"The doctor said he wants to keep me here tonight to make sure the poison is completely out of my system, but he thinks I should be out of here tomorrow morning."

Wade cupped her hand in his. "That's wonderful. I was worried about you. As small as you are, I was afraid the poison would overtake you."

Connie nudged next to Wade. "The doc said the EMTs did some quick thinking using the suction and the tourniquet. He doesn't recommend those anymore, but with the short time between the bite and the treatment, it was exactly the thing to do."

"Remind me to send them a thank-you card. It sure didn't take long for the whole town to find out about it. That parking lot was jam-packed."

Sam grimaced. "Wade, you've got to remember. There are no secrets in Evergreen."

Wade started to remind her that there were at least four: the shooter in the murder of Rachel, the identity of the murderer of Ed, the facts about the big project seemingly in the middle of all this and the identity of the person who put the snakes in Sam's car. But he decided now was not the time for that entire discussion.

"Do either of you know who around here would have access to a couple of rattlers? Someone might have been able to catch one on short notice, but catching two timber rattlers at one time doesn't sound normal."

"It wouldn't be that unusual, but this time of the year, they're hard to find. Most of them hole up and don't get out much."

Connie should know since she and Sam roamed through the woods at the Plantation when they were kids.

Sam thought for a few minutes before saying anything.

"There is one of those snake-handling churches out in the country, but I don't remember the name. Dad took us by there one time when a kid got bit in one of their services and the mother was thinking about pressing charges, but changed her mind before we got there."

Wade had heard of these churches, but had never been to a snake-handling service; nor did he have any desire to go to one now after his experience with Sam.

"Do you think you could find it again, Sam?"

"I think so. Between me and Connie, we should be able to get you close after we ask Dad where it is and if it's still in business. A lot of them quit doing the handling services after the publicity a few years ago about all the deaths. In fact, I think several preachers ended up in jail."

"Okay. Let's check on it when you get out of here and able to move around without an old-lady wheel chair."

Wade laughed and ducked. The pillow missed him by inches.

"By the way, girls. Do either of you know much about a City Councilman named Brogan?"

"Yeah," Connie answered. "He's a slime-ball."

"What makes you say that?"

"One year when I was a cheerleader at the high school, all the councilmen were asked to escort us on the field during halftime of one game. I had the misfortune of having Mr. Brogan as my escort. I swear he had more hands than an all-night poker game. Before halftime was over, he'd felt every part of my body at least twice."

"Did you say anything?"

"I didn't have to. When we came off the field, Dad met him in the end zone and they went behind the concession stand to talk. I saw him three days later, and he still had two black eyes and a swollen lip from that conversation with Dad. I don't think he's been back to a football game since."

Sam's eyes widened.

"You know what? He used to raise snakes as a hobby. I remember him calling Dad to see if he needed a license or anything. Dad told him he hoped one of them would bite him in the ass and hung up on him. But I don't know if he raised rattlesnakes or not."

Wade nodded.

"Maybe I should go pay a visit to Mr. Brogan."

Sam shook her head.

"Wade, you don't have any authority to investigate this right now. You'll have to wait until I can go with you."

Wade grinned.

"Well, Sheriff. I have the authority."

He showed her the badge he'd picked up from Judge Whittington on the way to the hospital.

"I'm now a Federal Investigator assigned to your case, thanks to your Father and his friend, the Judge. I believe this badge will supersede any authority of a mere County Sheriff."

He ducked another pillow as it whizzed by his ear.

"Now, Sheriff. I wouldn't want to arrest you in your condition for an assault on a federal law enforcement officer."

The next pillow caught him square in the face.

"But to show you I intend to work with the local authorities, I'll wait for you to get out of here."

He said as he ducked the glass that was about half full of water. *At least the snake bite didn't weaken her arm strength,* he thought as he grinned at her.

Connie was keeping her mind on the more important business as the two of them engaged in more horseplay.

"What would it gain Brogan to slip some snakes in your car?"

Sam threw an ice cube at Wade before turning to Connie.

"I don't know, Little Sis. Maybe we got closer than we know in one of the interrogations and somebody doesn't want us to find out any more about this deal."

"Or he still held a grudge against your Dad and thought this might be a good time to get even without arousing any suspicion of him."

Wade had assumed that the snakes and the murders were connected, but wasn't as sure now.

"The key thing right now is for you to get some rest so you can get out of this place tomorrow."

"Yes, Sir!" she answered as she threw the last ice cube she could find at him as he ducked out of the door. His phone beeped as he was leaving the hospital indicating a text message. The message was from Mindy and asked him to meet the twins for lunch at the Evergreen Café.

31 THEY WERE IN THAT ODD STAGE OF LIFE BETWEEN CHILDHOOD AND ADULTHOOD

WADE GREETED APRIL AND THE WAITRESSES WHEN HE got to the café and asked for a seat in the far corner where he would have some privacy. He was there for about twenty minutes sipping on some iced tea before the twins arrived. They had stopped by their house because now each dressed exactly the same in a light blue top with a dark blue skirt and black heels. They even had on matching jewelry; A silver cross necklace, diamond stud earrings and a silver bracelet. Wade had to focus hard to tell them apart.

"We found out some stuff about Mr. Brogan, just like you asked us to."

Wade was fairly certain that Mindy was talking.

"Do you want to know what we've found out so far?"

"Absolutely. Would you like to order something first?"

"We told the waitress on the way back here to bring us the lunch special since we've got to get back to the office. Can't waste any time."

The twins had evidently found a personnel file on William "Bill" Brogan somewhere in City Hall. He was in his mid-forties, married three times. He was now single and ran a Feed and Seed store on the outskirts of town and served on the City Council for his second three-year term. His hobbies included horse racing, gardening and raising exotic pets. His exotic pet collection included some snakes, but the data in the file was not specific enough to determine if the snake collection included any Eastern Diamondback Rattlers. The financial statement in the file listed his assets in excess of three million dollars, although these were not individually named in the file. Wade wondered how a Feed and Seed store could generate enough revenue to provide that kind of net worth.

The only connection to Rachel in the file was a notation of one meeting that included both Bill and Rachel along with Frank Davis, the Purchasing Manager and several others. The meeting lasted for two hours, but there were no notes or minutes of the meeting.

"Excellent job!"

Wade complimented the twins as they enjoyed the daily lunch special: catfish fillets and fries.

"You guys didn't get into any trouble or cross any lines getting this, did you?"

"Nope. But we've made a new friend in the Personnel Department."

Both of the twins giggled, and Wade knew he was better off not knowing the details.

Wade really liked the twins. Not in a romantic or sensual way, but more in a little sister kind of relationship. They were in that odd stage of life between childhood and adulthood that made them so sure of themselves that they had no fear. He once felt that way when he was their age, until he later discovered the realities of life.

Despite their idiosyncrasies, Wade thought the twins had something going for them that most people never have;

An inner belief that what they were doing would help someone else. Here, they were desperately trying to help their father avoid the consequences of having a relationship with a girl not much older than themselves. They didn't judge him or think less of him for his indiscretion and only wanted to help him through this ordeal.

Wade watched the slender frames of the twins easily wind their way through the tables and noticed the sharp contrast of their slimness to the prevalent obesity surrounding them. Their sleek bodies and graceful manner reminded him of the delicate movements of the whitetail deer at the Plantation crossing an oak-lined creek bottom. Both images evoked a smile.

32   WHO WAS OTIS ANDERSON?

After lunch, Wade dropped in on the Sheriff's office to find out if Gus had made any progress in his investigation of the source of the rattlesnakes. He waved at Wanda and continued back to the cluttered world that Gus called his office.

He stuck his head inside.

"Anything new on the snakes?"

"Hey, Pard. Come on in and sit down. Just push those papers over here. I've been meaning to get to them, but don't have the time right now."

Wade grabbed the pile of papers in the chair and looked around for a place to set them. He finally stacked them on another pile of papers, undoubtedly on Gus's agenda to peruse at a later date.

"We've got news, but I don't know what to make of it."

Wade settled in the chair.

"Whatcha ya mean, Gus?"

Gus picked up a file laying on top of the others.

"We found a fingerprint on the driver's window on

Sam's car, like someone was trying to jimmy the window down, you know."

"Great, that should help. Any luck finding out who the print belongs to?"

Gus held the fingerprint card up.

"We know exactly who it belongs to. Guy's name is Otis Anderson."

"Who's Otis Anderson? I've never heard of him."

Gus put his hand up to his chin.

"The question is not 'Who is Otis Anderson?'. The question is 'Who was Otis Anderson?' Seems like old Otis died two weeks ago and was buried in the Shady Grove Cemetery."

Wade sank in his chair.

"Are you sure it's the same Otis Anderson?"

"Yep. We interviewed the preacher and the family. It's the same guy. The family said he was deathly afraid of snakes and wouldn't touch one with a ten-foot stick."

Wade moved his chair over a little.

"Why were his fingerprints on file? Was he convicted of something?"

"Nope. Seems like he used to work in the financial industry, a stockbroker or something. Anyway, part of the requirements was to get fingerprinted, and they put it in the system. He'd never been in trouble with the law at all."

"How'd he die?"

"Long bout with cancer. According to his widow, old Otis smoked a couple of packs of cancer sticks every day for his entire life. It finally caught up with him and for the last six months, he's been pretty much bed-ridden. There's no way he put the snakes in Sam's car. How his prints got on the window is anybody's guess."

Wade was silent, thinking about the planted evidence at the scene in the National Forest. As he had predicted to Sam, the peanut hulls had produced a DNA sample, but so far that sample could not be matched to anyone in the system. The shoe print found close to the beech tree was made by a size thirteen wading boot. The manufacturer of the wading boot didn't have a distributor in Evergreen and had no way of tracing all the size thirteen boots it'd sold over the years across the United States. Both leads had produced nothing of value to the investigation.

Wade smiled.

"He made a mistake, Gus."

Gus looked up from the file.

"Who made a mistake, Pard?"

"The shooter. He made a mistake."

Gus shook his head.

"Pard, you've got to speak English if you want me to follow what you're saying. Sounds more like gibberish right now."

Wade put one hand on his chin.

"Gus, we figured, at least Sam and I figured the boot print and the peanut hulls were planted to mislead the investigation. We couldn't trace them back to identify anyone because they weren't in the system. The same is true of this fingerprint. The shooter planted it because he believed it we couldn't trace it back to anyone since the man it belonged to was dead. The shooter didn't know his print was in the system."

Gus nodded. "So now we just have to find out who borrowed one of old Otis' prints either before or after he died. Since Otis was only seventy years old and this print could have been lifted from him any time during his seventy years on this old earth, that'll narrow down the list of suspects, all right."

"You're right. That print didn't even have to be lifted from Otis. It could have been transferred from almost anything he touched. A glass of water, a tool, anything. It could've been taken from his file. I assume the file is at City Hall."

"Yep, that's an affirmative, Pard. They keep the originals down there in storage, just in case anyone ever asks to see them."

Wade put both hands on top of his head.

"Dang it, Gus. This might not be a mistake. This guy just might be smarter than all of us put together."

"What do you mean, Wade?"

"How long do you think it would take to track down all the places that the print could have been transferred from? The files down at the Hall, the hospital, his home, his friends, the morgue, the funeral home and dozens of other possibilities?"

Gus chuckled.

"Not more than six months if we assigned our entire force to it. I guess I see what you mean."

Wade stared at the ceiling.

"How about the snakes, Gus? Any idea where they came from?"

"Nope, we scanned them and neither one had a chip in them. If they were pet snakes, they should have had an RFID chip planted in them somewhere, but we didn't find one."

"Could someone remove the chips?"

Gus laid the file aside.

"Sure they could. And we're still waiting for you to volunteer to get them out of the cage and ask them to be real still while you look for a small slit that may or may not have held a computer chip at one time."

Wade laughed.

"I believe we should leave that job for Sam when she gets out of the hospital. I've got a feeling she's gonna get those snakes to be real still if she gets a chance."

"That'd be okay with me, Pard. Those things give me the jitters. As far as I'm concerned, they'd make a good rattlesnake boudin or jambalaya."

"Wouldn't that be poetic justice? They bite her and then she eats them. Then everybody's happy."

"Except the snakes."

33 I REALLY THINK SHE WAS TIRED OF THE WHOLE CHARADE AND WANTED A WAY OUT

THE HUNTER FOUND HIS PREY GETTING MORE AND more wary. He would try one and then another of his targets, but every time he thought he might have an opening, the predator found them protected under enclosed parking areas that he couldn't successfully penetrate without being seen. The hunter was not skilled at breaking alarm codes, so he had to rely on finding his prey in the open where they were easily accessible to him.

Today he was sitting outside of City Hall, disguised as an overweight senior adult, complete with a graying beard and a Panama hat. He saw several people he recognized, but none of them recognized him. He had become adept with the costume make-up kits he'd ordered over the internet. With these kits, he could add a scar, make his eyebrows thicker or change his complexion so much that even his closest friends couldn't recognize him.

He'd been sitting on the park bench in front of the Hall when two young ladies suddenly appeared out of nowhere and sat on the adjoining bench carrying their bags of lunch. The hunter kept his head down and closed his eyes, but he immediately recognized the Thomas twins. He also knew that most girls the age of the twins ignored the older generation as if they didn't exist. These two were no exception to the rule as he discretely listened to the conversation between them.

The twins were excited about working with the ex-FBI agent and his girlfriend, the County Sheriff, on the investigation of the two murders and the incident involving the snakes.

"Who do you think did it?" Mindy asked her twin.

Mandy grabbed half a ham sandwich out of her bag.

"We know it wasn't Dad, so that eliminates him. That leaves Mr. Grimes, Mr. Davis, and Mr. Brogan as the only suspects left. It has to be one of them."

Mindy pulled half a ham sandwich out of her bag.

"I'm thinking it's Mr. Brogan. He lives out in the country where he could get the snakes with no one knowing about them."

Mandy took a bite.

"I don't know. I don't like Mr. Grimes. Remember the time he grabbed your ass at the reception for the mayor. He was also involved with Rachel at the end. I didn't see Mr. Brogan together with Rachel that much."

Mindy took an identical bite out of her sandwich.

"I agree. But Rachel had a way of doing things without everyone else finding out about it. Dad still doesn't know she was sleeping with everybody at the Hall. It would kill him if he found out."

Mandy picked a carrot out of her bag.

"You're right. Since Mama left, I never saw him so happy as when Rachel came along. I don't even care if she was our age. She gave Dad a reason to live again."

Mindy grabbed an identical carrot.

"That's why I know he couldn't have had anything to do with her shooting. He'd give anything to get her back alive again."

"Why do you think Rachel did what she did? I mean, she could have had any of those guys or anybody else she wanted. Why do you think she slept around with all of those old guys down there?"

"Your guess is as good as mine. I don't know if it was the money, the prestige, the adventure or what? But do you remember the last time we had lunch with her?"

Mandy nodded while finishing her sandwich.

"I do. She seemed like she was ready to get out of all of it, at least to me."

Mindy devoured the rest of her sandwich.

"Me, too. I really think she tired of the whole charade and wanted a way out."

"I guess she found it, but not the way she wanted."

A tear came to the corner of the hunter's eye and, despite his best efforts to contain it, rolled down his cheek. The facts the sisters had and the accuracy of the list of suspects surprised him. Someone was smarter than he had given them credit, and he would have to adjust his plan if he was to be successful.

A chilly gust of wind sent the twins scurrying back inside the office building and reminded the hunter that winter was not that far away. The darkening skies cast a dim parlor over the immediate area and further added to his already falling demeanor.

Why did those two twins have to come out here on this date and sit on the very bench next to me of all the days possible? Why did they have to bring up all the other men Rachel slept with? Why did they have to mention Rachel's increasing sadness with her situation right before she died?

Now the hunter felt his anger growing against the twins.

How dare they talk about Rachel as if she were just another person? Rachel was special and nobody had the right to talk about her like that.

An inspiration hit the hunter in mid-thought. But first, he had much work to do and not much time to do it. He rose off the bench and was quickly striding across the lot in front of the building. Then he remembered the way he was disguised and slowed to a creaky waddle. He hoped no one had noticed.

34 OKAY, GUS. LET ME HAVE IT

Wade was in high spirits on this cold frosty morning, even as the sun rose above the horizon. The cool weather stimulated the rousing whistles of the bull elk, signifying their readiness to mate with any of the cow elk available. The deep roar of the European elk, more commonly known as the red stag, contrasted with the high-pitched whistles of their domestic cousins, but had the same meaning. Wade was constantly amazed at how similar the North American elk and the European red stag were, but how different their mating calls were. He often wondered if the difference resulted from the unique slight physiological characteristics of each animal or if they learned to call the opposite sex in different ways on each side of the big pond. Either way, he enjoyed the symphony of nature from the elk and the stags, along with the almost comical grunts of the Chinese Pere David deer, which looked like someone had tried to put a mule and a deer together without a lot of success. The subtle grunts of the whitetail, the fallow bucks and the axis bucks were much less noticeable to humans, but just as effective among their own species.

Unlike most of the other deer families except for the axis deer, the lowly Muntjac bucks will mate any time of the year. Known as the barking deer, the population of the Muntjac, native to southeast Asia, is quickly expanding in England and may soon become the most populous of all the deer there. A few escapees from a park in 1925 just kept procreating and with no hunting of them allowed for many years were now expanding into Scotland and Ireland. Their little barks didn't fit in with the rest of the deer, but brought a smile to Wade every time he heard one.

Wade's peaceful solitude was broken by the elk bugling tone of his cell phone, the only ring tone he was willing to pay extra from the long list available. It was Gus.

"Hey, Pard. Did I catch you with your pants on?"

Wade chuckled.

"Barely, Gus. What's got you up so early in the morning?"

"Son, I told you I gave up sleeping. I found out it's bad for my health. Anyway, we got one of those anonymous tips that I know you love, but this one sounds like it has some substance. So I thought I'd pass it on to you."

Wade sighed.

"Okay, Gus. Let me have it."

"The tip came in on one of those throwaway phones. You know, the kind you buy at the dollar store and prepay for so many minutes of call time. There's no way to trace them. Anyway, this guy or gal, we're not sure which because the caller disguised his voice. He said the snakes tossed in Sam's car came from the Blue Heaven Nature Church on Route 43 and bought by Councilman Bill Brogan in the last few days. They said we would find a receipt in the big Bible on the altar at the foot of the podium in the church."

Wade covered his eyes with his hands.

"And I guess he also told you where we could find a copy of the receipt at Brogan's place."

"Actually, he said we'd probably find it in the glove compartment of his truck. How d'ya know?"

"Just a lucky guess. Sam should get out of the hospital this morning. I'll see if she wants to take a ride out to the countryside."

Wade remained on the back porch of the lodge for another hour, trying to place all the pieces of the puzzle together. But some just didn't fit into the logical scheme that he was accustomed to analyzing. He was down to three or four suspects and all of them showed signs of fear of each other. One of them had to be guilty, or at least it seemed that way to Wade. Yet, Gus handed him a suspect on a golden platter and it didn't feel right to Wade. Maybe, after seeing more of the evidence against Bill Brogan, the ex-agent would feel differently.

Sometimes he wished life were as simple as that of the elk cow. Just mate with the biggest bull in the herd and that choice alone will give the herd the best chance to survive. In Wade's life, the choices were much more complex, but in this case lives were at stake. The more time it took to figure out who was behind these murders, the more other lives were at risk and the onus fell on him to solve the mystery.

35 YOU GUYS DON'T HAVE MUCH FAITH, DO YOU?

Wade waited by the front doors of the hospital as the nurse wheeled Sam down to the exit. He knew the policy of the hospital was to bring every discharged patient to the front in a wheelchair, so it didn't surprise him at all, but he still didn't understand the logic. If a patient could walk to the front door, why not let them?

"So how does the prettiest Sheriff in the world feel today?" He greeted Sam with a hug.

Sam walked with a noticeable limp. "Ready to get out of this place. Don't get me wrong. They treated me really well, but it's still a hospital."

Wade grinned. "Since you've been pent up for the last three days, why don't we take a drive in the country?"

Sam settled into the cab of the pickup.

"I don't suppose this drive in the country has anything to do with the tip Gus gave you, now would it?"

Wade sighed.

"So he told you, huh? And that was going to be my get-out-of-the-hospital present to you."

"At least it's cheaper than the flowers you forgot to send me while I was in there."

Wade's face turned red. He'd meant to send some flowers to Sam's room, but every time he thought about it, something else happened that took his mind off of it. Now, three days had elapsed, and he still didn't have any flowers for Sam. Wade's grin quickly faded.

"Relax, Wade. I'm just kidding."

She reached over and gave Wade a long, deep kiss.

"Besides, I had so much fun eating the candy you didn't send that I didn't have enough time to appreciate the flowers I didn't get from you."

She laughed as he stumbled to make up a good excuse.

"I didn't want to tempt you with candy, Sam. That wouldn't be fair, with you cooped up in that hospital room and bored with nothing to do except get fat."

Wade could see that, if anything, Sam had lost a pound or two from her petite frame, but he had to get back on the offensive. He also knew that almost every girl around Sam's age was sensitive to potential weight gain.

Sam called a truce by laying her head on his shoulder.

"Shut up and drive."

The directions Wade received to get to the Blue Heaven Nature Church weren't at all clear to him, but Sam interpreted most of the twists and turns necessary to find it. They ended up on an old logging road intruding deep into the dense forest. When they came to a swift flowing creek, Wade got out of his pickup to look.

"There's a rock bottom, so we should be able to make it without too much trouble," he said after surveying the situation.

"And if we don't?"

"Then the truck will end up somewhere down the creek

and one of us is gonna have a long walk back to town. And with you using your leg as an excuse, I'm guessing that's gonna be me." Wade chagrined.

"Good guess."

Sam laughed as he got back inside the pickup.

Wade eased the pickup across the steadily flowing creek and up the other bank without a lot of trouble. He surmised that there must be times after a hard rain that the creek would be too high to cross for the congregation of the remote church.

The trees closed in on each side of the old logging road, creating a foreboding atmosphere that overshadowed Wade with an eerie sense of peril. He could feel the tension in his body mounting as each subtle sound in the forest and movement among the trees caught his attention. Sam edged a little closer to him on the seat of the pickup. The whistling of the wind permeated through the treetops as though the spirits of the forest could not rest, further heightened the edginess of the young couple confined in the truck. Wade doubted the wisdom of coming out to this remote church with Sam.

When they broke out of the shadows of the old logging road into a small clearing, the couple both let out long sighs, as if each had been holding their breath without realizing it. In the middle of the clearing sat an old whitewashed building with the name 'Blue Heaven' above the door. Wade pulled the pickup right in front of the door and they waited for a few minutes before getting out of the truck.

Wade, with Sam limping closely behind him, walked up to the door and softly knocked. There was no answer from within the church. Wade tried to open the door only to find it locked.

"If you guys'll drop those guns you're carrying and step back to your truck, then we can talk."

The voice surprised both Wade and Sam as they whirled toward the side of the building, only to face the twin barrels of a long shotgun. They had no choice but to comply with the simple command, and each of them dropped their pistol on the steps leading up to the door of the church.

"You're making a mistake. I'm a Federal Investigator and this is the County Sheriff. We don't appreciate being held at gunpoint. You could go to jail for this, you know."

Wade put on a much braver front than he felt inside.

"Ya'll turn around and face the truck."

Wade and Sam complied, not knowing if they would ever get out of this little clearing alive. They could hear a scuffling sound as their weapons were being picked up. The man holding the shotgun then stepped up behind Wade and patted him down from head to toe, checking for any additional weapons he might have. Finding none, he stepped behind Sam.

"Ma'am, I'm going to ask you if you have any more guns on you. I don't want to disrespect you by touching you all over."

Sam reached inside her pocket and pulled out her Sheriff's badge.

"This is the only thing I have. You can see I'm the Sheriff of Evergreen County, and my name is Sam Cates. This is Wade Dalton, and he's a Special Investigator for the Federal government. We're looking into the murders of Rachel Chastain and Ed Moore."

"Sorry, Ma'am. Ya'll can have your guns back now."

They turned around to find a young man in his late teens with his arms outstretched with each of their guns in his hands. They took and holstered the revolvers and waited for the young man to decide what to do next.

"We ain't murdered nobody up here. We just ain't comfortable with strangers wandering around, that's all."

Wade could see the discomfort in the young man.

"What's your name?"

"I'm Johnny. Johnny Raymond. I'm the preacher's boy. Jack Raymond. He's my dad. He's the preacher here. He's been the preacher here for more than thirty years, even 'fore I was born."

"Is your dad around? Can we talk with him?"

"Nope. He ain't here right now. He's down at the sawmill working. He should be back tonight after he finishes working."

"Well, can we ask you a few questions, then?"

"No, Sir. I don't do good with questions and all. I ain't got a lot of schooling, you know. Mama, she's been trying to teach me herself, but I reckon I ain't cut out to be no bookworm."

Wade peered at the young man. "Is your Mama around?"

"No, Sir. But my little sister is here. She's better with questions than I am."

"Where can we find your sister?"

"Oh, she's already found you. She's had her shotgun pointed at you since you drove up here."

Johnny pointed toward the roof of the little church.

All Wade could see was the top of some beet red hair and the muzzle of a single-barreled shotgun when he looked up to where Johnny was pointing.

How could I have missed that when we drove up?

"Ma'am, can you come down here and talk to us?"

There was no answer, but the muzzle of the gun and

the red hair disappeared from view. A minute later, the front door of the church opened and a young girl no older than fifteen stepped out. Wade almost gasped when he saw the figure on the little girl. Skin and bones from her head to her toes, except for her breasts. She had the largest breasts Wade had ever seen on any live female, no matter what size or age they were.

The lad sidled next to his sister.

"That's all right, Mister. Everybody stares at Sarah's boobs. They got to be the biggest ones in the county. Dad says she got that way because we couldn't afford cow's milk when she was a baby, so Mama fed her with pig's milk. He says if every girl drank pig's milk when they was a baby, then they would all look like Sarah."

Johnny showed no hesitance in describing his sister's unusual physique.

Wade regained a little of his composure. "Miss Sarah, would it be all right if we asked you a few questions?"

"Sure." Sarah had a feminine, almost refined voice totally unlike her brother. "Are you two married?"

Sam answered, "Not yet, but we're engaged. We just haven't had time to plan the wedding and set a date yet."

"Why don't ya'll come in and we can talk inside?"

Sarah unlocked the door to the church and stepped inside.

"Johnny, you stay out here and keep watch in case somebody else shows up."

Wade wasn't sure what to expect when they entered the church, but was surprised to find it looked like most other small churches he had ever attended. There were a dozen rows of pews, the front altar with a few chairs for a choir behind it and the piano off to the side up front. On the drive up to the church, Wade had imagined a den full of creepy crawling snakes, but there was not a snake anywhere.

Sarah went to the front of the church and sat on the piano bench and motioned for them to sit on the first pew. She looked at Sam.

"Are you the one that got bit by that rattler?"

Sam hesitated, shocked by the question.

"I am, but how did you know?"

"Dad heard about it while he was at work at the mill. He figured we'd get blamed some way or another. That's why me and Johnny were watching out. To see if anybody would come up here to get even."

Wade was trying to keep up with the conversation, but couldn't keep his eyes or his mind off of Sarah's breasts.

Sam looked directly at the frail girl's eyes.

"We're not here to accuse anybody of anything. We have a tip that the church sold some snakes to an individual in the county, and we're here to follow up on that. Does the church still use snakes in the worship service?"

"Yes, Ma'am. We do."

"Does the church use rattlesnakes?"

"Yes, Ma'am."

"Do you know if the church or anyone related to the church has sold any snakes to anyone recently?"

"No, Ma'am. We don't sell our snakes to nobody."

"Sarah, we were told that the church did and that we would find a receipt for the sale in the big Bible right there on the table."

Sarah said nothing, but rose from the piano bench and picked up the big Bible. Thumbing through the first few pages, a sheet of paper fell out onto the floor. She reached down and picked up the paper, reading it to herself.

"I reckon this is what you're looking for. It says we sold

two rattlesnakes to a fellow named Brogan last week, but I know we didn't. It's my job to keep up with feeding the snakes, and I know we still got four rattlers and two cottonmouths in the box. That's all we've had for quite a spell."

"Are you sure they're all still there, Sarah?"

"I'm sure. But I can show you if you like."

Sarah didn't wait for an answer, but went to the alcove behind the piano and pulled out a large wooden box. When she opened the top end of the box, Wade and Sam could hear the distinctive rattling emanating from its interior. Sarah reached inside the box and took out a large Eastern Diamondback Rattlesnake in her hands. She gently laid the snake on the floor and reached inside the box again to retrieve another one.

As soon as the snake started crawling on the floor, Sam jumped on the pew as though her leg wasn't sore at all with her eyes wide open watching the snake's every move. Wade tried to be brave and manly, but that didn't last too long as soon as the second rattler moved toward him. He was standing on the pew right beside Sam.

Sarah laughed at them as the four rattlesnakes and the two water moccasins slithered across the floor of the old church.

"Ya'll ain't got much faith, do ya?"

Sam's voice was raspy as she replied, "You've got to remember. I was bitten by one of these things three days ago and just got out of the hospital this morning."

"And I was with her when she was bitten, and I'd just as soon never get that close to a rattlesnake again." Wade added.

"You didn't have to go to the hospital, Sam. Almost nobody ever dies from a snake bite. I've been bitten four times already, and now I barely feel it. Everybody in the church has been bitten at least once, and nobody's died in years."

Sarah's reassurance didn't make Sam or Wade much more comfortable, but when she gathered up the snakes and put them back in the box, they both relaxed.

"I just know it was painful, my leg swelled to about three times its normal size and I felt like I was going to die."

Sam rubbed her leg for emphasis.

Sarah closed the lid on the snake box.

"I believe you. That's how most people react the first time they're bitten. But every time after that, the venom has less and less effect on them."

"I trust you, but I don't want to try it for a second time. Sarah, how could the receipt have gotten in here without you or anyone else knowing about it?"

"I don't know."

Sarah stroked her long red hair.

"We lock the doors and the windows, and we didn't see any sign of anyone that might have broken in or anything when we got here this morning."

Sam thought for a little while before continuing.

"Do any of your church members collect or sell snakes?"

"Yes'm. Silas Williams. He's one of our elders and he catches snakes for our church and any extra snakes that he catches, he sells to other churches or whoever wants them."

"Does he have a key to the church?"

"Yes'm. He keeps a key in case he has to drop off a snake. He can just come by and drop it in the box."

"I see. Thanks for being so helpful, Sarah. Is there anything else you want to tell us before we leave?"

Sarah glanced at Wade and then back at Sam.

"Can I talk to you alone?"

Wade was still looking at Sarah's breasts and didn't comprehend the question until Sam nudged him and asked him to wait outside. He sheepishly excused himself and went out to the truck. There was no sign of Johnny, although Wade was certain that the boy was watching the pickup.

When Sam came out a few minutes later, she and Sarah were smiling at each other. When they reached the passenger side door of the truck, Sam turned and hugged Sarah and whispered something to her he couldn't hear.

They turned the truck around and headed back down the old logging road. Neither spoke until they were out of the clearing and back in the forest.

"What did she want to tell you that was so secret?" Wade asked.

Sam giggled before answering.

"She wanted to know how to get a boyfriend as handsome as you. She said that she'd never seen anyone like you except on television."

Wade was embarrassed and fumbled for what to say. When he couldn't come up with the right words, Sam continued.

"I told her not to worry. I said that you had plenty of faults that she couldn't see and that she could do a lot better than to get someone like you that just stared at her boobs all day long."

"You said what?"

Sam laughed.

"No, I didn't say that, although it would have been true. I just told her the right guy would come along for her and to be patient."

Wade tried not to show his interest in Sarah's physical attributes, but had to defend himself.

"You've got to admit, Sam. They are unusual."

"Unusual? Heck, they're huge!"

Then Wade said something that he should have kept to himself.

"You know what they say. '*Anything more than a mouthful is a waste*—"

He stopped knowing he had already said too much.

Sam looked down at her own chest and then stared at Wade.

"I hope you're not implying what I think you're implying!"

"Oh, no! Not at all! I was just repeating something I heard as a kid. Besides, I was talking about Sarah. It had nothing to do with you."

Sam glared at him.

Wade grinned.

"We have some pigs at the Plantation if you're interested."

They spent the rest of the ride back to town in silence.

36 IT WAS LIKE SMELLING THE ROSE AND IGNORING THE THORNS

Wade and Sam dropped by the Evergreen Café for some lunch after their morning trek to the Blue Heaven Church. Nodding to April on the way in, they wove their way to the usual back table.

Wade knew his ill-considered words still bothered Sam when she ordered the soup and salad du jour. Normally, she would take whatever blue plate special the restaurant was offering. The day's special was chicken-fried pork chops with mashed potatoes and gravy, which sounded a lot better to him than cauliflower and broccoli soup.

They hadn't been sitting there long before Frank Davis, the Purchasing Manager from City Hall, suddenly appeared at their table side. Unlike the confident manner that he had when he had come to the Sheriff's office, now he was reluctant and hesitant.

Frank stood at the side of the table.

"Do you guys mind if I take a few minutes of your time?"

Sam answered, "Not at all, Frank. What's on your mind?"

Frank took one of the empty chairs.

"First, I want to apologize for my behavior at the meeting in your office. I was ill-advised on my responses to your questions."

Sam forced a smile. "No problem. Would you like to have a cup of coffee with us?"

"Yes, I'd like that very much."

Frank settled into his chair and motioned with his cup he wanted some coffee. He turned back to the table and looked at Sam.

"First, I want you to know that I meant nothing personal when I met with you at your office."

"No offense taken. We assumed someone with a conflict of interest gave you some unsolicited legal advice."

Sam didn't hold a grudge.

"That is exactly what happened." Frank lowered his voice. "Now I want to talk to you without an attorney or the advice of one. I want to tell the truth."

Sam took a sip of coffee.

"I take it you might want to revise some of your answers."

Frank leaned closer to Sam.

"That is exactly what I want to do. Some of my answers before may have been vague or misleading, and I want to correct that."

Sam kept a stern countenance.

"Let's get to the heart of the questions and we'll see how sincere you are. Were you having a relationship with Rachel?"

Frank couldn't keep her gaze and looked at his empty coffee cup.

"We had an emotional relationship and a physical relationship. It started two years ago when she began representing Ed, I mean the mayor's office, at our monthly purchasing update. It was like night and day comparing her to the guy that used to represent the mayor's office."

"How do you mean, Frank? What was so different other than she was an attractive female?"

He looked up from the cup.

"That wasn't it at all, Sam. At least in the beginning that wasn't the difference. Before, Tom, that's the guy's name, always was pressing us to cut our budget and to buy whatever the city needed cheaper. Every meeting was the same. Where can we cut expenses and how can we buy cheaper?"

Sam continued to stare.

"And I take it that changed when Rachel started representing the Mayor's office."

Frank smiled.

"I still remember the very first meeting she came to when she replaced Tom. It was around Easter and she was wearing a beautiful pink dress that reminded me of the season. She had this effervescent smile that never left her face. She asked how much increase we needed in the budget for the rest of the year to properly do our jobs. I couldn't believe my ears! It's been a long time since anyone has asked me how much increase I needed. It seems forever since they weren't trying to cut my budget."

"So where did it go from there, Frank?"

Sam shifted in her seat.

Frank was in no hurry to get to the end, using this opportunity to reminisce about every moment Rachel touched his life.

"I heard nothing from her for the next four weeks until our next meeting she attended. When it was her turn to speak, she asked if we had gotten the numbers together for the budget increase. I hadn't thought to prepare for this request, so I just threw a number out on the table, almost one million dollars in increases. She smiled and asked if I were sure that would be enough. I wasn't sure if she was kidding or not, so I told her we might get by with eight hundred thousand. She just smiled and wrote that number down in her notes."

"Did you get the increase?"

Frank's eyes glazed.

"The very next day, she showed up in my office and told me we had gotten the first number I had thrown out, the million dollar one. I was absolutely shocked and I guess it showed on my face."

"Why is that?"

"She told me never to be surprised at good news if it came from the right source. I wasn't sure what she meant by that and didn't ask. She stayed in my office for almost an hour and I thoroughly enjoyed the conversation."

"Frank, when did it go beyond conversation?"

"Sam, it just happened one day. She had made a habit of coming by my office once or twice a week. A few times she wore some clothes that were on the edge, I guess you could say. When she bent over to get something out of her briefcase, I could see everything, if you know what I mean. I started getting thoughts in my head that someone my age should never get. One Friday afternoon, she came by right at quitting time. She wanted to show me some numbers from the budget. Well, by the time she pulled out the numbers, everyone had already left the office. You know how it is on a Friday afternoon. Anyway, she pulled out the numbers and came around the desk so she could point out the ones she wanted to talk about. She came right next to my chair and I just couldn't concentrate on those numbers at all."

Frank sweated and had a half smile formed as he recalled the events. He continued to recall each detail as though it had happened the day before.

"She was standing there next to the chair, and I put my hand on her lower back. She didn't resist or move at all, but just kept pointing out numbers. I moved my hand down to her backside, and she just kept looking at the accounting sheet. When she didn't resist, I slipped my hand under her skirt. She just turned to me and smiled and then kissed me on my forehead. I put my other hand under her skirt. From there, it wasn't long before we were on top of my desk. I couldn't control myself and I couldn't believe this was happening to me right there in my office. That was the first time, Sam and I still can't believe it happened."

"So you made the first advance on her? Is that correct?"

"I swear it was almost as if she planned it to happen. I know I shouldn't blame a kid and I should have known better, but I got caught up in the moment and I couldn't resist the temptation. From that day on, I wanted her so bad it hurt, and I wanted to quit having her so bad it hurt. I was torn up inside by the relationship, but I couldn't make myself stop it. I hate to say this, but it was almost a relief when I heard she was dead."

This was the second time Sam and Wade had heard this same sentiment about Rachel. Ed Moore, the Mayor, had said almost the same thing when they had met with him at the Gulf Club.

Frank paused in his recount of his encounters with Rachel, wiping his forehead with a napkin. His eyes had a glossy far-away look and his usually ruddy complexion turned ashen. Wade and Sam let him reflect without pushing for more information. They realized Frank was an emotional wreck and it would not take much more pressure to send him over the edge. He was at the far reaches of his capacity to cope.

The purchasing manager finally came back to the present.

"After the first time, we met every week, and I just couldn't get her off my mind. The relationship with Rachel was so addictive it was like smelling the rose and ignoring the thorns. I knew it was wrong, immoral, and the thorns would cut me some day, but I just couldn't stop."

"When did you execute a separate contract with Rachel for the Purchasing Department?"

Frank sighed, knowing the written evidence would seal his fate as the Purchasing Manager of Evergreen.

"Shortly after that first time, Sam. I wanted her so bad that I was willing to pay her to ensure that she wouldn't go away."

"How much were you paying her for that contract, Frank?"

"Three thousand a month, plus some incentives."

The twins had not mentioned the incentives in the contract that Rachel had with the Purchasing department when they had told Wade and Sam about all the contracts she had with the City.

"How much did she receive in incentives, Frank?"

"About ten thousand a month."

Sam frowned.

"And what were the incentives, Frank?"

"She had to attend two off-site meetings with the Purchasing Manager every month."

Sam wadded up the napkin by her plate.

"So, basically she had to sleep with you twice a month

for ten thousand dollars. Is that correct, Frank? Is that what we're talking about?"

Her voice was no longer low.

Frank looked crestfallen.

"That's the gist of it, Sam. I'm not very proud of my actions right now."

Frank looked around as though realizing for the first time that he was in a public restaurant.

Wade followed Frank's gaze around the restaurant and found only one patron looking directly at them. It was an older lady seated several tables away, but something about her was vaguely familiar. The old lady dropped head and began examining her menu while Wade looked at her. He could not recall where he had seen her before and made a mental note to ask Sam about her before they left.

Sam continued to get as much information out of Frank as she could while he was willing to talk.

"Frank, where were you the morning that Rachel was killed?"

"I was at home. My daughter had two friends spend Friday night with us, and we all rented a movie and watched it together. I got up around eight and did a few chores in the backyard until we all had breakfast together around nine."

"These friends of your daughter. Do you know their names?"

Frank nodded. "They work down at City Hall. In fact, you've already interviewed their father, Bruce. Their names are Mindy and Mandy Thomas, but I can't really tell them apart. They're identical twins, I believe."

Wade hoped the shock didn't show on his face as much as he felt it inside.

Why had the twins not mentioned that they were at

Frank's home the morning of the murder? Surely, they knew that Frank was one of Rachel's close acquaintances at work and that Sam would be questioning him at some date.

It didn't make sense to Wade.

Sam continued, "Okay, we'll follow up with them. One other thing. Tell us about the project all of you were working on together."

Frank looked around the restaurant one more time.

"Not here, Sam. I can come down to your office and tell you, but not here. I've already said too much, but I wanted to get it off my chest. But I can't talk about the project in public."

"When can you come by?"

"Let me get back to the office and check my schedule and I'll call you to set up a time."

As Frank left the table, Wade glanced around the restaurant and noticed the older lady that had been staring at them was no longer there. He hadn't noticed her leaving, and now it was too late to ask Sam about her. Something about the lady kept tickling the recesses of his memory, but he couldn't get it to come to the surface.

37 HOW CAN A COWARD LIKE THIS LEAD A CITY?

THE HUNTER COULDN'T BELIEVE HOW CLOSE HE HAD come to being discovered in the restaurant. The former FBI agent had caught him staring straight at the trio while they were in deep discussions. It was obvious from the emotions on Frank Davis's face that he was discussing his relationship with Rachel. The hunter wondered how Frank would have tried to explain his justification for a sexual bond between himself and a co-worker less than half his age. He wished he could've been a lot closer to the table to hear them, but knew he had taken a colossal risk being in the restaurant with them.

Frank had just elevated himself to next on the hunter's list, and the hunter couldn't wait long to act. He had to be more careful and quicker in dispatching Frank than he had with the Mayor. Thinking of the mayor brought back the memories of the night Ed Moore died.

The hunter regretted anything he'd done to the Mayor. After snatching him from the club, the hunter took him to his own secluded get-away and waited for him to regain his consciousness and recover from the anesthesia's effect.

The mayor recognized the hunter when he awakened and begged to know why he had been kidnapped and strung up like a pig on a hook. When he saw the razor blade in the hunter's hand, he cried like a baby. He urinated on himself before the razor blade even touched him. When the blade made the first incision across the mayor's stomach, Ed Moore let out a guttural groan and then screamed at the top of his lungs. In the hunter's opinion, the mayor had exhibited no bravery in his last hours on earth.

How can a coward like this lead a city?

As the hunter used the blade to extract every bit of pain and agony that he could, the mayor went in and out of consciousness, fainting several times from the fear of what he was being forced to endure. On a few cuts, Ed flinched at just the wrong moment and the blade made deeper incisions in his stomach and parts of his entrails emerged from the cuts.

After these deeper cuts, the hunter quit using the blade on the mayor and quietly waited for him to bleed to death. It was almost dawn before the hunter wrapped him up and took him to the hole in the ground that would be Rachel's final resting place, finishing him with a shot to the forehead.

The hunter did not intend to extract as much pain on the rest of the people on the list as he had with the Ed. In his mind, the mayor had been the instigator of the entire mess because of his own selfishness and greed. The others just continued what the Ed started, and they were less culpable. Even though they did not initiate the situation, they still had to pay for their deeds. And now it was Frank Davis's turn to pay. The hunter merely had to determine how to make that possible without being discovered by the agent, the sheriff, or those nosy twins that kept asking questions around City Hall.

38 HE SAID HE DIDN'T WANT TO SHARE HER WITH ANYONE ELSE

Wade and Sam went back to the Plantation for some time to digest everything they had learned from the Blue Heaven Nature Church and from Frank Davis without the interruptions that would invariably come if they went to the Sheriff's Office. Wade again saw the blue sedan parked outside his office. He immediately recognized the sedan as the one that belonged to the twins and cringed inside. He was not looking forward to having the twins and Sam together in a meeting at the Plantation.

Wade looked for the twins in the office, the den, the kitchen, and all the bedrooms and found no trace of them. Then he heard Sam yell for him from the back porch. He went out the back door, not knowing what to expect, but having a sense of apprehension at what the twins might be up to.

"Do you let all of your guests go skinny dipping in the lake while you're not here, or is it reserved for the special ones?"

Sam's gaze was on the lake.

As Wade turned his gaze to the lake, he saw the twins

playing at the end of the pier and neither had a stitch of clothes on. They were not aware that Wade and Sam were watching them and were engaged in various forms of horseplay, pushing each other off the pier and trying to outdo the other in diving acrobatics. Wade could only shake his head, not knowing what he could say to Sam that would come close to being intelligent or believable for this occasion. He decided it would be best if he went back inside instead of staring at the naked twins down at the lake.

Sam followed him back into the lodge, her expression telling Wade she was not too thrilled with this development. She paced around the den for several minutes saying nothing and then suddenly started smiling. Wade was not sure what she was smiling at and was not sure he should ask.

"They're crazy, aren't they?" Sam finally said.

Wade stumbled with his response.

"They don't do things the way other people do them, if that's what you mean."

"What I mean is that most of us have a filter in our conscience that tells us what is acceptable behavior and what isn't acceptable behavior. They don't have that filter, do they?"

"They have an unorthodox way of doing things. I think they have a filter, but sometimes it gets a hole in it. I think they mean well, but they don't know how to do things the way the rest of us do."

Wade knew he was rambling, but couldn't put his words in the correct order with Sam looking at him the way she was.

Sam laughed.

"What you just said is that they are crazy, only you

went around by China to get there. They've got to be freezing their butts off in this weather."

Wade relaxed and smiled, knowing that Sam was not holding him responsible for the actions of the twins.

"You're right. They're crazy. And they have to be insane to swim in that cold lake."

Sam shook her head.

"Do you think they'll put on their clothes before they come up to the lodge?"

"I'd say the odds are about fifty-fifty."

Wade remembered waking up in his bed to find the twins half-naked in bed with him.

"They can be a little unpredictable."

"So much for privacy. Do you want some coffee?"

Sam headed to the kitchen without waiting for an answer from Wade.

When Sam disappeared in the kitchen, Wade stepped to the back windows and stared at the twins, who were still playing on the pier down by the lake. He envied their lack of inhibition and freedom to do whatever they wanted to do without worrying about what other people thought. Sometimes he felt shackled by his conservative upbringing and his Baptist affiliation. He wondered how his life would have been different if he had been raised by different parents or taught in another religion. He stepped away from the window when he heard Sam coming with the coffee, not wanting to get caught staring at the bare teenage bodies frolicking in the lake.

Sam handed a cup of coffee to Wade. He took it and sat in one of the large recliners, expecting Sam to sit next to him. Instead, she went to the window he had just been staring out of and looked down at the lake. She didn't say anything, but continued staring at the twins.

She didn't turn around when she asked the question.

"Would you like it if I were more like them?"

The question caught Wade by complete surprise, but he was sure of his answer.

"I don't want you to change anything about yourself. You are the most beautiful lady I've ever met, and you're everything a man could dream of. You shouldn't change anything about yourself."

She turned and walked over to Wade.

"But I see you when you're around the twins and I know you enjoy being around them."

Wade told the truth, at least as much of it as he dared.

"I enjoy being around them where I can see what they do, only because I can't ever tell what they'll do next. I'm amused by being around a drunk at a party, but that doesn't mean I want to marry one. The twins bring a unique perspective to life and it's amusing, but not something I want to build my life around."

"I don't think the law would allow you to marry both of them at the same time anyway, unless you move to Utah. I don't think it's legal there, but they turn a blind eye toward polygamy because of the Mormons."

Sam laughed, glancing toward the pond.

"I already know who I'm gonna marry and there is only one. Not two or three or six, but we might have the twins as Maids of Honor at the wedding. There's no telling how that might turn out."

"Over my dead body. Actually, over your dead body. That's not going to happen."

Wade got out of the recliner and put his arms around her. He began kissing her on her forehead and then on her ears. He kissed her deeply on her lips and started caressing her body, pressing as close as he could to her.

"You guys need to move it to a bedroom. Don't you have any shame?"

Wade wasn't sure if it was Mindy or Mandy, but they had both come up to the lodge from the lake without Sam or Wade noticing. To Wade's relief, at least they put on their clothes before they did.

Wade and Sam did not release their grasps on each other.

Wade looked at the sisters.

"Since you girls were putting on a show down at the lake, we decided to put on one up here at the lodge."

"Oh, a love story. How cute?" Mindy was serious.

Sam responded to her. "Yes, it is. And it's our story, and he's hands off to both off you. He's all mine and I don't intend to share him with anyone."

Her eyes turned to Wade.

This was as open as Wade had ever heard Sam speak about their relationship, and he nodded in agreement before kissing her full on her lips.

"Yep, girls. I'm spoken for and paid for. So I can't even be rented by a lovely pair such as yourselves. But I have to admit, that was an interesting show you guys put on. Weren't you cold?"

"We meant nothing by that." Mandy explained. "We were here waiting for you to come back and got bored. Looking at the lake and with nobody around, we couldn't resist the temptation. It's a tad chilly, but nothing like when we jumped in a frozen lake in Colorado. That was crazy." She paused. "We didn't think you would be back until nearly dark, so we weren't expecting anyone to be watching us. But that's okay. It's not like you guys haven't seen naked girls before. Besides, that water is cold and I mean real cold. It'll make your nipples stand up and take notice."

Sam just shook her head and went back to the kitchen for more coffee. Wade sat back down in the recliner. He couldn't get the visualization of the twins' nipples out of his mind.

"So what brings you girls out to the Plantation?"

Mindy answered, "We've been snooping around the office and we think we know who killed Rachel. We also think he was the one that put the snakes in your car."

Wade stood erect and Sam walked back in the room. It was obvious she had been eavesdropping.

"Who do you think it was?" Wade asked.

"We think it was Councilman Brogan that did both. We found some things at the office that sure make it likely he had the motive to do it, at least to kill Rachel. We assume he thought you guys were getting too close, and he wanted you to back off."

Mandy was now speaking.

"What did you find that makes you think it was him?"

Mindy stepped closer to Wade.

"We found some emails, really just notes 'cause they aren't very long, but they are to the point about his feelings for Rachel."

Sam interrupted the girls.

"We looked at all the emails to and from Rachel at the office. The city provided us with a complete list and copies of all of them."

Mindy shook her head.

"What you saw were the emails sent to and from Rachel's official email address at the City Hall. She had several personal email addresses that she used for private notes to a bunch of folks. Did you know she was sleeping with almost everybody down at the office? She was quite a girl."

"We know she was active and got to know most of the men in the right positions to help her."

"You could say that again. You should read some stuff they wrote to her. She must have been a great lay in bed. These guys were all gaga over Rachel and every one of them thought she was gaga over them. They didn't know about each other."

Sam considered the long-term aspects of this additional information.

"I hate to ask this, but how did you find these emails when the City couldn't?"

"Don't kid yourself, Sam. The City can find anything it really wants to find. But Dad must have been the one to ask for the emails that the City supplied to you guys. He knew he'd sent Rachel some emails to a personal account of hers, so he probably was precise in what he asked for. He didn't want you to read his emails back and forth to her so he specifically asked only for the emails to and from her official email address. That way, he can say he fully complied with your request and he doesn't get embarrassed."

Sam paced. "I can see that as a possibility. But you still didn't answer my question. How did you find these emails if they were on her private accounts?"

"Sam, there's nothing private at City Hall. They log every piece of mail showing who sent it and who it was addressed to. And they log every email on a driver somewhere, just in case someone is sending out information that they shouldn't be sending. It's only a matter of finding which server was logging her so-called private emails and getting access to it."

"How did you find it and get access to it?"

Mindy and Mandy giggled as though it was a big joke.

Mindy responded, "Sam, have you ever seen the nerds

that work in our computer department. Most of them have never had a date, at least with anything other than a blow-up doll. When a live girl, actually two live girls, show a little cleavage up close and personal, they can get anything they want from one of them."

"And that's all you girls did? Show a little cleavage?"

Wade shook his head.

"We might have let him have a little closer look." Mandy said, looking down at her breasts. "But we didn't let him go any further than that. We didn't need to."

Wade instantly thought back to the first time he had met Mindy, and she had manipulated him into feeling her breast in the hunting stand. Evidently, the twins were not shy about using particular parts of their anatomy to get what they wanted. He felt a little sorry for the computer tech, but at least the tech got a momentary thrill out of it.

Sam was torn about how to proceed from this point. If she listened to any more information the twins had uncovered, a judge would probably rule it inadmissible in any trial proceeding and any information that would result from the investigation based on what they told her would also probably get thrown out. If she didn't listen, they might lose the crucial break they needed.

Wade seemed to read her mind.

"Sam, it might not be appropriate for you to be part of this conversation. Why don't you go in the kitchen while I talk to the girls? Then you might get an anonymous tip that we need to investigate someone further."

Sam gathered the two coffee cups and went back into the kitchen.

Mindy giggled. "You're smooth, Detective Ranger. Now you have us all alone with you. You didn't have to do that. We really don't mind a foursome if Sam's okay with it."

Mandy laughed. "She's just kidding, Wade. What do you want to know?"

"What makes you think it was Councilman Brogan?"

"All the men that Rachel was sleeping with at the office each thought they were the only one that had a relationship with her. Except one. We found some emails from Mr. Brogan that said he wanted to be the only one and asked her to drop her relationship with Ed. He said he didn't want to share her with anyone else. He specifically listed the mayor as the one he did not want her to see any more. He didn't list Dad or Frank Davis or John Grimes, but we're not sure if he knew of them or not. But her other emails back and forth to them are explicit enough that we're sure she was sleeping with them."

"Did the emails insinuate that he was jealous of the relationship that Rachel had with the Mayor?"

"More than that," answered Mindy. "He told her she had to quit seeing the mayor or he would take care of the situation himself."

Mandy continued, "Rachel wrote back that she had discontinued sleeping with Ed a long time ago and they were just friends. But we don't think Mr. Brogan believed her."

"So what makes you think he had anything to do with the snakes in Sam's car?"

Mindy looked around as if someone else might overhear before answering.

"We found some emails where they talked about the snakes he owned. He told Rachel he had some rattlesnakes that could take care of the problem with the mayor if he left them in his office one night. We figured he didn't use them on the mayor, but he might have used them on you and Sam."

"Dang it! You guys are good. Why are you doing all of this?"

Mindy answered. "We told you. We don't think Dad had anything to do with Rachel's murder, and we want to make sure he isn't hurt by the investigation. We're willing to do just about anything to protect Dad. If that means we have to flirt with a computer nerd to get information, then we're willing to do it."

"Does your Dad know what you're doing?"

"Heavens, no! He would kill us if he knew. He thinks we're still twelve years old."

The twins looked at each other and giggled.

Wade changed the subject of the conversation.

"You guys forgot to mention that the friend you stayed with the Friday night before the murder was Frank Davis's daughter."

"You never asked us. In fact, you never asked us where we were Friday or Saturday. You must have asked Dad, and he doesn't know who we're spending the night with most of the time. Besides, we didn't think at the time that it was important. We thought you might have asked if we could provide an alibi for Dad, but you never did."

Wade was trying to recollect if he asked the twins or asked Bruce where they were. Then he remembered that Bruce had told him the twins were out Friday night and Saturday morning, but it never dawned on him to ask the twins directly.

"Okay, my mistake. So, I'll ask now. Where were you Friday night and Saturday morning?"

"We were at Lindsay's house. She's Frank's daughter and we go over there all the time."

"Was Frank home the whole time you guys were there?"

Mandy giggled. "You mean the pervert? Yea, he was there."

"Why do you call him a pervert?"

Mindy looked at Mandy, insinuating that Mandy should answer this question.

"We've been going over there for a long time, since we were kids. They have a pool and we've always enjoyed it because we don't have one ourselves. So it's nice to go over to Lindsay's and swim in their pool. We kept noticing that whenever we went into the pool that Mr. Davis would go into the little workshop right next to the pool. One day I saw the slats on the blind on the window cracked a bit while we were swimming. The sun was shining just right, and we could see Mr. Davis's face peering out of the window. So we figured he was watching us swim in our bikinis and we were only fourteen or fifteen."

Mindy picked up the story from there.

"The next time we went there, we rigged the window opposite of the pool where we could look through the blinds. We all got in the pool and started playing, and sure enough, Mr. Davis headed to the workshop. We'd planned for this and I said I had to go to the bathroom inside the house while Mandy and Lindsay stayed in the pool. Mandy wrestled with Lindsay and pulling on her swimsuit. So Lindsay pulled back on Mandy's. We figured Mr. Davis would watch them and not pay attention to me. When I went to the other side of the workshop and looked in the window, there was Mr. Davis staring out his window watching Mandy and Lindsay. Not only was he watching them, he was pleasuring himself. If you know what I mean."

"I get the picture." Wade said, shaking his head.

"So we made a game out of it. We would play in the pool until Mr. Davis went into the workshop, and then we would take a break and go back in the house. We'd let him sit in there for a while and when he got tired and came out, we'd go back to playing in the pool. If we stayed in the pool while he was in the workshop, we kept our bodies under the water so he couldn't see them. It's been a lot of fun watching him get frustrated with us."

Wade marveled at the willingness for the twins to accept that they elicited powerful desires from older men and their ability to use these desires to manipulate them. But then, not much different from what Rachel was doing down at City Hall. The only difference was the degree to which Rachel played the game.

Mindy was continuing while Wade mused.

"We can't for sure say whether Mr. Davis was home all morning the day Rachel was killed, but we're sure it wasn't him. He's more of the kind of fellow that likes playing with himself in the workshop than one that would stalk Rachel in the National Forest."

"Okay, these emails. Did you make a copy of them?"

"That would have been against City policy and you know we would never violate City policy."

The girls giggled as Mandy handed over copies of all the emails sent between Rachel and Bill Brogan.

Wade stared at the copies of the emails, realizing that he shouldn't accept them, but knowing that he had to at least look at them to give him an edge in solving the murder of a nineteen-year-old girl and the Mayor of his city. The internal struggle between playing by the rules he had been taught at the Academy and solving the murders had his stomach roiling. He finally handed the copies back to Mandy.

"Why don't you girls hold on to these for now? I don't want to be in a position that I have to lie about having seen them. You've told me what they say and we can use that to get to the bottom of this case, but if I take them now, it could jeopardize the prosecution of Bill Brogan."

"No problem, Detective Ranger. Just let us know when you need them. Can I ask you one question?"

Mindy looked him straight in his eyes.

"Sure."

"Does this clear Dad, or is he still a suspect?" A tear rolled down Mindy's face and dropped from her chin.

He hugged both girls.

"I don't think your Dad had anything to do with the murders. I don't believe he is that type of man and unless some facts come out that contradict my beliefs he will remain a part of the investigation, but not a prime suspect."

Both girls had tears in their eyes and wrapped their arms around Wade in a big bear hug. Wade noticed Sam come into the room just as the girls were releasing him from the hug. He turned toward Sam.

"The twins have provided some information that should prove useful in our investigation. I'll share it with you later."

"It looks like they were sharing more than information to me."

Sam looked at them sternly and then broke into a broad smile.

"I'm just kidding. I understand you girls a little better now than I did and I want both of you to know I appreciate what you're doing to help us."

Both of the twins now had tears streaming down their faces, and they gave Sam a huge bear hug. While in their embrace, Sam looked over at Wade and winked at him. Wade felt relief that Sam now understood that the twins operated within their own ethical system and that it was a little different one than most other people would find comfortable.

After the twins left the Plantation, Wade and Sam sat on rocking chairs on the back porch holding hands. All the tension brought on by finding the twins skinny dipping in the lake had now dissipated.

"They are a seductive little pair, aren't they?"

Sam said this with no malice or ill-feelings prevalent in her voice.

"Yes, but it's almost like sometimes they know they are and other times they are without realizing it. I still think this is one big game to them and they don't follow the standard rules the rest of us follow."

"I know. At first, when I saw how you interacted with them, I was jealous. You really seemed interested in everything they did and how they looked. Then I realized that you were more like a big brother to them, trying to guide them into the adult world."

"Thank you, Sam, for trusting me." Wade squeezed her hand even tighter. "And you will never have any reason to be jealous of any other girl, I promise."

39 WRITTEN IN WHITE POWDERED SUGAR BENEATH THE TOWEL WAS "H E L P"

THE MORNING SUN BORE THROUGH THE WINDSHIELD and quickly warmed the interior of Wade's truck as he and Sam climbed their way up the hill to Bill Brogan's farm. The cool fresh air invigorated the forest around them and they witnessed rabbits, squirrels and an occasional whitetail deer stirring on this frosty morning. Sam had called ahead to ensure that Bill would meet them at his farm.

They pulled up to the old farmhouse sitting amid picturesque scenery. Bill was evidently a very organized fellow, meticulously maintaining his place. The wooden fence around the ranch-style house looked brand new with a fresh coat of white paint. The shudders sported a recent coat of a dark green hue that blended nicely with the dark cedar exterior. The brown fallen leaves were raked up next to the tree trunks, providing added nutrients for the expected spring growth as they again became part of the plant cycle. Sitting behind the neat farmhouse was a crimson red barn, making Wade wonder if Bill was a closet Crimson Tide fan among all the State and Ole Miss fans of Evergreen.

Behind the barn was one of those fences that Wade had now become accustomed to in this part of Mississippi, an eight foot game proof fence indicative of keeping alternative livestock. Wade wondered what type of exotic animals Bill had penned up and why Bill had never contacted him to buy some of them for the Plantation.

Stacked behind the other side of the house along an old fence row were several rows of bee boxes. This was one industry that Wade had never had an inkling to get involved with. He loved fresh honey and knew there was some serious money to be made in the honey gathering industry, but he couldn't make himself comfortable around a horde of swarming bees, no matter how much smoke he could spray at them.

When Wade drew close to the farmhouse, a young man stepped outside with a chocolate Labrador Retriever by his side. Wade had never met Bill Brogan and had assumed he would be much older, an idea supported by the ages of the rest of the men that Rachel had formed a relationship with. Sizing him up, Wade figured Bill could not be over thirty years old and was in great physical condition. He could have been mistaken for a college athlete if not for the corncob pipe dangling from his mouth.

"Sam, welcome to the Evergreen Magnolia. And who is this handsome young man on your side?"

"Hello, Bill. This is Wade Dalton. He is a Special Investigator for the Feds working on the case of the recent murders in Evergreen."

"Good morning, Wade. Welcome to my home. I hope you guys had a delightful ride up here, but I'm sorta baffled about why you would want to see me. All of my business with the mayor was strictly business. I rarely saw him outside of a council meeting."

Neither Wade nor Sam responded to Bill's comments, and he motioned for them to enter the farmhouse with him. The interior of the house met if not exceeded the exterior. Every piece of furniture strategically placed and not a single dust particle in sight.

Bill sat in a cherry rocking chair and he motioned for Wade and Sam to settle into one of the double cherry rockers on the other side of a coffee table with a mounted bobcat inside a glass wall.

"Would you guys like some coffee or hot chocolate? Suzee Mae just made the coffee and I have to say, she makes the best coffee in these parts. She adds a little chicory to give it an extra boost."

Sam nodded. "I don't think I've met Suzee Mae."

She was trying to get some information without being too obvious.

Bill laughed. "It's not what you're thinking. Suzee Mae and her brother, Trahan, help me around here. She does the inside work, and he does the outside work. In exchange, I provide room and board and a little paycheck. I couldn't ask for a better couple to help around here than those two."

"I didn't mean to insinuate anything. I don't remember Dad mentioning anything about them, and he usually gets around to mentioning everything. I guess he didn't know about them either."

"They don't get to town much."

Bill took a puff on his pipe.

"I pick up whatever they need when I'm in town, so they stay here pretty much all the time."

Wade changed the subject.

"I'll have some of that coffee with the chicory. I like the extra twang the chicory gives it."

Bill called out toward the kitchen and a young Creole

girl came out. Wade guessed she couldn't be more than twenty years old and had that Cajun complexion that other girls dream of. Her dark black hair flowed down below her shoulders and glistened even though she was indoors.

"Hey, Suzee Mae, this is Wade and Sam. Would you mind bringing them some of that wonderful coffee you make?"

"Yes, Sir. I just put some beignets in the grease when I heard them drive up. Do you want me to bring some with the coffee?"

Wade loved beignets. The Acadians introduced the delicacies to south Louisiana, and Café du Monde in New Orleans made them famous. The café has been around since the late 1800s and has attracted hundreds of thousands of tourists and locals over the century and a half it has been in business. Wade had heard that they filled the original beignets with fruit, but now they were commonly square pieces of dough, deep fried in hot grease and covered with white powdered sugar.

"I saw your game fence in the back. Do you mind me asking what you raise?" Wade asked.

"Not at all. I raise some of the best bison in North America. As you know, most people call them buffalo, but they're actually not buffalo, but a separate species."

"What got you into raising bison?"

"My dad bought a calf from the Plantation a long time ago and gave it to me as a birthday present. I named him Huey, and I loved that little calf. Over time, I've added one or two a year and now I have a herd of about two hundred head."

"Man, I wouldn't want to have your feed bill. I know how much my elk and red stags eat. I can't imagine how much two hundred head of bison eat every year."

"It's really not that bad, Wade. As you two already know, bison are grazers, not browsers, which means they feed primarily on the grasses available to them. So as long as I can provide enough graze for them in the summer and hay in the winter, they get along fine. But I'm reaching my limit on what my acreage can support, so I'm gonna have to sell part of my herd soon. Are you interested in buying some for the Plantation?"

"Sure, if the price is right."

"I usually get five hundred for the cows and one thousand for the bulls. You can triple your money on those pretty easily, especially in this economy. Hunters will look at getting a six hundred to eight hundred pound cow for fifteen hundred dollars as a steal. Same with a fifteen hundred pound bull. Three thousand for that much meat, a trophy for the mantle and a rug is a bargain in today's hunting prices."

Wade nodded. "I have to agree with you there. I can sell those all day long."

"And I have a special surprise for you if you ever get one of those hunters that has taken every trophy imaginable."

Wade squinted.

"What do you have, Bill?"

"White bison. There was a movie a long time ago about a white buffalo, they called it. But most people think they're a myth. But I've been raising a strain of white bison for about six years now. They are gorgeous."

Wade had never described a buffalo or bison as '*gorgeous*', but then, he had never seen a white one.

"Do you sell many of them, Bill?"

Bill took another puff on his pipe.

"They're too expensive for most folks. Wholesale price on them is around forty thousand dollars each, but I guarantee you none of your customers have ever killed one."

"You're probably right. I've never thought about it before."

Suzee brought in the coffee and beignets and set them down on the coffee table in front of Sam and Wade.

Sam looked at all the powdered sugar.

"There's no way to eat these without getting that sugar coating everywhere. Do you want us to go out on the porch?"

"Goodness, no. We're used to it around here. Suzee always puts twice the amount of sugar than most people do. But that's part of what makes them special."

Wade grabbed one and quickly bit into it trying not to spill much of the powder. The pocket in the fried beignet popped in his mouth, releasing a little of the hot grease inside it. His taste buds, euphoric from the bursting sensation of hot oil, sweet sugar and baked dough at once, sent his brain a signal of a combination of pure delight and pleasure. The powder coated his mouth, making it more difficult to swallow, but making the taste linger even longer. He washed it down with a gulp of the coffee with chicory. The added dash of chicory provided just enough bitterness to offset the sweetness of the beignets. Wherever Suzee had learned to fry beignets, she had mastered the art.

"My compliments to Suzee. These are wonderful."

"I told you they were the best. I'm lucky to have Suzee and Trahan helping."

"How long have they been here?"

"They came here after the storm in New Orleans. They lost their parents and were fairly young, but they were both of legal age and were looking for work and a place to stay. I made a deal with them that if they would fix up one of the old slave quarters in the back, they could stay in there and I would provide meals and a small salary. It's been the best deal I've ever made."

"You still have slave quarters?" Wade was incredulous.

"I haven't updated them and no one else has over the last hundred years. They were pretty run down before Trahan got hold of them. Now I've got three of the buildings left and he's got them looking better than when they were first built."

"That's unbelievable. This was actually a slave plantation?" Wade had no idea.

"Don't look too surprised. The Evergreen Plantation, which I understand you now own, was one of the largest slave farms in the South. My dad told me that Mr. Teddy, who owned it for several years, tore down the old quarters because it bothered him so much that his land had been a place that treated people so badly and so inhumanely. He didn't want to be reminded of it every time he saw those buildings."

"Doesn't it bother you to have the old quarters on the Magnolia?"

"That's why I keep them here, Wade. It reminds me of how cruel and hateful mankind can be if we get rid of all the evidence of our past wrongdoings. Every time I see those old quarters, it reminds me to treat every other human being with respect, regardless of what color or religion they are. And even with those reminders, I sometimes forget when it comes to the Arab folks and their religious beliefs these days."

Wade instantly appreciated Bill's tolerance and wished he could build up that same respect for his fellow man. He kept trying to picture Bill killing Rachel and the Mayor and then putting rattlesnakes in Sam's car, but the image didn't fit with the man in front of him. He was trying to figure out a way to make a segue into the investigation when Bill did it for them.

"I know you guys didn't come all the way out here to find out about my bison or to sample Suzee's beignets. I assume you're here about the Mayor. What questions do you have for me?"

Sam answered, "We're here about Ed's murder and also about Rachel Chastain's murder. You knew both of them, correct?"

"I've served on the city council for the past three terms and worked with the Mayor and his team to get some things done in Evergreen."

"Did you have any problems with Ed?"

"No, not really. We disagreed on the budget priorities, but that's fairly common between city councils and mayors in most towns, I assume."

Sam placed her cup on the coaster.

"Did you have any problems with him outside of the official business down at City Hall?"

"We weren't social friends and I pretty much keep to myself out here. There's plenty to do between here and the Feed Store and not enough time to do it, so it keeps me from mingling with most of the politicians in town."

"Do you know of anyone that had a reason to kill Ed?"

Bill laughed quietly.

"Not more than a couple of hundred. Ed was not the most beloved mayor Evergreen has ever seen."

"Is there any way you can narrow that list down a little for us? Is there anyone that wanted Ed dead and had the wherewithal to kill him?"

Bill sat back in his rocker and took a deep draw on his

pipe. His forehead wrinkled and his eyes had a deep, far-away look. After several minutes, he finally spoke up.

"How far have you gotten in your investigation, Wade?"

Wade hesitated to tell Bill everything that they had uncovered, especially the facts about Rachel's relationships with most of the Managers at City Hall.

"We've come a long way, but there are still several pieces missing."

"Do you know about the project that Ed was pushing for Evergreen?"

"We know there is, or was an extensive project being discussed, but we don't know the particulars of it. Would you like to tell us about it?"

"I can't do that. I can only tell you it involves big money. I mean more money than Evergreen has ever seen or will see any time."

"Who's involved in the planning for the project?"

"Let's see: there's the mayor, Rachel, Frank Davis, me, Bruce Thomas and John Grimes, the City Attorney. Bruce was only on the periphery of the project and wasn't in on the specific details. Unless Rachel told him."

"Bill, does it bother you that two of the people on the project are dead? That only leaves you, Frank Davis, Bruce Thomas and John Grimes as, shall we say, persons of interest in this case." Wade was looking for some sign of weakness in Bill but didn't see it. Instead, Bill took a long draw on his pipe and tapped his fingers on the arm of his rocker.

Suzee silently appeared in the room to pick up the coffee cups and saucers. She picked up Bill's and Wade's before getting to Sam. When she got to Sam, she slightly tilted up the tray carrying the dishes and moved the big dish towel over. Written in white powdered sugar beneath the towel was *"H E L P"*.

When Sam placed her cup on the tray, she nodded imperceptibly to Suzee, then placed her saucer over the message and maneuvered it closer to the center of the tray, destroying the message entirely. Suzee quietly took the tray full of cups and saucers back into the kitchen.

Bill finally answered, "I'd say your list is mighty narrow considering how many people knew Rachel in town and how many people had a severe dislike for our beloved mayor. I'm not sure the two cases are even linked."

"We're not sure they are, but we have to follow every lead we have. Given that they worked together, and we found the mayor in Rachel's grave before she was buried in it leads us to strongly believe the two are linked, however."

"That makes sense." Bill was still drawing on his pipe. "If you want to see one of those white Bison before lunch, we'd better hurry."

"I'd love to see one, but we'd better start back to town. There's no telling what's going on down there with Gus watching over everything." Wade wanted to see one of the rare white bison, but was sure Sam was ready to leave. Her response caused him to hesitate.

"Let's take the time, Wade. How often are we going to get this way and now is the chance for you to see an animal very few people ever get the chance to see?"

40 I'M GOING TO NOTICE YOU NOW

Trahan drove with Sam in the passenger seat beside him, with Wade and Bill in the back seat of the open-topped Jeep. Wade had grown accustomed now to the smoother ride and relative quietness of the Mules and found it difficult to maintain a conversation with the noise and rough ride of the old Jeep.

When they came up out of a creek bottom into a meadow on the other side, Wade saw the first white Bison of his life. There were a dozen mixed in with a herd of thirty or forty normal brown Bison. One of the white Bison was just a calf, and Wade thought it was one of the prettiest animals he had ever seen. It wasn't as majestic as the axis bucks or as regal as a monarch elk, but it was still so unique that Wade knew eventually he would have to have one.

Sam got out of the front seat and intertwined her arms with Wade's.

"We've got to have some of these on Evergreen. They are so different and so beautiful."

"We will eventually. I've got to save up some money to buy one, though. Remember, I was living on an agent's salary before I got the Plantation and I haven't found that money tree yet growing hundred-dollar bills."

"You know that Dad, Connie and I can help you if you weren't so stubborn. Ol' Moze has been good for us over the last few years and we wouldn't mind helping a little."

Wade knew what Sam was talking about. Moze was the breeder buck on her father's ranch with more antlers on his head than Wade could count. Sam and her family were selling each straw of semen from Moze for about six thousand dollars each, and they were getting over two hundred straws of semen from him each year. Moze also bred fifteen does each year, producing twenty-five to thirty fawns, each worth more than ten thousand dollars. This one deer was worth around one and one-half million dollars per year for the Cates' ranch. Now, they could sell semen and fawns from Moze's offspring, both the does and the bucks from his pedigree. He was known to have the kind of bucks that hunters craved, wide and tall with lots of antlers.

"I know you and Sam wouldn't mind helping, but I'm determined to make Evergreen work on its own."

"Okay, but you never know what Santa may bring you. I can't control him, you know." Sam smiled and kissed him on the cheek and slipped back into the front seat of the jeep with Trahan.

Sam was quiet on the way back to the Magnolia, and Wade wondered what she was thinking about. Suzee was not in sight when they arrived back at the Magnolia. Sam was trying to figure out how to get her alone to find out about the mysterious plea she marked on the tray. But she was not in sight, and Wade was already headed to the truck. Sam followed quickly, bidding farewell to Bill and Trahan, thanking them for the hospitality and the beignets.

They had not gone far before Wade slammed on the brakes. "What the—?"

Sam looked over at him and saw that he was looking in the rear-view mirror. She looked back to see Bill's SUV following close behind them with the lights blinking on and off. Wade pulled over to the side of the road and got out of the cab of his truck. Bill jumped out of his. They approached each other at the rear of Wade's pickup. Sam exited the passenger side of Wade's truck.

"Wade, I'm sorry to bother you, but I can't find Suzee and I was wondering if she somehow slipped into your truck without you knowing about it."

"She's not with us. Why would she want to run away like that without telling you?"

Bill glanced over the tailgate.

"Suzee has a vivid imagination. Sometimes she likes to make up stories and pretends that she's been mistreated at my ranch. Nothing could be farther from the truth, but she's so convincing sometimes that people believe her."

Bill looked in the bed of Wade's truck even as he talked to Wade. He started for the cab of the truck before Wade leaned against the bed, blocking his approach.

Bill bowed his shoulders and clenched his fists.

"You really don't want to do this. This is between me and Suzee."

"I'm not sure exactly what is between you and Suzee, but based on your reaction something untoward is going on and Sam and I need to find out what it is. We're gonna follow you back up to your ranch and ask Suzee about all of this."

"You don't need to do that, Mr. Wade. I'll go back with him so no one gets hurt because of me."

Wade looked back at his truck, at the small head that

had popped up from the floor of the back seat. He didn't see the blow strike the base of his head, crumpling him to the ground.

In one smooth motion, Bill somersaulted in the back of Wade's truck bed and out the other side, landing directly on Sam as she was trying to retrieve her gun from the truck. The weight of Bill's body and the impetus of his jump were too much for Sam to handle as he drove her into the loose gravel along the side of the road. He was lying on top of her, reaching for her handcuffs on the belt around her waist. Even as he was doing this, his hand slipped down between her legs.

"We might come to some sort of agreement that will keep you alive for a little while, Sam. I've always kinda liked the way you looked, but you never even noticed me."

"I'm going to notice you now."

Sam butted Bill's head with the back of hers and rolled her body into a ball, lashing out with her feet into his midsection. One of her feet found the target she was trying to strike, eliciting a long groan from Bill. He bent over at the waist and she kicked with the other foot, again finding the target, but this time with even more force. Two more quick kicks to the same vulnerable area had Bill on the ground writhing in pain. Sam raced around the end of the truck to check on Wade. He was trying to stand on his feet, but his legs wouldn't cooperate. Slowly, she half dragged up in the bed of the truck. With a little help from Suzee, she managed to get him nestled in the long bed. Sam grabbed her cuffs and jumped over the side of the bed to where she had left Bill writhing on the ground, but he was no longer there. She grabbed her gun from the cab of the truck and checked the entire interior of Bill's truck, finding nothing. He had disappeared.

Sam jumped behind the steering wheel on Wade's truck and spun gravel in her haste to get off this little road to hell. Running off the road on one side and then the other, she regained some of her composure and slowed down. No one on foot could have come close to keeping up with them at the pace she was driving. When the three of them finally arrived at the main highway, Sam was conscious of her breathing for the first time since jumping in the truck. Tears started rolling down her cheeks as she glanced in the rear-view mirror at the man she cared about more than anything in the world in the arms of a beautiful young lady, but she was so glad she was there to help him.

Sam drove quickly to the hospital, but when they arrived, Wade refused to go in. He kept arguing about some other unfortunate incident that had occurred there the day they had first met, and he didn't want to repeat that situation. All three ended up at the Cates' ranch house.

41 SAM, YOU'RE A GENIUS

"Jeez-um, Pete's He sure had me fooled! I never dreamed Bill could be capable of such madness and evil. He seems so down-to-earth and peaceful, talking about how the old slave quarters reminded him to treat all of his fellowman with respect. What a bunch of Hooey!"

Sam was still irate. She and Wade had been digging through Bill's house, barns, and outbuildings for the past week with no sign of Bill or Trahan. But there were signs of his abuse of Suzee and Trahan. Shackles, handcuffs, dark rooms with no lights, windows, beds, or toilets with massive locks on the outside doors.

From the story Suzee told, the abuse started almost immediately after Bill had approached the siblings at the free shelter they had temporarily moved into while the hurricane-ravaged New Orleans. No one found their parents and Suzee still didn't know their whereabouts or even if they were alive. While they were grateful for the shelter, they jumped at the chance to move in with Bill. In a real house with real furniture and a little freedom to move around. The freedom didn't last long. Bill shackled both of them the very first night at his house, and used them in any way he saw fit since then. Suzee was only eleven years old at the time and was not prepared for the torturous life brought onto her by Bill. She serviced his every need, from maid and cook to sex servant. After a while, the shackles were no longer necessary because Suzee and Trahan had nowhere to go and no one to turn to. They accepted their fate in life until Sam showed up and Suzee saw her badge. A flicker of hope sparked within her and she had hidden in Wade's truck, hoping to escape this unbelievable nightmare. She saw Sam as her last chance to return to the outside world.

Sam climbed down from the small attic in an outbuilding, sat down in one of the small rocking chairs that was still in amazingly superb condition, and wiped the sweat and a few spider webs from her forehead.

"Where could they be?"

Sam looked up at Wade when he climbed the three steps to the small porch.

"I wish I knew." Wade replied. The search for Bill and Trahan was getting frustrating.

"What I don't understand is why Suzee and Trahan didn't just walk away while Bill was in town at one of the town hall meetings.

"Walk away to where?" Wade responded. "Most people need somewhere to walk to before they can walk away from where they're at in life."

Sam pulled another cobweb from her hair. "Anywhere would have been better than here."

"Did you notice that the only television was in Bill's study? He probably didn't allow them to watch TV or get on the computer, so Suzee and Trahan would know very little of the world outside of this plantation other than what Bill told them."

Sam shook her head, unconvinced.

"I still can't imagine they thought this was right."

Wade thought back to some case studies the FBI forced him to review at the Academy.

"This may be a classic case of the Stockholm Syndrome."

"I've heard of that, but I'm not sure what it is."

Wade replied, "There's a theory a hostage or captive over time will take on the cause or at least become sympathetic with the cause of the captor. But that's usually a case where there is a political or religious basis for the kidnapping. It usually isn't implied when the purpose is personal or sexual, although a lot of experts thought the girl that was kidnapped in Utah demonstrated some symptoms of the Stockholm Syndrome."

Sam whistled.

"So what you're saying is that over time Suzee believed what was being done to her was right and not the evil actions of a pervert. And she became so inured to the situation she accepted it without the chains and locked doors."

Wade nodded. "That's the only way I can explain it from what I've seen so far. But when she saw you, something snapped in her mind and she decided that the situation wasn't right and now was the time to make a break."

Sam rocked in the chair.

"I wish I had come up here years ago if that's the case."

"She might not have been ready to decide years ago or even weeks ago. Sometimes, we just show up at the right time."

"Do you think Trahan is on Bill's side or his sister's side right now?" Sam asked.

Wade shrugged.

"I don't know and that's what makes this dangerous. We don't know if we're looking for a kidnapper and a hostage or two guys on the wrong side. I suppose we'll find out when we find the two of them."

"How does all of this fit in with the murders of Rachel and the Mayor?"

"I'm not sure of that either, but somehow I believe Bill was tied into this whole thing somehow. Either he murdered Rachel and Ed, or at least one of them, or he has a good idea who did. My guess is that he murdered both of them."

"Why?"

Sam raised her gaze to look directly at Wade.

"First, Bill thinks he is smarter than anyone else. He thinks he could get away with it. My guess is that he found out about the other men in Rachel's life and became jealous. So he first took his jealousy and rage out on Rachel and then went to the highest profile of the other men in her life, which would have been the mayor. From what he told us, he had some conflicts with Ed and didn't particularly care for him anyway, so why not start with him?"

"So what you're saying is that Bruce, Frank Davis and John would have been on the list if we hadn't interfered."

Wade nodded. "My guess is that they're still on the list until we catch Bill."

"You don't think he'll still try to kill them with us knowing about him now, do you?"

"Sam, something isn't right about a man who would kidnap two teenagers, use one for a farmhand slave and the other one for a sex slave for many years, and still show up for the town council meetings as though he led a normal life. Bill thinks the rules that apply to the rest of the world don't apply to him. He thinks he is intellectually superior to us and will always be one step ahead of us."

Sam looked around the empty farm.

"So far, I'd agree with him. We haven't seen a trace of him in over a week and we've looked everywhere. He just might be too smart for us."

Sam dropped her head in disappointment.

Suddenly a wide smile crossed Wade's face.

Sam saw it and looked up expectantly.

"Sam, you're a genius, but you already know that."

"You've figured something out, haven't you, Wade?"

"What you said made sense. We've been looking all over his property and haven't seen a hair or any trace of him."

Sam stopped rocking. "I don't see what's so ingenious about that."

"You also said he was smart and was staying one step ahead of us all the time."

"Yes, and it's true."

Wade grinned.

"So how is he staying ahead of us all the time?"

Sam shrugged her petite shoulders.

"I don't know."

"He would have planned on this happening way before it happened. He had a contingency plan for getting exposed. He may not have known how it would happen, but he knew it was a distinct possibility."

Sam rose from the rocker. "So how does that help us? We still don't know where he is."

"If I wanted to just fade out of sight for a long time, I would do one of two things. I would have an identity in another country or I would go underground."

"So he's in Europe, Asia, Belize or Africa or he's in the underground community in the USA. Is that what you're saying?"

Wade shook his head.

"The first part is right. Either he could be in a foreign country under an assumed name, but that doesn't fit his profile to me. He thinks he's too smart for us and would want to show us up. When I said underground, I meant that I believe he's right here on the property, but not on the property. I think he is under the property."

Sam's eyes widened.

"That means he would have had to dig a cave and furnish it with food and water for a long time."

Wade was more sure of this than ever.

"Have you seen some of these doomsday bunkers, where people were planning on the end of time with the Mayan calendar running out?"

Sam nodded. "I've seen a couple of news spots on them."

"Some of them are set up for folks to live several years underground with all the comforts of home, but with the safety of being underground. They have enough food and water to last several months, if not years. They also have at least one filtered air vent to allow oxygen in." Wade explained.

"So now we're looking for an underground bunker. Do you know how many acres he has here to hide a bunker?"

"I do, but my guess is that it's close to his house. A lot of these things are set up to tie into the existing water supply, so the users can use that to flush the toilets and take showers. Then they get to use the stored water for drinking only."

A thorough search of the interior of the house didn't

lead to any trap doors that hid a bunker. Wade and Sam sat on the front porch to decide their next move.

Sam sighed.

"You know this is like looking for that proverbial needle in a haystack, don't you?

Wade looked over at her, but not directly at her, as his thoughts turned to thinking like Bill Brogan. He tried to imagine what Bill was thinking when he put in the bunker.

If I were Bill, where would I put it? I'd want a place where other people either wouldn't think of or would be afraid to go. Where would that be and still be close to the house?

"I've got it!"

Wade yelled as the realization came to him. Sam jumped at the excitement in his voice.

"What do you have?"

"I know where the bunker is!" he exclaimed.

Wade strode confidently toward the small barn and turned directly toward the cage holding the rattlesnakes. When he got to the cage, he scrutinized examined the bottom and then reached down and lifted the cage which then rested on three hinges in the back of it.

Below the cage was a door with a lock on the outside, which didn't fit the scenario Wade had imagined.

Why would there be a lock on the outside? Normally, the lock would be on the inside to keep people from entering, not on the outside to keep someone inside from leaving. Something was wrong.

42 PROTOCOL, HELL. THERE ARE SOME THINGS MORE IMPORTANT THAN PROTOCOL

WADE DUG AROUND THE BARN AND FOUND A BOLT cutter and removed the lock from the door of the bunker. By now, half a dozen deputies gathered around the opening. Although all of them were saying encouraging things to Wade, none volunteered to be the first to enter the bunker. Wade knew the difference between bravado and true courage, and Sam's deputies had lots of bravado, but very little courage. He lifted the door to the bunker, unsure if he had true courage when in a situation where he was forced to act, since nobody else volunteered to lead. The hair on the back of his neck stood straight up and a queasiness in his stomach threatened to buckle his knees.

A series of descending steps led to the darkness below. Wade asked if anyone had a flashlight and was answered by a half a dozen shaking heads. Then Sam took off running toward her car and returned with a long, high beam light. Wade felt much better with it in one of his hands and his pistol in his other hand as he edged down the steps, shining the light in front of him. When he got to the bottom of the steps, he moved the light so it shined on the large room that was probably described as the living area in the brochure about the bunker.

Just as he placed a foot off the descending steps, Wade heard the rush from behind right before he felt the bone-jarring crush of another body slamming into his. He dropped the flashlight and the pistol, trying to focus on getting some air back into his lungs even as his body drove into the floor of the bunker. Fists pummeled his face and body seemingly from everywhere, and Wade could not fashion of defense from the violent assault.

Desperately trying to draw in a little breath between the blows being delivered on his body, Wade heard a piercing scream from the steps and felt another body slam on top of his and the assailant's. Through the fog, Wade felt the blows become less and less frequent until they finally stopped and the two bodies on top of his rolled to one side, allowing him to inhale some precious air, slowly at first and then in deep gulps.

Wade scrambled in the dark and regained his pistol and the flashlight. When he turned on the light, he gasped, seeing diminutive little Sam sitting on top of his assailant with her pistol stuck in his nose. Wade could not imagine little Sam overpowering someone that had just mauled him, but was glad and grateful she had.

"Don't stick that barrel too far up his nose. He won't be able to smell anything for a month as it is."

Wade focused his flashlight on the face of his assailant only to find not a confident Bill Brogan, but a trembling Trahan.

"What the heck are you doing down here in the dark, Trahan?"

"I was waiting—for Senor Bill. I was going to ask him—where Suzee was."

Trahan was still gasping for breath from the impact of Sam.

"You sure have a funny way of starting a conversation. I thought I was a goner until Sam jumped in."

Turning his flashlight on Sam, "By the way, thanks for the help. I didn't know you were a wrestling champ along with all of your other talents."

"There are a lot of things you don't know about me yet."

Sam removed the gun from Trahan's face.

"But if you stick around, I might teach you a thing or two."

Wade smiled and turned his flashlight back on Trahan.

"How long have you been down here?"

"I'm not sure, Senor Wade. Ever since you and Miss Sam came and left. I don't have a clock down here. I'm not sure if it's night or day."

"Trahan, that means you've been down here for a week. Are you okay?"

"Yes, I found food and water when I turned on the stove for light. I didn't want to leave it on because I didn't know how much gas it had. I didn't want to run out."

Wade could only imagine Trahan stuck in this jail below the earth, having no idea how long he might be here and the only source of light that he found was a gas stove. He felt sorrow for Trahan and extreme anger at Bill Brogan for leaving him here with no explanation.

"Trahan, let's get you above ground. We need to ask you a lot of questions."

Wade led Sam and Trahan out of the survival bunker and back to fresh air. The cool crisp breeze coming off the tree tops never felt so good to him and he swore silently that he would never take this wonderful gift of nature for granted again.

Looking around at the half a dozen deputies, he wondered why none of them had descended into the bunker to help. He turned to the nearest deputy.

"Jesse, why didn't you come down there and assist us?"

The deputy looked down at the ground, nervously digging the toe of his shoe in the dirt.

"It happened quick and from the way it sounded, we weren't sure what was down there. We took cover just in case there was something that wasn't human that had you and Sam, and we were ready to shoot it when it came out of the hole."

"Jesse, remind me not to depend on you if anything important comes up. You know, like a life or death situation or something like that."

The deputy never lifted his gaze from his boots.

"You don't understand. We saw Sam go down there and she let out a blood-curdling scream like we ain't never heard before. That scream just froze us in our tracks. Then we heard all hell break loose down there. Besides, we're not in love with you like she is."

The tension slowly released.

"That's okay, Jesse. I'm not sure I would have reacted any differently than you did had I been in your position."

He then turned to find Sam. He saw her leaning against her patrol car, taking in some deep, deep breaths. Wade walked over to her car and put his arms around her.

"Thanks for saving my bacon down there. But you realize that wasn't exactly protocol on how to handle that situation."

"Protocol, hell. There are some things more important than protocol and I happen to think your life is one of those things, Mr. Dalton."

"And you will never know how much that means to me,

Sheriff Cates. But you need to protect that pretty little body of yours, and that means following protocol. Besides, I was just letting him tire himself out before I got after him."

Sam shook her head.

"From what little I could see and hear, the only thing he was tiring out was his knuckles upside your hard head. I should have let him alone for a while so he could beat some sense into it."

"That might have taken a little too long."

Wade took in another deep breath.

"How did you learn to take a guy down like that, anyway?"

"I'm not sure. I just reacted when I heard him blindside you and then pound on you. I think adrenaline had a lot more to do with it than training."

"Whatever it was, I truly appreciate it. But it always seems like you're saving my big backside. I always thought the hero was supposed to save the damsel in distress, not the other way around."

"Welcome to the twenty-first century, Mr. Dalton. Don't you know that damsels have equal rights now and we can save the big bad heroes if we want to?"

He gave her a big hug and wondered how he could be so fortunate to have discovered Sam in this tiny Mississippi town.

43 DESTINY AND DISASTER ARE NEVER FAR APART

THE EXTENSIVE INTERVIEW WITH TRAHAN TURNED UP very little fresh evidence for Wade and Sam in their investigation of Bill Brogan. He had never seen Rachel Chastain at the ranch and could not pick out her picture from a lineup of six photographs. He feared rattlesnakes and stayed away from them and had no idea how many Bill normally kept. He had no knowledge of Rachel's rifle. Nor would he have known because Bill kept all of his guns in a fortified built-in gun safe with a combination lock. Trahan did not know the combination, even though Wade had figured it out rather easily by knowing one trait of a self-centered man was to create passwords and combination codes that reflected them. Wade entered Bill's birthday broken into three numbers for the month, day and year, and the doors swung open to the gun vault. Although he and Sam found a treasure trove of information and over twenty rifles, shotguns and pistols, Rachel's rifle was not among them.

"Is there anything else that you know that would help us find Bill, Trahan?" Wade asked.

The shy young man shook his head.

"Not that I know of, Wade."

"Did he ever mention friends or family to you he might go see if he needed any help?"

"No, Senor. I never gave it much thought, but he had no family over and the only friends he ever invited up to the ranch were the preacher and his kids."

"Do you know the name of the preacher?"

"Mr. Bill, he called him Brother Jack. I don't remember the boy's name, but the girl's name was Sarah."

Wade instantly recalled the trip he and Sam made to see the Raymonds, where he had encountered both Sarah and Johnny. Recalling the image of Sarah provoked a brief smile. The image might have been too pleasing and the smile a little too obvious since Sam kicked him under the table on his shin, bringing him back to the present.

"Can you describe the girl? I believe you said her name was Sarah."

"Si, Senor. She was skinny as five-day-old road kill, except for her pechos." Trahan grinned.

"I'm sorry, Trahan. My Spanish isn't that good. Did you say pechos?"

"Si, Senor. Teta's, I mean breasts, uh boobs"

Trahan pointed at his own chest, somewhat embarrassed by his inability to describe the unique characteristic he had seen in Sarah.

Wade just smiled more, knowing they were talking about the same girl. Trahan looked down at the table, not wanting to make eye contact with Sam. After a minute or two of awkward silence, Sam spoke.

"I believe you might be talking about Sarah Raymond, daughter or Reverend Jack Raymond. She has a brother named Johnny."

"Si, Miss Sam. That is the one." Trahan sighed in his relief that he didn't have to further describe Sarah to Sam and Wade, mostly to Sam.

44   DOES A BOYFRIEND REALLY MAKE YOU FEEL SPECIAL?

SAM AND WADE DECIDED NOT TO MAKE THE TRIP BACK to the Blue Heaven Nature Church by themselves. Instead, three patrol cars accompanied them, each with a pair of deputies. They had no way of knowing if Bill Brogan was there or what he'd told the Raymond's and the rest of the congregation if he was hiding up there in the hills. They wanted plenty of firepower for the worst-case scenario, although neither expected this situation to escalate to that point. Both Wade and Sam were skeptical that Bill would hide out with the Raymond's or would resort to gunplay.

As they meandered through the overgrown road on the way, each of them remembered the somewhat eerie experience of their previous visit and wondered if they would have the same feelings on this trip. As they neared the opening where the little church sat, Wade could feel the tension mounting in his body and glanced over at Sam. She was sitting almost stiff from head to toe, exhibiting an angst that Wade fully understood. He felt there was just something different about this place other than Sarah

Raymond with her big boobs, although he would enjoy seeing them again.

The four patrol cars eased into the clearing and parked a good way from the church. Wade and Sam got out of their vehicle and surveyed the situation. Wade spotted Johnny on top of the church in almost the same location he had seen Sarah when they came the first time.

"Hey, Johnny! It's Wade and Sam here."

Wade relaxed and walked toward the church.

Suddenly, Johnny fired a shot at Wade's feet. Wade instinctively jumped backwards towards Sam's patrol car. He then realized it was just Johnny's way of telling him he wasn't welcome.

Sam realized the same thing and yelled to the six deputies, all of whom crouched behind their patrol cars.

"Don't shoot! Don't shoot!"

Just as she said it, Johnny fired another shot into the branches above Wade's head. Johnny then stood up, grinning at Wade and Sam. Wade grinned back until he heard a shot from the direction of the deputies and saw Johnny grab his side.

Johnny lifted his rifle and fired at the patrol cars protecting the deputies. Wade didn't know if the wound in Johnny's side was affecting his aim or if he was intentionally missing his targets, but the shots from Johnny's rifle were nowhere close to hitting any of the deputies.

Wade yelled at the deputies to cease firing, but to no avail. None of them had ever been in a gunfight before, and they were intent on finishing this one. Wade saw Johnny grabbing at his stomach again and then watched as he folded and fell from the roof of the small church into the dirt right in front of the steps. His last couple of breaths were filled with the same dirt he played in so many times as a child.

Sam first noticed the door of the church opening and feared what would happen next. To her dismay, she saw Sarah running out of the church toward her wounded brother. The deputies to Sam's right, filled with adrenaline, did not stop firing their rifles and pistols. Sam watched in horror as a bullet hit Sarah in the upper leg and Sarah catapulted forward. As she struggled to get up off the ground, another shot hit her squarely in the midsection and she fell backward, resting on the church steps not six feet from her brother.

Sam, without thinking, sprinted toward the frail fallen body. The deputies, seeing their leader charging toward the church, quickly followed with their guns ready to fire at anything or anyone that might present a danger. Wade, his mind still in a haze about what he had just witnessed, raced up to Johnny and kicked his rifle away from the body. He knew that Johnny was in no shape to use the weapon, but his prior training was controlling his actions now until his mind could regain control.

Sam cradled Sarah in her arms with tears running down her cheeks. She looked at the holes in Sarah's pants and her shirt and took off her jacket and pressed it against Sarah's midsection to slow the bleeding. Sarah's eyes flickered open, and she smiled at Sam.

"Oh, Sarah! I didn't mean for any of this to happen."

Sam was in tears.

"It's okay, Miss Sam. Is Johnny going to be okay?" the frail girl asked feebly.

Sam glanced at Johnny's crumpled body and knew he was already dead, but did not want to tell Sarah in her condition.

"He's gonna be okay. We have to get the two of you to the hospital where they can take care of you."

Sam could not control the avalanche of tears streaking down her face.

"We both know I ain't gonna make it to no hospital, Miss Sam. I've shot enough critters to know when they're done fer, and I'm hit worse than most of em'. Just tell Johnny to keep fresh flowers on my grave, will you?"

"Sarah, don't talk like that. You're going to live to be an old lady."

"I wish, Miss Sam. I don't reckon I'll ever know what it's like to have a real boyfriend like yours. Tell me, Miss Sam. Does a boyfriend really make you feel special?"

With those words, Sarah's eyes closed for the last time and her ears could not hear Sam's reply.

"Yes, Sarah. He makes me feel really special."

Sam whispered, knowing that Sarah would never experience a relationship like she had with Wade.

Sam looked down at her blood-soaked jacket, still pressed firmly against Sarah's stomach even though there was no more blood flowing from the wounds. She gently raised Sarah's head and laid it on the steps of the old church. Then, in an instant, she turned and sprang at the nearest deputy, clawing and beating him with an uncontrollable rage.

Wade jumped from the ground next to Johnny and grabbed Sam from behind, trying unsuccessfully to pin her flailing arms against her side. Sam's rage was too much to control until another Deputy came to Wade's rescue and helped him subdue Sam. Finally, Sam stood trembling and shaking in front of the six deputies and Wade.

"What the hell were you doing? You just shot an innocent boy and an unarmed girl?"

Sam stared at them.

"Sam, they was shooting at Wade and then they started shooting at us. What did you expect us to do?" One deputy stammered.

"If Johnny had been trying to shoot Wade, then he'd be dead right now. If he was trying to kill one of you, then you'd be dead right now. He wasn't shooting at you. He just was sending you a message, you morons."

"How were we supposed to know that?" The same deputy asked.

Sam ignored the question. Instead, she moved to within inches of the deputy and placed her face almost touching his.

"And what was the girl going to shoot you with, you idiot? Her finger? She didn't have a weapon!"

"I just saw her running out of the church right at us. I didn't know she wasn't armed."

The deputy was obviously the one that shot Sarah. He hung his head, unable to look Sam in her eyes. Wade almost felt sorry for him until he looked at the two dead kids lying on the ground in front of the church.

He watched as Sam slowly regained her composure as the deputy sheepishly shuffled off toward his patrol car. He had no idea what to say to Sam to make this inane, senseless act more acceptable in her mind. To justify the killing of the two kids by her Deputies could be easy in a court of law since Johnny fired in the general direction of the officers, but Wade and Sam knew he wasn't trying to kill them or even come close to them. Wade walked over to Sam and put his arms around her and squeezed her tightly. Sam accepted his embrace as her tears could no longer be held in check, slowly rolling down her soft cheeks. Wade pulled her even more tightly to his body, not caring what the other Deputies might think of the situation.

The shot shattered the quiet, and Wade jerked his head around.

45 WE JUST KILLED AN ENTIRE FAMILY

H<small>E HAD ASSUMED ALL THE GUNPLAY WAS OVER AND WAS</small> not expecting the loud report of a weapon so close to him. In the confusion, he wasn't even sure from where the shot came. He just reacted and pushed Sam to the ground with his body on top of her to protect her from more shots. A second shot pinpointed the location of the shooter right behind the corner of the Blue Heaven Nature Church. He rolled his body to that side, putting it between the shooter and Sam.

With gun in hand, lying on the ground, Wade took his first survey of the situation. The deputy that had been making his way toward his patrol car was in a heap in the dirt halfway to the car, either immobilized or dead. Wade assumed the latter, given the amount of blood already seeping into the dirt around the body. None of the other deputies seemed harmed as they scattered to find cover from the shooter. Wade could not see the shooter from his vantage point, only the end of the rifle barrel sticking out from the corner of the building.

As he watched, fire exploded from the barrel with the

third shot. Wade heard the thud of the bullet striking flesh and another deputy cried out in pain. A quick glance toward the sound told Wade that the deputy was not dead, but was in no condition to continue trying to defend himself or his fellow Deputies. Wade realized that he had to act quickly or almost the entire force of the Evergreen County Sheriff's department would be decimated.

A fourth shot silenced the injured deputy as Wade heard his bullet laden body hit the ground. Wade leaped from his kneeling position at a right angle to the corner of the church. As soon as he came even with the sight line of the shooter, he dove to the ground, rolling over in the dirt. As he rolled, he fired three quick shots at the figure behind the rifle. His first two shots hit the shooter squarely in the chest, and his third shot was high as the shooter fell backward. It hit the shooter in the throat and blood gushed from all three wounds. Any of the three shots would have been fatal and the combination of the three completely incapacitated the shooter immediately.

The shooter's body twisted and fell face down next to the church building. Wade slowly stood to his feet and slowly inspected every corner of the area within his eyesight and saw nothing else that would indicate any further danger from sniper fire. As he turned back toward the clearing, he was dismayed to see the two deputies that had been hit were not moving at all. Sam had re-positioned herself at the top of the steps with her pistol drawn and aimed at the corner of the church. The four remaining deputies were cowering behind their patrol cars, afraid to even peek out above their shelter.

Wade eased up to the body of the shooter and gently rolled it over, expecting to see the face of Bill Brogan.

Instead, he was staring in the dead eyes of Jack Raymond, Pastor of Blue Heaven Nature Church.

"We just killed an entire family."

The soft voice behind Wade startled him. He pivoted to see Sam, her pistol still in her hands, staring down at the dead Reverend. His gaze followed hers back to the body on the ground, but he felt no remorse for his part in this senseless circumstance. He knew that if he had not acted, the other four deputies of the Evergreen Sheriff's department would now lay on the same ground as their two deceased companions.

"Yes, Sam. We did."

Wade put his pistol back in its holster and embraced Sam again. Her arms hung limply by her sides with her pistol still clutched in her right hand. Wade gently took the pistol from her hand and tucked it in his belt.

"You can't blame yourself for this, Sam." He whispered in her ear. "Sometimes things happen outside our control and this is one of those things."

Three of the other four deputies were slowly approaching Wade and Sam. The fourth deputy was on his knees next to the tree line of the clearing, regurgitating his stomach contents.

Wade spoke to the nearest deputy.

"Get the coroner headed this way and tell him he needs to handle five bodies. I don't think we'll need an ambulance."

The deputy nodded and started talking into his microphone at once. The other deputies stood in a daze, waiting for someone to give them instructions.

"Don't touch anything." Wade said. "Call the State Troopers and have them send an investigator out here so there won't be any question of what happened and our role in it. Also, get in touch with a judge and get us a search warrant for this church."

With that, Wade strode up the steps of the church building. Sam followed closely.

"What are you doing?" She asked. "We have to wait for the warrant."

"I'm going to do what we came here to do. Find Bill Brogan!" He had barely finished the sentence before he leaped in the air and kicked the right side of the double doors leading into the church. The door gave only less than an inch and repelled Wade backwards. He slipped on the steps and fell on his back, sliding down the incline. He came to rest staring at the blood-soaked face of Sarah Raymond.

He then heard the soft giggle from Sam.

"These doors pull out, Agent Dalton." She said quietly. "They don't push in."

She pulled on one door, and it opened easily with little effort.

Wade looked down, or rather up, at his belt and realized he still had Sam's pistol tucked in his pants. He scrambled up, pistol in hand and through the door that had bettered him only moments before. He found Sam only a step inside the church, staring at the rattlesnakes in the cages along the walls. As Wade handed Sam her pistol, he eased past her into the main Sanctuary. There was little light and an eerie feeling crept up the back of Wade's neck. He felt like he was being watched, but saw no one in the building other than Sam. He motioned to Sam to search the left side of the room, and he watched the right side as they inched their way down the center aisle. He carefully scanned the floor between the pews as they neared the pulpit. A fast movement behind the pulpit in the baptism pool caught his gaze. He turned and fired at the movement, amazed when a small bird flew out of the baptism area.

Wade hadn't known just how tense he was until he saw the bird fly off. Now he better understood how the deputies must have felt when Johnny was firing rounds in their general direction.

"You missed him, Agent Dalton" Sam giggled.

"Yeah, but I didn't miss the other one."

Wade pointed at a dead bird floating in the baptismal pool.

"*Damn*" was all that Sam could say.

"Didn't your Dad teach you not to cuss in church?" Wade grinned.

Three of the four deputies burst through the doors of the small church with their guns drawn. Wade wondered if the fourth deputy was still puking his guts out down by the tree line.

They inspected the rest of the small church and found nothing else.

46 WHO KNOWS WHAT THE TWINS ARE THINKING?

THREE DAYS PASSED SINCE THE TRAGEDY AT THE Blue Heaven Nature Church, and Wade still had no solid lead on finding Bill Brogan. It seemed Bill disappeared into thin air. A constant check of his credit cards and cell phone records turned up nothing. The deputies posted at his farm got bored sitting there all day with no one else around except for the bison. They particularly didn't appreciate the long nights that far away from the city with no way to entertain themselves. Their complaints fell on deaf ears at the County Sheriff's office. Sam wanted to find Bill Brogan and make him pay for all the heartache and grief he caused.

The joint funeral service for the two deputies and three members of the Raymond family was scheduled for the early afternoon at the First Baptist Church, and Wade didn't want to attend. That he killed one of the deceased weighed heavily on his mind. He wasn't sure how he would react when he looked into the coffin of Brother Jack Raymond, knowing he was the one that put him there. Going over the circumstances of the situation time and time again in his mind told him he had no better choices available to him at the time than the one he chose, but that choice ended in the death of another person and that bothered him greatly.

Wade drove to the Sheriff's office and picked up Sam. She looked pale and drawn, as though she had not slept for many days.

"Are you okay?" Wade queried.

"Not really. We lost two deputies for the first time in the history of Evergreen County, and it was on my watch. I'm responsible and now I'm going to their funerals. I feel like a hypocrite."

"Sam, it wasn't your fault that Johnny started shooting at us and it wasn't your fault that one of your deputies disobeyed your orders and fired at him and Sarah. It also wasn't your fault that Reverend Raymond decided to get revenge himself and killed your two deputies."

"Then why do I feel so bad?" Sam sighed.

"Because you're just like me. You wish you could undo it. That it'd never happened. But it happened and the best thing we can do is learn from it. One of those caskets we'll be looking at today is directly because of me. Don't you think I've tried to figure out if I could have done something different?"

"But what do I say to the families of the two deputies? They were depending on me to keep their husbands and fathers safe, and I blew it."

"Sam, when they pinned that badge on their chests, they knew there might be a day coming when they would risk their lives for the safety of the residents of Evergreen County. That day came three days ago and as much as I would like to change it, two of your officers didn't make it through the day. It wasn't your fault."

"I keep telling myself that, but it'll take time. Officer Howard resigned yesterday."

Wade assumed Officer Howard was the deputy that threw up by the tree line after the gunfight. Wade assumed he wouldn't last on the force for long when he saw his reaction to live combat.

"That has to be a decision that he makes with his family, Sam. I'm not sure it's our place to influence him. Some people aren't meant for certain jobs. I would suggest that the department offer the other officers and him psychological counseling. They need and deserve that."

"We've already set it up for the entire department, not just the other four Deputies on the scene. I scheduled a psychologist for tomorrow to interview everyone and he'll be here for the next few weeks to follow up with those that need it."

"And let me guess. Your name isn't on the list?"

"I'm going to talk with Brother Jeff down at the church tomorrow. I trust him more than some geek trying to determine if I beat my dog by showing me a bunch of dots on a piece of paper and my interpretation of what those dots look like."

Wade laughed.

"I understand that. I'd hate to see his evaluation of me when I tell him the dots look like a bunch of dots on a piece of paper. He'd probably have me locked up."

"No, Agent Dalton, he'd just you categorized as a sexual deviant with a perverted sense of humor. But the Thomas twins already know that, don't they?"

Wade winced. He hadn't even thought of the twins for several days now and was surprised that Sam still had those thoughts lingering in her mind. He decided not to confront her directly.

"Who knows what the twins are thinking? It'd be interesting to see a psychological evaluation of them, wouldn't it?"

"I'm not sure that a psychologist could make an evaluation of what's going on in their minds because what's going on now may or may not be what's happening in their minds a few minutes from now."

Wade chuckled. "You're right. They aren't confined by the community mores and ethical platitudes that most of us concern ourselves with. They're more like the free spirits that we hear so much about but never meet."

47 YOU KNOW HOW SECRETS AREN'T SECRET LONG AROUND HERE

THEY ARRIVED AT THE CHURCH, AND BROTHER JEFF greeted them on top of the steps.

"Good afternoon, Sam. Hello, Wade. I'm glad you came. I know how difficult these circumstances must be for both of you, particularly you, Sam."

"Yes, Brother Jeff. I wished none of this had happened and today's service wasn't necessary, but there's nothing I can do now to change anything. Given the circumstances, looking back on it, I understand better why everyone did what they did."

"I still think we should talk tomorrow."

Brother Jeff put his hand on Sam's shoulder and patted it the way her father had many times when she was a girl. Even though Brother Jeff was not much older than she was, he seemed to her so much wiser and more mature for his age.

"Thanks, Brother Jeff. I still plan on meeting with you. Would it be better if Wade and I met with you together or separately?"

Wade jerked his head in Sam's direction. He had not

discussed meeting with the Pastor, either with Sam or apart from Sam. He did not look forward to either scenario. He glanced at Brother Jeff and saw a look of understanding his predicament.

"I think you and I should meet first, Sam. Then we'll see if Wade wants to meet with us or with just me. Wade, you might handle this by other means, but I want you to know I'm available if you want to talk."

Before Wade could answer, he felt four arms surround his waist. He knew immediately they belonged to the Thomas twins and a strained look crossed his face, knowing how awkward this could end up.

"Hey, Wade!" they said in unison.

Then they turned to greet Sam and the Pastor.

"We think we have some good news for you, Wade."

"And what would that be, Mandy?"

"We think we can find out where Bill Brogan is hiding. But we'll have to wait until the Clerk of Court opens tomorrow to find out.

"What are—? Where did—?"

Wade stammered, trying to compose himself. This was the last thing he expected the girls to say. He and Sam searched high and low for any sign of Bill and came up empty-handed.

"How did you girls get a lead on the whereabouts of Bill?" Sam asked.

"Let's just say that sometimes being a good listener is better than being a good talker. Then putting two and two together, we came up with five, one more than the average bear."

Mindy beamed at their accomplishment, and both were genuinely proud.

"But we still have some work to do to find out if the story we heard has any validity."

"Would you like to share that story with us?"

Mandy cut in.

"It would take too long to tell you everything, but we have a legal address, you know, the address with the longitude and latitude and all that. We just have to convert it to a street address so we'll know where we're going."

"I hate to interrupt you, but we must get the service going." Brother Jeff cut in.

"Oh, we're sorry!"

Again the girls were in unison.

"We were just so excited about what we found, we couldn't wait to tell Wade and Sam. Let's go inside now and we'll tell you the rest after the service."

Brother Jeff looked at Sam.

"You're more than welcome to use my office to meet with them so you won't be disturbed. You'll just have to move some of my clutter out of the way."

"Thanks, Brother Jeff. I really appreciate that. You know how secrets aren't secret long around here."

Wade and Sam, along with the Thomas twins, entered the church and took their seats directly behind the families of the slain deputies. The attendees from the remainder of the Raymond clan took the pews on the other side of the aisle, not mixing in with the relatives of the deputies. Wade was concerned with the possible repercussions of the joint funeral, with all the loved ones from each side of the battle in the room with each other.

Sure enough, each side glared at the other, blaming each other for the death of their own loved ones. Wade was glad he brought his revolver and hoped Sam had one also hidden somewhere on her person. He felt like this situation could get ugly in a hurry.

Brother Jeff rose to the podium and looked out over the standing-room only crowd. He looked down first at the Raymond clan and then toward the families of the deputies.

"Let us turn to a song that I believe is appropriate in a time like this. Please open your hymnals to page three-seventy-five."

Wade and Sam shared a hymn book and opened it to "*Victory in Jesus*" on page three-seventy-five.

Wade wondered how singing a song together would make everyone feel better.

Brother Jeff paused.

"Instead of singing this song today, let us just read the words out loud. Eugene Bartlett wrote it in 1939, but somehow I feel like it is appropriate today."

The entire congregation read the entire lyrics of the old song including "*And then I cried, Dear Jesus, Come and heal my broken spirit*".

After the congregation read the song, Brother Jeff spoke again.

"There are a lot of broken spirits here today. Some of you blame others in this same room for your circumstances, for the loss of your loved ones. I don't know the whole story and I'll guess none of you here today know the whole story of why each of the participants did what they did. Even those of you that were there and saw as much as you could see will never know the motivations that caused the actions that took place. But I know that if you let those feelings fester, then you'll always look at that day with hate building in your heart. You won't remember the good times you had with your loved ones and the blessings you received by having them around, only the vile disgust for others in the room that you blame for their demise."

Brother Jeff paused for effect.

"But you can release that venom building up inside your body. Just as our Lord forgives us, let us forgive our neighbor and understand that our neighbor is also mourning. Will you let the victory take place in your life or will you let the hatred destroy you?"

The Pastor waited and looked left and right at the opposite sides in this affair. No one was budging.

"Are you really going to continue to hate for the rest of your lives?" he implored.

Still no one moved, although tears formed on both sides.

Brother Jeff fell on his knees by the pulpit and prayed out loud, but so softly that Wade could not make out the words. The suffocating tension in the Sanctuary bore down on the congregation as the minutes elapsed, each passing moment ratcheting up their emotions.

Sam, with tears streaming down her face, was the first to act. She slowly stood and sidled to the end of the pew. Then she crossed the aisle and walked to a spot directly in front of the matriarch of the Raymond clan.

She mouthed the words, "I'm sorry" and continued to cry.

After several long seconds passed, the older graying lady reached out to Sam and hugged her tightly, and then the avalanche of tears began across the entire congregation. People from each side of the aisle crossed over and hugged each other. Wade felt awkward and just stood where he was. He felt a small hand take his, and he looked down to see what seemed like a smaller replica of Sarah Raymond. The girl was obviously related to Sarah, but could only be six or seven years old.

"Hi, I'm Sue. I know you shot my uncle, but I just wanted to tell you I forgive you and that I love you."

The little girl squeezed Wade's hand tightly and smiled up at him through her own tears.

Wade put his arms around Sue and gave her the biggest bear hug he could without hurting her. With all the adults in the room, this small child had touched his inner being more than he could have imagined.

He whispered in the child's ear, "Thank you. I'll never forget your kindness."

He lowered Sue back down to where her feet could touch the ground and slowly released her. Although tears were still streaking down her small gaunt face, she still smiled.

She mouthed the words, "I love you" and returned to the other side of the isle.

Wade marveled at the wisdom of Brother Jeff. Now he saw the benefit of the unified service in a way that no one would have been able to explain earlier. He knew that the Pastor brought a feuding community together by this simple act of faith, and only through the eyes of one as faithful as the Pastor could this have been envisioned. Wade's respect and admiration of the Pastor reached all-time highs.

Wade saw that Brother Jeff was still on his knees by the pulpit, continuing to pray for this unification of the people. He walked up to this man of God and put his arms around him.

"Thank you, Brother Jeff. Thank you, thank you, thank you!"

The Reverend just smiled, almost abashedly, and nodded. He rose and stood again behind the pulpit, observing the mingling congregation and the rising emotions prevalent among it.

After several minutes, he said, "Thank you, everyone. If we could return to our seats for a minute or two."

The Pastor waited for everyone to take their seats. He then spoke again, but the tenor of his voice was different to Wade. It seemed to have softened dramatically.

Brother Jeff was looking directly at Wade, or so it seemed.

"As we seek answers to the riddles of life, sometimes the answers are directly in front of you. Remember, the wise men had only to follow the star, and they reached their destination. We sometimes have only to follow the obvious signs to reach our destination."

Wade remembered nothing else from the rest of the service, which lasted for another twenty minutes. He knew by now that the Pastor never said anything off-the-cuff, and that everything he said had a deeper purpose than the words themselves. But Wade could not decipher the meaning behind the obvious words from this wise man. He had no doubt that the Pastor had intended those particular words for him and him alone. Or had he? Did everyone in the congregation feel like the Pastor was speaking directly to him or her? Wade had heard of some preachers that purportedly had this skill. Talking to the entire congregation while to each member separately.

Was the Pastor trying to give him a lead in the case from something he heard through a confession?

Wade knew that the Baptists didn't confess to their Pastors normally, but did someone say something to Brother Jeff that he couldn't pass on to Wade because of his position in the church?

48 WE'VE GOT BOOBS, WADE

After the service, Wade and Sam gathered with the Thomas twins in the Pastor's office. Wade was eager to see what the twins had uncovered and if it would be of any use to the investigation.

"We kept looking for ties to Bill Brogan in the old city records," Mindy explained. "We found a sale for an old tract of land with a house that his uncle bought almost twenty years ago. His uncle died and his brother inherited the tract. That was Bill's father. But the records were never updated to reflect the change in ownership. So when Bill's father died, Bill must have inherited the house and the land, but his name isn't anywhere on the records, just his uncle's and his dad's. We figured he might hide out there since no one knows to look for him on his own property."

Wade could only shake his head and admire the detective work the twins performed.

"I don't know what to say, girls. This is outstanding work, whether Bill is there or not. You should be proud of what you've discovered here and the obvious effort and hours you spent digging for this information."

Both girls grinned.

"What's wrong? I just gave you a compliment." Wade asked, his exasperation clear.

"Wade, you don't know how City Hall works, do you? Even when you've seen how Rachel could manipulate the entire staff, you really haven't caught on, have you?"

"I guess not because I don't know what you mean." Wade wore a confused look.

The girls grinned again.

"We've got boobs, Wade. We don't have to spend hours looking through files and computer records. When you've got boobs, there are plenty of nerds that will do that for you." Mindy explained to Wade.

Mandy added, "So far we just have a legal description, but one nerd is supposed to have us a street address tomorrow morning. And as much as Mindy has flirted with him, I bet he has it when we get to work."

"Those guys don't have a chance with you two around, do they?" Wade smiled at both of the girls.

"Nope." Mindy answered. "And neither would you if you weren't so madly in love with Sam."

She changed her focus to Sam.

"But we understand. It's not your fault. Heck, if we'd found him first, you wouldn't have a chance either."

Sam looked at Mindy and then grinned at Wade.

"I'm not sure that was a blessing or a curse. I may want to trade him to you guys if a better offer comes along later."

Wade deflected the conversation to another subject before it became too personal.

"You girls do know, don't you, that if you plug in the latitude and longitude numbers into the GPS on your cell phones, it will direct you to the location? The GPS system can use either those or the street address to guide you there."

"We haven't figured out how to use that yet." Mandy spoke up. "Maybe we'll have to get one of our new friends in the IT Department to show us how."

Both of the girls giggled.

"If you'll share it with me, maybe I can look it up on mine."

"We don't have it with us, but we can get it to you first thing after we get to work tomorrow. But then, we should have the street address from our new friends."

"Will you call me with it?"

Wade already knew the answer, but asked anyway.

"Nope; you'll to have to take us with you." Mandy answered, her face trying to show how serious she was. Wrinkles covered her forehead and her lips were drawn.

Wade consented, "Okay, you guys can go with us, but you have to promise to stay in the car until we make sure it's safe. We don't need another incident out there."

Both of the twins laughed.

"You betcha, Detective Ranger."

49 WE SHOULDN'T HAVE BROUGHT THE TWINS WITH US

Wade and Sam picked the twins up just before noon the next morning. Mandy confirmed that the twins obtained the street address from their new friends at City Hall.

"Let's go over this one more time, girls. You will stay in this vehicle until either Sam or I tell you it's safe to get out. Are we clear on that?"

Wade used the sternest voice he had, lowering his voice when he said 'you' or 'we'.

After he finished, Sam took over.

"We don't know if Bill is at his uncle's place or not, but we have to assume he's there and that he's armed and dangerous. I know you helped us find this place and I'm still not sure it's appropriate to bring you guys along, but we are responsible for your safety as long as you're with us. Do you understand?"

Both twins nodded in unison.

Wade was nodding also, hoping the twins would show a modicum of maturity. He and Sam discussed the decision to allow the twins to accompany them at length the previous evening. Both of them realized the ultimate decision to let them come was against department protocol and may put the twins in unnecessary danger. But they reasoned that Bill was probably not there, and they both wanted to keep some friendly ears at City Hall.

The coordinates provided by the twins led the foursome to a cabin nestled next to the Pearl River that ran out of the National Forest. A deep slough on one side of the property and the river on the other side made the site a virtual peninsula, impenetrable except down the narrow path barely visible from the county road.

Wade pulled up to the railed gate made with remnants of oilfield tubing. When the car came to a stop, he again addressed the twins in his sternest voice.

"You guys have to promise me you'll stay in the car until either Sam or I tell you it's okay to get out."

Wade arched his eyebrows, awaiting a response.

The twins looked at each other and then both nodded somberly, as if Wade hurt their feelings and did not completely trust them. Each of them looked down at the floor of the patrol car and then sheepishly back at Wade and nodded again.

"We promise."

The giggles did little to build Wade's confidence in their words.

Wade drew his revolver as he exited the vehicle and walked up to the gate. Sam, her gun also drawn, exited the vehicle, but stayed behind the open door in case she needed it for cover.

"There has been activity here this morning." Wade announced after a brief visit to the closed gate. "The same car passed by here twice, entering once and leaving once. I'm not sure of the order. Whether it left and returned or it came and then left. My guess is that it came and then left."

"Why do you think that?" Sam queried.

Wade motioned toward the ground.

"Do you see the mud on this side of the gate where it appears the car sat for a little while and the mud dropped off on the ground? There's one or two partial footprints in that mud. I didn't see any footprints on the other side of the gate. I'd take from the prints that the driver of the car opened the gate on his arrival and left it open until he left. Then he got out of the car and closed the gate when he left."

"No wonder they call you a Detective Ranger." Mindy piped up from the back seat.

Wade's jaw dropped a little because he momentarily forgot the twins could hear him. Wiping his forehead to stall until he could get his thoughts together, he shrugged his shoulders and continued.

"My assumption now is that Bill is here or at least was here and somehow somebody found out we were coming and beat us out here to warn him."

Sam blinked before staring directly at Wade.

"I didn't even tell the deputies where I was going this morning. Besides, you and I didn't know the location until after we picked up the twins."

Wade looked somberly at the twins.

"I guess that narrows it down, doesn't it?"

"We didn't tell anyone except you guys. I promise."

Mindy looked like she was on the verge of tears.

"One of those techs at City Hall may have said something to someone, but we didn't say anything."

"Should we call for backup?"

Sam had not forgotten the tragedy at the Blue Heaven Nature Church.

"We probably should." Wade shrugged. "But I seriously doubt if Bill's still here."

Wade paced in front of the railed gate, looking for any indication of the identity of the person or persons that had beat them to the location. After a few minutes, he strode to the back of the police car and addressed the twins directly.

"Are you sure that you didn't notice anyone take a special interest in your activities this morning? You know, asking what you were up to or where you were going?"

The twins looked at each other, each simultaneously shaking her head.

"We didn't notice anyone paying any more attention to us than normal, but we probably wouldn't have noticed, anyway. Men are always staring at us because—well, you know why. You're a man."

Wade nodded without even glancing at Sam, who was listening to the conversation. She knew the twins were well aware of the attention they drew from most men and the reasons behind it.

Wade continued to pace back and forth, barely able to contain his anxiety as he waited for the backup deputies to arrive. His furrowed brow revealed the unease he had with this entire situation.

We shouldn't have brought the twins with us. It's not protocol and nothing good can come out of this situation with them along.

Gus and three other deputies pulled in behind Sam's patrol car, bringing a smile to Wade's face. Sam greeted the deputies and filled them in on the circumstances leading up to the morning activities.

Gus, his old body creaking but full of confidence,

turned his attention to the back seat of Sam's patrol car, where the twins whispered with each other. He winked at Wade and turned to Sam.

"Sam, I know our budget is tight, but I didn't know we hired school girls for deputies. I guess that's what happens when people get tired of paying taxes."

"Gus, I just told you why they're here. Don't you listen?"

"I listen, but I wanted you to know that when these two apply for my job, I want to provide the '*hands-on*' training, if you know what I mean."

Mandy couldn't resist.

"Gus, we might teach an old goat like you a thing or two."

Gus grinned. "Don't let my age fool you girls. There's still plenty of spark left in this old body."

Mindy laughed. "But we're not looking for a spark. We're looking for a bonfire."

Gus guffawed. "That's the trouble with you girls. You're in too much of a hurry."

Sam interrupted them. "If we don't hurry down this road, we'll all be looking for a job. Gus, did you bring the bolt cutter?"

"Sure did, Sam. Hey, one of you lazy buffoons get that chain cutter out of my trunk and take care of that gate." Gus was motioning toward the other deputies.

"Did you get the warrant?" Sam looked at Gus expectantly.

"Quit worrying. I've got it. Everything is legal and above board." Gus looked at the twins and laughed. "Almost everything, anyway."

The deputy cut the lock on the rail gate and swung the gate wide open. Wade, Sam, and the twins led the procession in their car up the narrow path to the cabin. Wade and Sam were much more cautious exiting the vehicle and approaching the cabin than they had been at the Blue Heaven Nature Church. They could only hope this trip turned out better.

50 NOW WHAT THE HELL DO I DO?

Wade could not see any other vehicles parked next to the sun-bleached wooden shack. His eyes strained for any movement within the enclosure or outside near the century-old live oaks that provided shade for the structure. The moss laden limbs of the oaks bowed to the ground and then rose back up to the sun, inviting adults to sit on them and kids to climb on them. Wade became so engrossed with the serenity and beauty of the setting that he jumped when startled by the blare of a bull horn next to him.

"Bill Brogan!" Wade heard Sam through the amplified voice box. "Come out with your hands up. We have blocked the exit, Bill. You have no way out."

Sam glanced over at Wade and shrugged her shoulders.

Wade gave her a thumbs-up and waited for a response from inside the shack. Beads of sweat formed on his forehead even though the temperature for South Mississippi was cooler than normal. He wiped his clammy hands as he fumbled with his gun.

Looking over at Sam, he gave her the walking fingers sign with his pointer finger, and his middle finger and then pointed to himself. She nodded and then passed on the message to Gus and the other deputies.

Wade felt his quadriceps tighten and then explode as he leaped toward the little shack, covering the distance between the cars and the hut in a few long strides. He did not exhale until he had reached the safety of the trunk of the biggest live oak, only three steps from the front door. From this vantage point, Wade motioned for Sam to once again try the bull horn.

"Bill Brogan! Put down your weapon and come out with your hands up. If you don't come out, we're going to come in after you, Bill."

Wade cocked his head to one side and strained his neck to get his ear as close to the structure as possible. He heard a slight brushing sound from inside the building. He quickly motioned for Sam and the other deputies to remain where they were and stay hidden behind the cover of the vehicles.

Now what the hell do I do? If I rush in, I'm liable to get myself shot. If I stay out here, Bill line up a shot at Sam or one of the other deputies while I'm only a step or two from preventing him from shooting.

Motion from behind the vehicles forced Wade to decide. Glancing to see what caused the motion, Wade saw one twin standing straight up, her cell phone in front of her face while she was taking a picture of the front door.

Seductive little pair, hell! They're about to get some people killed out here!

With a curse under his breath, Wade bull-rushed and crashed down the door with his shoulder. He regained his balance instantly and waited for the milliseconds for his eyes to adjust to the darker interior. A louder brushing sound came from his left and he whirled in that direction and went down on one knee, his firearm extended toward the sound. His pupils widened as he strained to focus on the source of the subtle noise. His sight narrowed to a lump of humanity in the fetal position lying in a pool of blood on the hardwood floor.

Wade crept over to the heap and turned it over. It was Bill Brogan.

Just as he discovered the identity of Bill, Sam and Gus burst through the now open door, guns drawn and pointing all over the room as their eyes adjusted to the darker surroundings.

"Over here." Wade rasped, his nerves still on edge.

The irony smell of blood enveloped the room. Quickly scanning Bill's body, Wade saw several gouges up and down the torso and what appeared to be a gunshot wound in the lower stomach or crotch area.

Bill's face bore no resemblance to the vibrant, healthy young man Wade and Sam had visited just several days prior. His fallowed cheeks sank and wrinkles covered his entire forehead. Will's noticed that Bill had not shaven or combed his knotted hair in days.

"He's not going to make it, is he?" Sam inquired.

"It doesn't look that good." Wade replied, his finger on Bill's faint pulse.

"If you two will 'cuse me for a minute and leave me with him, it'll look a lot better in a minute. I'll make sure he never bothers another girl around here again."

Gus edged next to Bill.

"Gus, you know we can't do that."

Gus roared. "The hell you can't! This guy isn't getting a plug nickel's worth of effort from me to get him any better. Just let him go on to that judgment in the great beyond. Ain't no doubt in my mind where he's gonna end up."

"And if you don't help him, you might find yourself

right along beside him. Now get on that radio and tell someone to get an ambulance headed this way."

The firmness in Sam's voice left no room for rebuttal.

The grizzled old deputy shuffled out the door, mumbling under his breath about the old ways of dealing with perverts was better.

Sam turned her attention back to Bill. The gunshot wound released fresh blood every time Bill attempted to move.

"Wade, hold him where he can't move. Wait, first hand me some of those wash cloths and towels off that shelf over there. We've got to stop the bleeding if he's going to have any chance at all."

Wade grabbed a handful of rags and towels and started pressing them into the seeping wounds. He leaned over Bill with his mouth right next to Bill's ear.

"Bill, do you know the person who did this?"

There was a perceptible movement of Bill's head.

"Bill, can you tell me who it was?"

Again, the slightest hint of a nod, but too much blood had spilled onto the floor. Bill tried to mumble, but he garbled the words. Wade strained to make some sense of the barely audible attempts by Bill, but could not understand any of it.

"Bill, do you know why this happened?"

Wade could see Bill straining to inhale as much oxygen as possible before trying to respond. After a few seconds, which seemed like hours to Wade, Bill eked out two words.

"For her."

Bill's body caved in and his breathing ceased. Sam pushed Wade aside and frantically administered mouth-to-mouth resuscitation. Wade watched tensely, anticipating a response from Bill's body. His shoulders sagged when he realized that Sam's efforts were futile.

"It's too late, Sam."

He helped her get to her feet.

"Did you hear what he told me?"

Sam wiped her mouth.

"No, he didn't say it loud enough."

"When I asked him if he knew why this happened, he said it was '*For her*'. I assume he's talking about either Rachel or Suzee."

Sam looked down at her uniform, now splotched with Bill's blood.

"If it was for Suzee, then Trahan would be the one we're looking for. But a deputy is supposed to be keeping an eye on him."

"If not Suzee, then he must have meant Rachel."

Wade could hear the wailing of the siren as the ambulance approached the old shack. He glanced toward the open door, his body stiffening when he saw the twins standing inside the room.

"How long have ya'll been there?"

"Long enough to know somebody did this because of Rachel." Mandy answered.

Wade was still furious with them and wasn't sure which one of them was speaking.

"Which one of you stood up out there? Didn't you realize you might have been killed or gotten somebody else killed by being stupid?"

Wade's body visibly shook with anger.

"It don't matter none." Gus had re-entered the room. "I'm going to take 'em both outside, pull their britches down and give 'em a good spankin'. Then maybe they'll learn to mind their elders."

Gus latched onto an elbow of each twin and pulled them out the door.

"So much for keeping facts internal to the investigation. We might as well broadcast it on the ten-o'clock news."

Sam sighed, "You know what they say. There are no secrets in Evergreen. I believe that'll be the case here."

51 AS WE SEEK ANSWERS TO THE RIDDLES OF LIFE, SOMETIMES THE ANSWERS ARE DIRECTLY IN FRONT OF YOU

AFTER THE OTHER DEPUTIES LEFT ESCORTING THE ambulance with the body, Wade and Sam were left alone in the shack with the twins. Wade occasionally glared at them while Sam attempted small talk as she and Wade looked for clues.

"Can we ask a question?" Mandy was hesitant, considering Wade's mood.

Wade stared at her before nodding.

"Where's the car? I mean, how did he get here without a car? How did he get groceries without a car?"

Wade's gaze softened, and he glanced at Sam. She shook her head.

"I honestly don't have a clue, Mandy."

"Well, he couldn't have walked from his ranch to here and there's no convenience store or grocery store for miles." Mandy continued to muse out loud.

"Maybe somebody helped him. You know; drove him out here and brought him food." Mindy jumped into the conversation.

Wade's mouth fell open, showing his surprise at the apparent logic of the twins.

Where was this logic when one of them stood up, making her a perfect target if Bill had shot? Does it just come and go like a wisp of smoke on a breezy day? Can they turn it on and off like a light switch or does it just appear at random?

These thoughts flooded Wade's mind, preventing him from immediately responding. He plopped down in a chair beside the vinyl-topped table.

"Excellent conclusions."

He nodded toward the twins. Their ear-to-ear grins showed how much his affirmation meant to them. They hugged each other as if this was the first time anyone had ever taken them seriously.

"You're right. Why didn't I think of that?"

Wade then remembered the words of Brother Jeff.

'As we seek answers to the riddles of life, sometimes the answers are directly in front of you.'

He said at the joint funeral.

What is wrong with me? I should have thought of those conclusions way before the twins did. If the answers are so obvious, why can't I see them?

"Humbling, isn't it?"

"Huh?" Wade's deep thought was interrupted.

"I said, it's humbling for a couple of teenage girls to think of something before you do, isn't it?" Mindy smiled.

Wade's eyes widened, and his cheeks reddened.

"Was I thinking out loud?"

"You might as well have been. What you were thinking was written all over your face."

Wade glanced at Sam for confirmation and she nodded.

"I don't know what's wrong with me."

Sam replied, "There's nothing wrong with you, Wade.

You just risked your life busting down a door and then watched a man die. It's okay for someone else to make some observations every once in a while."

Wade dropped his head for a minute or two. He raised his gaze and looked directly into the eyes of each of the twins and Sam.

"I'm sorry. I'm sorry that I let my ego impede progress in this case. Of not taking all of you seriously enough."

All three girls had tears welling at the corners of their eyes. Mindy was the first one to let hers flow freely, quickly followed by the other two. All three went to Wade and hugged him tightly.

After the embrace, Wade's voice was low and somber.

"Unfortunately, this puts us behind where we were before."

"What do you mean?" Mandy asked.

"Before an hour ago, I thought Bill had killed Rachel and I'm still not sure that he didn't. He fit the profile."

Wade made sure the young ladies were in agreement with him so far.

"But he couldn't have shot himself, Wade. There's no gun here." Sam was looking for holes in his hypothesis.

"True. We didn't find a gun, and there's no doubt in my mind that somebody else shot Bill. But do you remember what Bill said? He said '*For her*' when I asked him why this happened. This means someone is out there avenging Rachel's death."

Sam pressed her fingers into her temples.

"That only leaves Frank, the purchasing guy and John Grimes, the City Attorney. If I remember right, there was another city councilman on the project."

"Don't forget Dad. He was working with Rachel, or at

least sort of working with her." Mandy whispered quietly, almost feeling embarrassed about saying it.

"That's right. I had forgotten about Bruce." Sam nodded.

"And there's another name we haven't brought up in a while."

"Who's that?" Mindy asked, hoping the suspicion landed anywhere but with her father.

"Luke Chastain." Wade answered. "He could be out there taking revenge on whoever might have killed his daughter. He may not know which one killed her, but he may be going down the list."

Sam's brows arched.

"Do you remember how cut up Ed was? If he had known anything, he would have told Luke or whoever was torturing him. Since Bill is now dead, it wasn't Ed that killed her. Maybe Ed told Luke that Bill did it."

"That sounds as plausible as anything I can come up with right now."

"Then, hopefully, the killing has stopped, at least for this case."

"I don't think so, Sam. Did you see how cut up Bill was? He was probably asked all the same questions as Ed. He also probably gave the killer the same answers, which means Frank, Bruce and John are still on the list if Bill didn't admit killing her."

Wade heard the twins whimpering beside him.

"Geez, I'm sorry. We shouldn't have been discussing this in front of you two. I guess I'm still not thinking clearly."

"What can you do to help Dad?" Mindy asked.

"Sam can offer some protection, but I don't know how much."

Sam's gaze searched the ceiling for answers.

"We don't have enough manpower to offer around-the-clock protection. I don't think anything will happen to them at City Hall. It's too public. We can escort them to and from work if they want and we can have a deputy give rolling surveillance on their three homes at night. That's probably the best we can do."

"Ya'll know that Dad couldn't kill anyone, don't you?" Mindy implored.

"Mindy, I don't think your Dad killed Rachel or Ed or Bill. But we have to go where the evidence leads us. If it leads us to Bruce, then we have no choice except to go there. Do you understand?"

"The evidence won't take you anywhere near Dad. If it does, then something is wrong." Mindy said defiantly.

Both twins turned in unison and strode out into the sunlight.

"I really feel bad for them. I couldn't stand them at first and now I like them." Sam whispered to Wade.

"I know. I've kinda grown fond of them myself, and not for the reasons you're thinking."

"I know you're just admiring their inquisitive minds. You just forget their minds are located sometimes." Sam smiled as if she had a secret and wasn't telling.

"Sam, you are the most suspicious woman I've ever met."

"It's not that I'm suspicious, Wade. I remember something my Mom always told Dad."

"And what might that be?"

"She always told him, 'I know you're gonna look at other ladies. I know you'll even think about doing things with other ladies. Just remember, I know how to cut up a chicken and I know where you sleep.' Even when I was a little girl, I knew what she meant and so did he."

"I wish that I would have had the chance to meet your Mom. Speaking of your Dad though, how do you think he would get past our dilemma here?"

"I don't know, but I know how to find out. Come over to the ranch tonight for supper and we'll ask him."

"Sounds good to me. Besides, this place gives me the creeps."

52 SHE REALLY DIDN'T FIT IN WITH THE REST OF US THERE

"Dang, Son. You've got yourself in a spot all right."

"Yes, Sir. We do, Sheriff." Wade always called Sam's dad, 'Sheriff' even though he retired and Sam was now the Sheriff of Evergreen County. He felt the elderly gentleman sitting at the kitchen table with him deserved the respect for his many years of public service.

The old ex-Sheriff rubbed his grizzled chin with his wrinkled hands as he considered the situation.

"From what you've told me, you have two lists, one of the potential future victims and one of the possible perpetrators. The problem is that the same names are on both lists, except for Luke Chastain. He's only on the perp list. Have I got that right, Son?"

"Yes, Sir."

"And you've interviewed all these people?"

"Yes, Sir. All of them except John Grimes, the Attorney. He won't even return our calls. We eliminated one of the city councilmen from both lists, Joe Thigpen. We considered him along with the others, but he was on a four-month assignment in New Zealand when Rachel was murdered and when Ed was found in her grave. He just got back a few days ago, so he couldn't have done these things himself. We took him off both lists. He could go back on the victims list, depending on what we find when we get around to interviewing him."

"Good work, Son. But that still leaves you with Frank Davis, John Grimes and Bruce Thomas on both lists, and you added Luke to the suspected perp list. And you haven't spoken to John?"

"No, Sir. He's refused to speak to us and we don't have any real evidence against him. We were told by some confidential informants that his office had a contract with Rachel. We assume she was performing some personal services for him like she was the others, but we don't have an admission from him on that."

"You ain't likely to get one neither. John is like most lawyers I've ever met. His only interest in the entire world is hisself."

"Yes, Sir." Wade shifted uncomfortably in his chair at the broad generalization of the legal profession, but didn't want to upset the Sheriff.

Sam poked her father.

"Dad, shame on you! Don't paint the whole world with one broad brush of your prejudice."

Wade almost forgot that Sam was part of the conversation since she had been so quiet.

"Girl, when you two have dealt with as many of those pigs as I have, you'll get to draw your own conclusions. And I'll betcha, your conclusions won't be a gnat's hair different than than mine is now."

"Okay, Dad. But we're getting off base. Let's get back to figuring out where to go with all of this."

Sheriff Cates took a puff on his huge cigar. "Okay, but I still hate those pigs! Now, where were we?"

"John Grimes, Sir. The City Attorney. We still haven't been able to interview him."

"Hold on."

Without saying anything else, the old Sheriff picked up his cell phone and quickly dialed a number. Wade listened intently to the one side of the conversation he could hear.

"John, Sam."

"Yep, doing okay."

"They're doing fine, John. Look, let's cut to the chase. I understand you have refused to meet with Sam down at the Sheriff's office."

"Yep, I understand that, but you're not going to have a choice, John. It might look better for you if you volunteer."

"I know, John, but the judge assigned a Federal Investigator to the case, John. You ain't got enough stroke in Evergreen to fight the Feds."

"I just telling you, you stubborn pig, that you will testify one way or the other. I thought I'd give you a heads-up and let you make yourself look a little more cooperative, that's all."

Long pause. The old Sheriff winked at Sam and Wade.

"I tell you what, John. You head on over to my house and I'll get Sam and that Fed over here."

"Yep, everything will be off the record. Just get your ass over here."

The old Sheriff grinned at the two young officers.

"Now that's the way to get results. You can send those letters and subpoena's all day long, but if you pick up the phone and call them, it's gets real personal in a hurry."

Sam hugged the old man.

"Thanks, Dad. You always have my back, don't you?"

"Yes, Hon. If there's anything you can be sure of in this world, it's that I'll always be there when you need something. At least as long as you're not leading me around in a diaper and I don't know where I am."

Wade and Sam laughed, trying to visualize that image.

When the doorbell rang, Wade was just finishing his cup of coffee. He fidgeted on the kitchen chair as he waited for Sam to usher John back to the alcove.

53 I WON'T PRETEND I'M A PURITAN

"Hello, John. Good to see you again."

"You too, Wade. I wish it were under more pleasant circumstances. Before I sit, I want your assurance that this entire conversation is off the record. Nothing said here tonight can or will be used in a future filing in this case concerning Rachel."

"That's correct, John. We just want to talk to you about the case so far and how your name has come up in the investigation."

"Fine, as long as it's not on the record."

The old Sheriff stuck his head in the kitchen.

"Hey, John. Glad you could make it. I believe this way will be better for all concerned. Now I'm going out back and smoke a cigar. If any of you need me, just call."

All three sets of eyes watched the old man disappear before turning to each other.

Wade was the first to speak.

"John, your name has come up a couple of times in our investigation and we'd like to get a few answers."

"Okay."

"First, you knew Rachel Chastain, didn't you?"

"Let's skip the preamble and get down to what you want to know."

"Fine. You probably already know the questions I have to ask. Why don't you just tell us about your relationship with Rachel from wherever you want to begin?"

John Grimes put his hands on the kitchen table.

"Fair enough. I met Rachel at one of Ed's boring staff meetings that none of us wanted to go to. She was like a mirage in the desert. You really couldn't have suspected a young lady that looked like Rachel to show up at one of Ed's meetings. She really didn't fit in with the rest of us there."

A slight upturn at the corner of John's indicated his pleasure of the reminiscence of his first meeting with Rachel. Wade squirmed in his chair, wanting to ask for more details, but resisted the temptation.

"I could not believe one so young could have so much poise and be so confident without being arrogant. She was completely at ease among us, which was a rare thing for most people, especially young staffers and interns. She had an innate quality that drew others into her. That made one seek to know her better and get closer to her. It seemed as if she and I were the only people in the room and she was speaking in a language only we could understand."

John paused and looked at Wade and Sam.

"I was smitten at first glance. By the end of the meeting, I knew I had to have her, no matter what the cost." Glancing at Sam, "Uh, we still agree everything I say is off the record, don't we?"

Sam nodded.

"I won't pretend I'm a puritan and that I've never cheated on my wife before, but my relationship with Rachel was different. The others times were simply for sex. You know, just to have someone different. With Rachel, I wanted to have her completely. Her body, her mind and her soul. And I believe the feeling was mutual. She could have had any man. I mean, every man in that room was admiring her. But she chose me. Out of all the guys in the room, she chose me."

John took a sip of the tea that Sam had quietly set in front of him.

"I started making up meetings just so I could invite her to them. At first, she didn't attend every one of them. I guess Ed had her tied up on other business. But I didn't give up. One day I had a meeting late one afternoon. To my surprise, she showed up for that one. As I recall, the meeting didn't last long at all. When it was over, she stayed in the room until it was just the two of us. I don't remember how it happened or who said what, but we ended up in the hotel next door to City Hall. That was the beginning of the most extraordinary relationship I've ever had."

John undid his tie and took another sip of tea.

"One thing led to another, and I tried to occupy as much of her time as possible. I even gave her a consultant agreement with my office so she would have a reason to spend time with me. She told me she didn't need one, but I convinced her to sign it. Besides, what young lady couldn't use a little extra money?"

Wade glanced knowingly at Sam. The twins told him that the agreement between the Attorney's office and Rachel was around seven thousand dollars per month, hardly 'a little extra money' as John had phrased it.

"I won't bore you with the details, but we had a wonderful time together. I can't imagine two people being happier together. She made me feel young again and made me want to go to work just so I could see her and talk to her.

I was on the verge of telling my wife about us when this awful thing happened to her."

John's countenance fell, and he took a long swig of the sweet tea. His voice was much more subdued when he continued. "I was at the Evergreen Café that Saturday morning having brunch with my wife when the waitress told us about Rachel. I couldn't believe it. I went to the bathroom and threw up. How could something like that happen to someone so precious?"

John grabbed the napkin under the glass of tea and wiped his nose. After a long pause, he dabbed his eyes with the napkin and continued.

"You see. That's why I can't give you a deposition. I know how many leaks there are at City Hall and also in your office, Sam. Hell, half of the people in town would know about my relationship with Rachel before you even filed it. I just can't afford for my wife to find out, especially now that Rachel is—gone."

Sweat spread from John's forehead to his shirt.

"And, yes, I know the next couple of questions you need to ask. To the first one, I have an alibi for the time Rachel was killed. My wife got up before I did, around eight. I read the paper and watched the sports station on TV until we did brunch. She was with me in the house and at the café the entire morning. To the second one, I had no reason to kill her. She is, uh, was so special. I would give anything to have her back with me today."

Then in a barely audible voice, he whispered, "I loved her."

Even Sam was dabbing her eyes with a tissue.

John leaned back in his chair and closed his eyes as though he could relive every moment he had shared with Rachel.

Wade gave him a minute or two before asking.

"John, do you know if Rachel had any other contracts with the department heads at City Hall?"

"I'm sure she had one with Ed. I don't recall seeing it, but that would have been standard procedure. None of the other departments had any reason to give her a special contract, though. The one with Ed would have covered any work capacity at City Hall the other managers would have required."

"Okay. The next question is a little tougher. Do you know of any other relationships, I mean physical relationships, that Rachel might have been engaged in at the time of her death?"

"That's not tough at all. We were absolutely committed to each other. She wasn't seeing anyone else or I would have known about it."

"Fair enough. How about past relationships? Did she ever mention any old boyfriends or other guys that she might have been close to?"

"We didn't talk much about that. I mean, seriously, I was married at the time. I mean, I'm still married, but I couldn't very well probe into her past when I was married to someone else."

John's glass of tea was empty, but he put it up to his lips, anyway.

"There was one time that she said something rather odd, but I don't know if it means anything or not."

"Please, go on. You never know what bit of information might be the break we need."

"One night we were lying on the beach right after we'd had a great time together. She had reached over and was massaging me and suddenly she quit. When I realized she wasn't going to keep going, I looked over at her. She was staring up in the night sky. She said, *'I hope I'm not letting Bro' down too much.'* I didn't have a clue who she was talking about. As far as I know, she didn't have any brothers, so I assumed he was a boyfriend in her past. But I didn't ask, and she never mentioned him again."

Sam refilled John's tea glass.

"John, do you know anyone that would have wanted Rachel dead?"

"I don't. You never met Rachel, did you?"

"No, I never had the pleasure."

"Wade, she was the sweetest, most sensitive person in the world. There were times that I wondered if she was an angel sent from heaven, especially for me. I can't imagine anyone ever finding any fault with her."

Wade nodded. "I wish I would have had the opportunity. From what I've heard from everyone that knew Rachel, she was a unique lady."

"She was."

John tried to sip more tea from the empty glass.

"Okay, let's look at this from a different perspective."

John nodded. The relief of having told someone about his relationship with Rachel was evident in his demeanor.

"We have three dead people that had some connection with City Hall. Ed, Bill and Rachel were all involved in some project that nobody wants to talk about. Are you aware of that project?"

"I know of several projects we were working on. I'm not sure which one you're talking about."

"C'mon, John. This is off the record, remember. Nobody will ever know what you tell us here in this room."

"I wish I was naïve enough to believe that. But I'm not. Any discussion of a project we were working on is strictly confidential. I can't disclose the particulars of any projects.

But I can assure you that no project we were working on would have led to murder. Of that, I'm confident."

Wade leaped out of his chair.

"You might be next on the list of victims if it's about this project. Three people are dead! You've told us you cared for Rachel. Don't you want to know who killed her and why?"

John remained calm.

"Yes, I want to know. I can assure you that any project at City Hall has nothing to do with the murder of Rachel or the others. Now, I need to get back home before my wife gets suspicious. I wish you the best of luck in your investigation."

John abruptly rose and started walking toward the front door.

Wade quickly followed him. "I don't know what this project is about and really don't care unless it will help us solve this case. But I won't know that until I know what everyone is hiding."

Grimes looked over his shoulder. "Again, it has nothing to do with your investigation."

Wade added sarcastically, "If you think of anything that would be helpful, let us know."

"I will."

John closed the door behind him.

"Doesn't sound like he had anything to do with Rachel's murder, does it?"

The old Sheriff's voice surprised Wade and Sam.

"Dad? You were listening?"

"I can't help you if I don't know what is going on with the suspects."

"Dad, that wasn't very nice of you. You shouldn't be listening in on other people's conversations."

"What conversation? It was off the record, remember."

Sam smiled.

"You are impossible. I hope Wade doesn't turn out to be as stubborn as you are. Anyway, I agree with you. I don't think he had anything to do with Rachel's murder."

Wade shrugged his shoulders, indicating to Sam that it was a local matter.

"I'm not sure whether or not to believe him. How could he not know about the other managers' relationships with Rachel? Looks like none of them knew about each other. At least it seems that way."

The old man took a long drag on his cigar.

"Wade, men can block out a lot of information that doesn't fit their way of thinking on how it's supposed to fit in. We tend to come to conclusions and then make the data fit the conclusion rather than the other way around."

"I know, Sheriff. But how do we reform our hypothesis?"

"Your what?"

Wade laughed. "Our hypothesis. Our conclusion. If it's wrong, how do we go back and make it right?"

"Just go back to the beginning. What did you do first in the investigation?"

"We interviewed the hunters out at the scene."

"Then go back and do it again. This time, you know more about Rachel and maybe you'll pick up on something you missed before."

"We were thorough with them. I'm not sure we'll gain much by talking with them again."

"Give it a try. You never know what you'll pick up on. What did you do after that?"

Wade put his hands on his temples.

"Well, let's see. The mayor interviewed us at the Gulf Club. That was interesting, to say the least. We can't go back and interview him, but I'll review my notes from our conversation."

"All right, and after that."

"We talked with Luke and Carla Chastain. They didn't have a clue their little girl had been more generous than Santa Claus with her body. I'm not sure if they do now or not. You know as well as I do there aren't many secrets in Evergreen."

"There has to be something you guys are overlooking. There has to be something that ties this all together."

"The preacher said the same thing. He said that the answer was right in front of us. But I can't see it."

Wade shook his head in frustration.

"I don't know what it is, but I agree with him. Go back and talk to Luke and Carla and see if you can find the missing piece."

54 ONE DOWN AND ONE TO GO

THE HUNTER WAITED IN THE LONELINESS OF THE home, eyes already adjusted to the darkness.

I wonder which one will show up first. It really doesn't matter. I'm going ahead with the plan, regardless. Is that sound one of them arriving? Not yet. I can wait. I've waited this long. A little longer won't hurt.

The hunter crouched in the hall closet. This was the first time he had been inside the house, even though he watched it on several occasions from across the street.

Another sound.

Yes. One of them is coming in the front door. I wonder which one it is.

The sound of steps drew closer and closer. The hunter feared that one of the intended victims would open the door and discover him there.

Whew! That was close. A lot closer than I expected. When will the other one come home? How long before they are both asleep? Why didn't I wait outside? It would have been much more comfortable.

Again, the hunter heard footsteps outside the door to

the hallway. Now he was certain which intended victim the step belonged to. He heard the steps go into a bedroom, and the door closed.

Good! One down and one to go. It shouldn't be much longer now.

More than an hour passed before the hunter heard the front door open and more footsteps. He was less anxious about these than the first ones. He knew this victim occupied the bedroom right next to the closet.

Oh, she's going to the kitchen first. Don't these teenagers ever eat when they're out with their friends? I wonder what kind of snack she's having. Nothing that needs to be cooked, I'm sure. Today, teenagers don't know how to use a stove top or an oven. If it weren't for fast food, they'd starve to death.

The hunter waited patiently in the closet for the teenager to finish her snack and put the dishes in the dishwasher. He heard her feet pat past the closet door into the bedroom. When he heard the bedroom door close, he let out a long sigh.

It shouldn't be long now until she's asleep, although sometimes a teenager can stay up for hours texting or on one of the social sites on the computer. I'd better wait for a little while before I make any noise. It wouldn't be good for her to hear me out here. I should have brought my Kindle to pass the time.

The hunter waited for another two hours before exiting the closet. He had his bottle of chloroform and a rag. He tiptoed to the bedroom door and put his ear to the door. The slight sound of a soft snore brought him great relief. Slowly, ever so slowly, he eased the door open. He slipped out of his shoes and quietly stepped inside the room. He heard his own heart pounding and was concerned that the young girl would awaken because of it. Once inside the door, he paused for more than a minute, his eyes adjusting to the soft light emanating from the radio and alarm next to her bed.

Okay. There's not much between the door and her bed. There's a footstool that won't be a problem and a dresser next to her at the head of the bed. Neither of those should cause me any problems. Her pants and shirt on the floor. Typical teenager. Hope there isn't anything in them that would make any noise, but just in case, I had better avoid them.

The hunter took three small steps closer to the bed.

Good! She's on her side, facing away from me. That will help. I've already got the chloroform on the rag, so this shouldn't be that hard.

The hunter took two more tiny steps to the edge of the bed. He bent over the teenage girl and slowly lifted the rag right over her face. In one quick motion, he put the rag to her nose and mouth and fell with all his weight on top of her.

She awoke with a startled reaction, but in only seconds succumbed to the sleep-inducing drug. Her eyes closed, and she became a puddle underneath his weight. He quickly rolled off her to the other side of the bed onto the floor in case the other intended victim had heard the ruckus.

Wow! Talk about a rush of adrenaline. That was unbelievable. I'm not sure how long she'll be out. Probably not too long, so I'd better get to the next one.

He paused and looked at the young girl lying helpless in her bed. He stood by her bedside for more than a minute as a new plan emerged.

Yes, that would be more appropriate. It fits the circumstances so much better. I must have subconsciously planned for this all along. I came prepared. If I hadn't planned it all along, why would I have brought this with me?

The hunter reached inside his pocket and pulled out a

small vial. He smiled, although no one could see it in the glimmering light of the radio and alarm.

When he reached the other bedroom, the snoring on the other side of the door was much more pronounced. The hunter had not replaced his shoes. After quietly opening the door, he crept right next to the bed. He repeated the actions he had already performed in the other bedroom, except with much more confidence. The victim didn't put up much of a struggle. The hunter had assumed that a long night of drinking had made the victim less likely to wake up.

Now the hard part starts. Should I go with my original plan or the one I thought of a little while ago? I don't really want to do either, but I must. The second will be more appropriate, so I guess that's the one I'll go with. It will probably be easier to move the girl to this bedroom and then go from there.

The hunter spent the next thirty minutes preparing for the victims to wake up. When they became aware of their surroundings, the hunter reluctantly but precisely executed his secondary plan.

55 HOW CAN A FATHER ENDURE THAT?

"The pig raped Lindsay right in front of him. He tied her to the bed, tied Frank to the chair and forced him to watch while he raped her."

Sam slammed her fist against the wall.

"Looks that way to me too."

Wade was just as angry, but more subdued in his outward manner.

Wade surveyed the rope still clinging to the chair and the bed. The investigator would want to preserve the evidence for the case file, although Wade was fairly certain the perpetrator would not leave it behind if there was even the slightest of chance that it could lead the investigation to him.

What torture Frank must have gone through. Watching his teenage daughter being raped in his own bedroom and helpless to do nothing about it. Did he talk to Frank and Lindsay while he was committing the rape? How can a father endure that? Then Frank would have watched the rapist pick up the gun and put the barrel up to his head. I wonder what he said to Frank before pulling the trigger.

Sam continued to rage.

"And then he shot him right between the eyes at close range. At least he didn't kill Lindsay. I guess he figured she couldn't identify him since she was drugged and blindfolded. Probably GHB. I'm going to skin that sorry piece of human flesh alive when we catch him!"

She slammed her fist against the wall again.

I've never seen Sam so out of control. It's almost as if she's lost her sense of balance. I've got to calm her down.

"Sam, the wall is going to win no matter how many times you hit it. Relax and let's see if we can find something that will help us identify who did this."

Sam glared at him.

"The investigator found a pubic hair with a follicle on the bed. Want to bet whether it's his? I bet the pig planted it there just like he planted the boot print and the peanut hulls where he shot Rachel. Want to bet?"

"Sam, we don't even know if the person who shot Rachel is the same one that did this. We've got to wait for the evidence to lead us, not tell the evidence where we're going."

Sam was still boiling.

"We've got four dead people in Evergreen. Four of my friends are dead and one has been raped. We don't have any more time for the evidence to lead us. We've got to find out who is doing this and stop him!"

The shrillness in her voice highlighted her frustration.

So much for calming her down.

Wade stepped close to her, put his arms around her, and gave her a giant bear hug. He could think of nothing that would ease her pain at this moment.

"Why don't we take a break for a few minutes while you calm down?"

"I don't want to calm down. I want to catch this, this, this—pervert."

"I know you do. So do I. But we've got to think clearly if we're going to have a chance of getting him."

Sam spun out of his bear hug and hit the wall again. This time she put a small dent in the wall. "Who is it, Wade? Who would do such a thing? Whatever the motive is, surely Lindsay had nothing to do with it."

"That has me buffaloed too. I don't see how Lindsay fits into this puzzle."

"She doesn't. She doesn't work at City Hall. She hasn't worked on the big project, whatever that is. She barely knew Rachel or the other guys involved. She just doesn't fit. Hell, the twins fit into this plot more than Lindsay does."

Wade drew in a deep breath.

How would I feel if this happened to one of the twins instead of Lindsay? Would I be as outraged as Sam? Would I react like Sam was reacting now? Sam is right. The twins fit better in any scenario I could imagine for this situation than Lindsay. How would I protect them if I have no idea who's behind this?

"Let's not go there yet. Let's go sit down for a few minutes, catch our breath and see if we can make some sense out of some of this."

Wade led her to the kitchen table. Sam's petite body was trembling from head to toe, unable to steady itself from the internal turmoil.

Wade helped her into a chair and found a glass in the cupboard. He filled it with ice water from the refrigerator.

"Drink a little. It'll help calm your nerves."

"I'll need something stronger than water to calm me right now."

Wade went to the liquor cabinet and started searching.

He was not a drinker himself and was unsure what to give her. He finally settled on a brand name whiskey. After filling the rest of her glass, he sat back.

Sam gulped down the whiskey with no obvious effects.

"You're going to have to do better than that, Big Boy."

Wade found a much smaller glass in the cupboard and poured straight whiskey into it.

"Try this, Sam. See if it does a little better."

After inhaling the shot of whiskey, Sam shoved the small glass back toward him, indicating for him to fill it up again.

"That's enough for right now. Let's give that a little time to calm your nerves and then we'll see."

Sam's eyes bore directly into Wade, but she slowly withdrew the shot glass. She rose from her chair, sat in Wade's lap, and then unleashed a cavalcade of tears.

"Dad would have already caught whoever is doing this. Lindsay wouldn't have had to go through this if Dad was still Sheriff."

Aha! Now I understand. She is blaming herself for not figuring out who is killing these people and what it's all about. For all of her outward confidence, Sam is as vulnerable as we all are. Heck, I'm an ex-FBI agent and now a Federal Investigator and I don't have a clue. What does that make me?

"Sam, this isn't about you and me. It's about finding out the reasons behind the murders and the rape. Then we'll know who's doing them."

"But Dad would have already found out."

"I'm not so sure. We've talked to him, remember. Whoever is behind this is plenty smart. He's not leaving us a bunch of clues; at least that I've been able to figure out."

"But we don't know where to go from here, Wade."

Her tears continued to flow.

"Why don't we follow your Dad's advice and go back and talk with Luke and Carla? That's what he suggested, isn't it?"

"Yeah, it is." Her tears were ebbing and her voice became steadier.

Wade wasn't sure if the calmer Sam resulted from his words or the whiskey, but either way was better than the irate Sam of earlier.

"Before we talk to them, I need to get my thoughts together. I think it's obvious now that I've been on the wrong track all along."

"What do you mean, Wade?"

"Well, all along, I've assumed that we had a list of suspects and a list of potential victims and that the two lists were virtually identical."

"Yeah, three of them on that list are dead. So I don't see how you were wrong."

"I don't believe our suspect in on that list, Sam."

"Well, there's only two people left on the list; Bruce Thomas and John Grimes. The rest of them are dead."

"That's what bothers me. I don't see either Bruce or John as murderers."

Sam pulled her hand through her hair.

"I don't either, but that doesn't leave us much, does it?"

"Unless one of the five on the original list killed Rachel and the killer of the three on the suspect list is out for revenge. Only he doesn't know which one killed her, so he's eliminating all of them to be sure he gets the right one."

"I assume you're talking about Luke."

Wade nodded.

"I don't really know Luke that well, but from what I know about him, I'm not sure he could do this."

"Who knows what we're capable of when our daughter is murdered and we think we know who might have been responsible?"

"Man, I know how mad I am right now. If it were my daughter that was shot in the woods, I'm not sure I'd be able to control myself if I thought I knew who it was that did it."

"Unfortunately, me too. Let's go through this scenario and see if it makes sense."

Sam was thinking more reasonably now. "One of the five City Hall guys shoots Rachel in the woods because of some project down there."

"Right. Somehow, Luke finds out about the project and who's been working on it with Rachel. Or maybe he only knows about Ed. Do you remember how the killer tortured Ed before he killed him? With all the little cuts all over his body like he was trying to get some information out of him?"

"Yeah, that's right." Sam rose from Wade's lap and began pacing back and forth in the kitchen. "Ed would have told him everything he knew. He was not the bravest man in the world, to say the least."

"Under those circumstances, I probably would have told him anything I knew also, Sam."

"Okay, so let's assume Ed gave Luke the other four names on the list. I believe we can also assume Ed didn't kill Rachel because Luke would have stopped there if Ed had confessed to killing her."

Wade stared at the pool in the backyard.

"I think you're probably right. There wouldn't have been a need to go on with the others if Ed had confessed. Which also means Ed didn't know who killed Rachel. Only a list of potential suspects."

"Okay, so Luke has this list. He kills Ed and then kills Bill. But how did he know where to find Bill? We only knew about the shack in the woods that morning. The twins only knew where the GPS would take us that morning also."

"I don't know how he found out. But under this scenario, he somehow found out, beat us out there and almost killed Bill. He left in a hurry before finishing the job and left him almost dead, but not quite. He was there long enough to find out that Bill didn't kill Rachel, so he has to go on down the list."

Sam nodded. "That makes sense so far."

"Well, I'm leaving out some things that don't fit our scenario, but we'll get to them later."

"Okay, where are we? Oh yeah, Luke killed, or at least almost killed Bill and found out that Bill didn't kill Rachel."

"So then, he gets to Frank. He sneaks in the house and ties Frank up. Either Lindsay wakes up while Luke is struggling with Frank or she was part of the plan all along."

"She had to be part of the plan all along, Wade. The blindfold was custom made and didn't come from anything in the house. If Luke hadn't planned on raping Lindsay, why would he have brought the blindfold with him?"

"Excellent point. Unless he had originally planned to use it on Frank. But I agree with you. Lindsay was part of the plan, but why?"

Sam's rate of pacing increased in the large kitchen.

"All right, how about this? If Luke knew before he came here, either from Bill or some other way, that Frank was the one that shot his daughter, wouldn't he have wanted revenge? That's what this is all about, right?"

"Yeah, you're right."

"And Luke is a religious man. You know, an 'eye for an eye' and that sort of thing."

"He assumes—or knows that Frank was guilty and takes

revenge by making him watch Luke abuse his daughter right there in front of him without being able to do anything about it. That's the last thing Frank experienced on this earth before Luke killed him."

"Wade, I'm betting that all three bullets came from Rachel's rifle. The one we couldn't find in the woods."

"That would be poetic justice, wouldn't it? Getting revenge with his daughter's rifle."

"Yeah. Hey, can we go get something to eat? That whiskey isn't sitting well on an empty stomach."

"Sure. Let's go down to the Café."

56 THIS MUST BE IMPORTANT

THE AROMA EMANATING FROM THE KITCHEN AT THE Evergreen Café changed Wade's mind about what he would have for lunch.

"I think I'll have the fried catfish and sweet potato fries."

"And I'll have the usual."

Sam meant the country-fried steak with white sausage gravy.

"Okay, Sam. We have this scenario, but a couple of things don't fit."

"Like what?"

"First, Rachel's hunting license showing up at City Hall. There was someone with Luke the whole time from when Rachel was found until the twins found the license at City Hall. How could he have gotten it there?"

"Hmm. I hadn't thought of that."

"Second, how did he get the list of the suspects? The twins are the ones that let us onto the list and they haven't talked to Luke, at least as far as I know. Surely, they wouldn't give him a list with their father's name on it."

"We talked about that at Frank's house this morning. He could have started with the mayor. How he knew about Ed is beyond me, but let's assume he somehow found out about Ed. Then he could have gotten the rest of the names from Ed. Remember, Ed was cut up pretty badly."

"Third, how did—?"

The buzzing of Sam's cell phone interrupted his sentence. He only heard Sam's side of the conversation.

"Yes?"

"What did you find?"

"Are you sure?"

"For how long? Two to three weeks?"

"How could you tell?"

"Small doses? How small?"

"What would have been the effects?"

"How much more would it have taken to kill him?"

"Okay, thanks. Let me know if you get anything else."

Looking at Wade, Sam summarized the call.

"They found arsenic, probably from rat poison, in Bill Brogan. Looks like he took it in over the last three weeks of his life. They can tell by his fingernails and his hair, but you already know that. It was in small doses, not enough to kill him, but enough to make him awfully sick."

Wade rubbed his temples.

"That would have been painful. Lots of stomach pains and headaches. No wonder he looked like a mess when we found him. The poor guy was being tortured and didn't know it by whoever was feeding him."

"Over a three-week period. How does that fit into the scenario we've developed?"

"I'm not sure, Sam. Finding Bill was going to be one of my points. How did Luke know where to find Bill?"

"Still can't answer that one."

Their food arrived at the table, temporarily interrupting the conversation.

"April has done a good job taking over for Gabe at the café. The food is better than it was when he had it."

"I wonder if that catfish came from Dixon's farm."

"Bet it did. I still like the catfish at Middendorf's a little better, but this is getting a lot closer than before. How's your steak?"

"Great. As good or better than before."

"I think we ought to tell her." Wade motioned to the waitress. "Can you ask April to drop by our table if she gets a chance?"

"Sure," nodded the waitress. "Can I get you anything else?"

Wade and Sam shook their heads. It was only a minute before April appeared at their table side.

"We wanted to let you know how good the food is here, April. You've done a great job since taking over." Wade rubbed his belly for emphasis.

"Thanks. If it weren't for you guys, I don't know where I'd be right now. I owe you a lot that I can't repay."

"Forget about that, April. We're glad everything worked out for you." Sam was all smiles.

April started to leave the table, but then hesitated and returned.

"There is one thing I think I should tell you."

Wade's eyes arched in anticipation.

This is so unlike April. She is usually straightforward. This must be important.

"When you guys were here last, there was someone watching you."

"Who, April?" Sam asked.

"I don't know. The only thing I know is that it was a

man dressed up like a woman. When I gave him his change at the register, he forgot to raise his voice. You know, like a woman. He knew it too and almost ran out of here before I could tell you. I didn't know what to do, so I kept it to myself until now. I didn't want to get involved."

"How do you know he was watching us?"

"Because something was different about him. One thing is that he was wearing men's shoes under his dress. Guess that's what caught my attention first. Then, when I started watching him, he was staring at you guys the whole time he was in here."

Wade remembered seeing the old woman across the room with the familiar eyes. He had forgotten all about her.

"Did you recognize him, April?"

"Goodness, no. I don't know that many people in Evergreen and most of them only by their faces, not their names. He paid in cash and I didn't get a look at his face. His voice sounded familiar, though."

"Thanks, April. We really appreciate you telling us. And keep up the good work with the food."

Sam shook her head. "That's strange."

"Yes," Wade agreed. "Why would someone be watching us? And I remember seeing the lady or the man dressed up like a lady. I remember her eyes. It wasn't Luke."

"That doesn't help support our scenario, does it?"

"No, not at all. Luke didn't need to be watching us. If I remember right, that was the day Frank came up to our table. Luke would have already had the list from Ed. Unless she or he was following Frank."

Sam ran her hand through her long hair again.

"So where do we go from here?"

"Well, if it is Luke, and he believes Frank was the one that killed Rachel, then the murders are probably over. We need to build a case against Luke for the murders of Ed, Bill and Frank, and the rape of Lindsay."

"And if it's not Luke?"

"Then we'd better go talk to Luke and warn John and Bruce one more time."

57 YOU'VE GOT THIS FIGURED OUT, DON'T YOU?

"Carla, thank you and Luke for letting us visit again. Are you doing okay with all of this?"

"It's tough, Sam. Every time we go somewhere in town or even to church, we see something that reminds us of Rachel. You know, little things like the playground at the elementary school, the candy shop in the mall or the dress shop where she picked out her prom dress. When I remember the good times we had, I often wonder what we would be doing today if she was still with us."

"I can't say I know how you feel, Carla. I have no children, and I can't imagine losing one if I did. Especially the way you guys lost Rachel."

"Sam, at first that was big for us. You know, the way she was taken from us. But now, that is almost immaterial. We miss her. That matters. There's a big vacuum in our hearts that can't be filled with anything else. We've tried, but there is no replacement for a daughter we'll never get to hug or speak to again."

"I'm sorry, Carla." Sam wiped tears from her own eyes.

"Again, I won't pretend to know how you feel, but we do want to express our sympathies again."

"Thanks, Sam. Are you making any progress in the investigation?"

"A little. We had a good list of suspects. Unfortunately, three of them have been murdered themselves."

Luke interrupted his wife's response.

"That would be the Mayor, John and Frank, I assume."

"Yes, Luke. Those are the three. And we've lost two deputies and three other citizens of Evergreen County during our investigation."

"What's it all about? I know the three worked at City Hall, or at least had influence there. Rachel was just an intern there. She wasn't tied in with the politicians. How are the other three citizens related to this case?"

"We were looking for Bill Brogan and unfortunately, there was a misunderstanding about our intentions when we got to their church."

"The Blue Heaven Church, or something like that."

"That's the one. The Blue Heaven Nature Church. Brother Raymond and his children were killed while we were looking for Bill up there."

"I see. We don't want to keep you with our questions. We want to get everything as straight in our own minds as possible. As you've probably guessed, there are a ton of rumors on the streets. We're trying to ignore most of them, but it's difficult."

"We've heard a few of those, Luke. We also are trying to get to the bottom of all of this and it all seems to start with Rachel."

Luke's body stiffened, and Carla looked down at the floor. Luke was the first one to speak.

"It's the money, isn't it?"

"We don't know, and that is the truth. The money is a concern, but the truth is that we haven't been able to tie the money into a direct threat or cause for someone to kill Rachel."

"Three hundred thousand is a lot of money for a nineteen-year-old intern, Sam. It is still in her account. We haven't touched it and we figured someone would want it back one of these days."

"Again, I'm not an attorney, Luke. From what we've found, Rachel did nothing illegal that would warrant taking back the money from her account. As far as I know, you can do anything you want to with the money."

"Are you sure, Sam?"

Sam looked questionably at Wade, who only shrugged his shoulders.

"Go ahead, Luke. I'll send you a letter stating that I authorized you to use the money any way you want since we have no way to determine if it's evidence of a crime."

"Thanks, Sam. So you will know, Carla and I have discussed what to do with it if we're able to keep it. It's going to a good cause. We'll donate it."

"Awesome, Luke. There are a lot of good charities out there that can use that kind of money."

"We agree. But we've discussed one that is local and was close to Rachel's heart. As you know, the church was her focal point when she was a young teenager. So we'll donate the money to the Youth Ministry at the church. They did so much to help Rachel when she entered the teenage years, we want to give back to them."

"That's awesome, Luke. I'm sure Brother Jeff will appreciate the donation. I know they can use it. With the economy the way it is, I wouldn't be surprised if donations were down a good bit."

"Luke, can I ask you a question?"

"Sure, Wade. Go ahead."

"How would you feel if one of those three men from City Hall was the guy that killed Rachel?"

"Well—" Luke rubbed the crown of his forehead with both hands. "I guess I would still like to know why. Carla and I assumed the money was the reason, but you guys are telling us it may not be. So my biggest issue would be '*Why?*'. Why did one of them have to take Rachel's life? Wasn't there another less painful way to get whatever they were after? If it wasn't the money, then what was it?"

"That's what we don't know, Luke. Do you mind if we take another look at Rachel's room to see if we can find anything that will help us?"

"By all means, Wade. We've had our time in there to make peace with ourselves. If anything in there helps you figure out why she was taken from us, then please use it."

Wade and Sam rose from their seats and quietly headed for Rachel's bedroom. Luke and Carla remained seated, seemingly reluctant to once again enter the bedroom that brought so many memories back to the surface.

"What are we looking for?"

Sam pulled some of Rachel's belongings out of the closet.

"I'm not sure."

"So how are we going to know when we find it?"

Wade shrugged. "I'm not sure of that either."

"So what are you sure about?"

"I'm fairly sure Luke didn't had nothing to do with the murders. He's too, uh—he's too pure if that makes sense."

Wade went through some old shoe boxes.

"If it makes you feel any better, I agree with you. I don't think he had anything to do with them either. Besides, I didn't want to be the one that had to arrest him if he had. I don't know if the word 'pure' is the right one to use, but it fits the whole family." Sam paused. "Even Rachel somehow fits that word, even with all she did."

"I don't blame you for not wanting to arrest Luke, but that doesn't leave us with much. If Luke didn't do it, murder for revenge is no longer a motive. The money doesn't seem to be the motive. Jealousy doesn't look like the motive because they didn't know about each other. We've got four murders, two dead deputies, three dead civilians and a rape victim and we don't even have a motive yet."

"We make a helluva team, don't we?" The sarcasm was clear in Sam's tone.

Wade laughed, if nothing else to ease the tension in his shoulders. He kept looking in every box he could find in Rachel's closet.

Sam sat on the edge of the bed, looking around the room for a secret hiding place where they might find the secret to this mystery.

"I don't want to give up, but I'm not seeing it, Wade. Whatever '*it*' is."

"Me either. Your dad said the answer would be right in front of us. The pastor said the answer would be right in front of us. What do they know that we don't know?"

"Well, Dad had almost forty years of experience. He saw things from a different perspective than most of us." She paused before continuing. "The pastor also looks at things a little differently than most of us."

"Yeah, I remember him saying something good would come out of all of this. I'm not seeing that either. Maybe we need a different perspective on this case. We aren't making much progress."

"Are you suggesting that we give up and turn the investigation over to the State Police?"

Wade looked around the small bedroom one more time.

"I honestly don't know where to go next with it, Sam."

"I guess there comes a point when it's useless to go on. It's better to cash in whatever chips you have left and let someone else play if you find yourself in a hole you can't get out of."

Wade put his arm around Sam.

"Do you think we're in a hole we can't get out of?"

"It looks that way. You know, Rachel was probably thinking the same thing."

Sam stared at a picture of Rachel at her high school graduation ceremonies.

Wade stared at a photograph of fourteen-year-old Rachel singing in the choir. A broad smile crossed his face, and he almost jumped.

"Sam, you are a genius. Did I ever tell you that? You are a genius."

Sam looked at him as if he had gone crazy. With her mouth still wide open, she had to close it to answer her ringing cell phone.

Wade paid no attention to her conversation on the phone. He was busily scanning every photograph in the room. When he turned back to Sam, he stopped abruptly. The look of shock on her face as she held the phone told him that his worst fears were realized.

"It's the twins. I mean, that was Bruce and the twins are missing."

Sam's voice trembled as she recalled the torment Lindsay had endured.

"Get Bruce back on the phone! Hurry! Hurry!"

"Hey, Bruce. Wade wants to talk to you."

Sam handed her phone to Wade.

"Listen to me carefully. Are you listening, Bruce?"

"Okay. I know you're upset, but you have to listen to me if you want to find Mandy and Mindy safe and sound. Nothing will happen to them if you will listen to me, Bruce."

"All right, are you at home or at the office?"

"Good. Who's in the office with you?"

"No, I don't mean in your office. I mean in the office building."

"Okay, take your cell phone and take the stairs down to the lady's room two floors below you. Sit in one of the stalls until we get there. I don't care who comes in. Do not open that stall for anyone."

"I can't tell you, Bruce. Sam and I will be there in a few minutes. Don't look out a window or open the door to the stall for anyone until we get there. Understand?"

"Good. You've got to believe me, Bruce. As long as he doesn't have you, nothing will happen to Mandy and Mindy."

Wade frantically motioned to Sam to gather her files and other paraphernalia, even as he hung up with Bruce.

"C'mon. We've got to get to City Hall."

As they raced to Sam's patrol car, she yelled at Wade. "You've got this figured out, don't you?"

"Yep!" was his only reply, but his huge grin told Sam all she needed to know.

58 I GUESS I JUST DIDN'T WANT TO BELIEVE YOU

Sᴀᴍ ᴘᴜʟʟᴇᴅ ɪɴᴛᴏ ᴛʜᴇ ᴇᴍᴘᴛʏ ᴘᴀʀᴋɪɴɢ ʟᴏᴛ ɪɴ ꜰʀᴏɴᴛ of the building, and Wade exited the car and strode confidently to the front door. Finding it locked was not that much of a surprise, so he gently rapped on it until someone opened it from the inside.

"Please, come in. I've been expecting you."

"We had to make a stop or two. I'm sure you understand."

Wade sat in the closest seat.

"I understand. That means you picked Bruce up at City Hall and he is now safe and sound at the Sheriff's office."

"That's correct."

"And now you want me to release Mandy and Mindy?"

"You no longer have a reason to hold them. You can't get to Bruce through them."

"Wade, I want to explain why I did the things I did before I release them. After I release them, I'm afraid you might be in a hurry to lock me up and won't listen to me."

"I think I pretty much have it figured out, but I'd love for you to fill in the blanks for me."

"What have you figured out?"

Wade closed his eyes and tilted his head back.

"Rachel was the most precious young girl you've ever met. She was precocious, sweet and provocative all in one package. Sam used the word 'pure' when describing her dad a little while ago, and I believe that would be the word that you would have used to describe Rachel. These qualities attracted you to Rachel. And that she was attractive didn't hurt. Somewhere in your relationship with her, you crossed the line, and it became a physical relationship even though she was much too young to consent to one. She made you feel you were the only person on earth that she could relate to and you felt like she was the only person on earth that understood you despite her age. She started calling you 'Bro' and I'm sure you had a pet name for her."

"You're right so far, Wade. I called her '*Baby*'. Please continue."

"Okay, but please let me know where I'm going astray. Much of this is mere speculation based on the facts as we know them."

"No problem. So far, I'd say you were accurate."

"All right. A few years ago, Rachel became more distant. You didn't like it, but you assumed that eventually she would come back to you. Now the next part is extremely speculative, but again it fits the facts."

"Please, go on."

"A couple of months ago, Rachel came to you and told a story you had a hard time believing. She told you she'd been having physical relationships with a number of older men, most of them politicians down at City Hall. She admitted that she initiated the relationships and led these gentlemen on somewhat of a lurid trek. She made a lot of money, but realized that she couldn't buy peace with the money. She was absolutely miserable and saw no way out of the mess she had created. She wanted to keep her reputation intact with her parents and the community, but didn't see any way for this to happen given everything she'd done. She was at her wits end trying to somehow turn back the clock to where she had been with you, but didn't couldn't find a solution. That's why she sought your help."

"My oh my, Wade. You've given this some thought."

"Yes, I have. But for a long time, I thought it was a matter of revenge. But it was really a matter of salvaging her reputation, wasn't it?"

"Yes, although that may split hairs a little."

"I agree. But before, I thought one man may have killed Rachel, and another was seeking revenge. However, you killed Rachel because that was the only way to save her reputation and restore her dignity. You believed you could bury her past only if she was no longer with us, but had become a victim. Almost a martyr. You loved her too much to have her reputation sullied."

"That was my concern. Yes."

"Then you had to eliminate the men she had relationships with so that none of them could tell about her past."

"They would have ruined her, Wade. Don't you see? They would have sat around the water cooler or conference table and eventually one of them would slip up and tell the others. Then they would compare their stories with each other, and where would Rachel be then? I had to stop them before it went any further."

"I see that. The one thing that got in the way was when you poisoned Bill Brogan and raped Lindsay Davis. I had to think long and hard about that. But it finally came to me. That part was revenge."

The man slumped.

"You know. I don't regret poisoning Bill. I helped Bill, or at least he thought I was helping him for the last three weeks of his life. In fact, I slipped rat poison in his food and enjoyed watching him suffer. He deserved that for what he did to Rachel and the girl on his plantation. As far as Lindsay, that was the one thing I did that was the hardest. Lindsay was an innocent casualty in this. But Frank had to see what it meant to have someone he loved so dearly to be abused and disgraced like he did to Rachel. That was the memory Frank took to his grave with him. That is the only reason I did what I did with Lindsay. But I didn't kill her."

"And you were going to do something similar with Mindy and Mandy. You were going to make Bruce watch as the twins were abused so he would also know the pain of seeing his daughters abased before he died. You loved Rachel more than if she were your own daughter. You couldn't stand the fact that these men had taken advantage of her."

"Yes, Wade. That was the plan."

"Did I miss anything?"

"The only part you missed is that I tried to tell you. I told you the answer was right in front of you the whole time, but you didn't hear me."

"I heard you, Brother Jeff. I guess I just didn't want to believe you."

Wade saw the preacher reach inside his pocket. He leapt and slammed Jeff down to the floor. Then he heard the screams from the teenagers and smelled the smoke.

59 SOMETIMES THE LORD NEEDS A LITTLE HELP

THE FIRE ERUPTED BY THE DOUBLE FRONT DOORS, THE side door and behind the baptismal pool. The screams came from a door behind the organ. Wade knew it led to the church basement. His first instinct was the strongest. He jumped toward the organ.

"Let us out." both twins shouted in unison from behind the locked door.

Wade pulled on the door handle to no avail.

"Step back," he yelled.

Then he saw smoke coming from under the basement door. Jeff had set fire in the basement also.

Using more power than necessary, he took two steps forward and kicked. The door flew open, splinters flying everywhere. The twins stumbled off of the stairs leading to the basement and the fire below. Flames flickered only feet behind them.

Wade pulled Mindy and Mandy across the church floor. Smoke filled the sanctuary. He looked at the double doors first. A wall of flames hid the front of the church. The side door had flames standing guard.

The heat became unbearable. Wade went to his knees, trying to escape the plumes of smoke. Then he jumped up and raced to the dais behind the pulpit. Holding his breath, with tears running down his cheeks from the thick smoke, he grabbed the chair of the choir director. Without pause, he ran to the wall next to the piano.

Using most of the strength he had left, Wade slammed the chair through the window. With a couple of sweeps, most the shards of glass fell onto the yard outside. The ex-FBI agent dragged both twins to the window. He picked up Mindy and shoved her through the opening. Then he did the same with Mandy.

When both were clear, he went for Jeff. The smoke prevented Wade from seeing the pastor slumped on the front pew. Feeling his way along, the agent found him and dragged him toward the window. Using the last reservoir of strength, Wade lifted the pastor and shoved him outside. Then he followed.

Unseen hands grabbed Wade and pulled him away from the smoke. One gave him a cup of water, which he eagerly gulped.

Then he saw Jeff lying on the grass a few feet away. A shard of glass protruded from the pastor's neck.

In a hoarse whisper, he said, "I thought I cleared all the glass from the window."

Mindy leaned in close. "Sometimes the Lord needs a little help."

The End

Dear reader,

We hope you enjoyed reading *The Girl In The Woods*. Please take a moment to leave a review, even if it's a short one. Your opinion is important to us.

Discover more books by Jim Riley at https://www.nextchapter.pub/authors/jim-riley

Want to know when one of our books is free or discounted? Join the newsletter at http://eepurl.com/bqqB3H

Best regards,

Jim Riley and the Next Chapter Team

You might also like:
Murder by Moccasin by Jim Riley

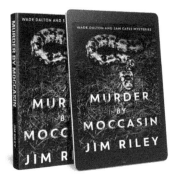

To read the first chapter for free, please head to:
https://www.nextchapter.pub/books/murder-by-moccasin

NOTES

The Girl in the Woods is the second of four books in the Wade Dalton and Sam Cates series. It features the dynamic duo with even greater challenges.

I have taken great literary license with the geography and data of south Mississippi. They are wonderful and a great way to experience the deep South culture. I lived there for over five years and found it to be one of the most desirable places on earth if you enjoy the outdoors, great cuisine and remarkable people.

There are so many people to thank:

My family, Linda, Josh, Dalton & Jade
David and Sara Sue
C D and Debbie Smith
My brother and sister-in-law, Bill & Pam
My sister, Debbie
My sister-in-law and her husband, Brenda & Jerry
The Sunday School class at Zoar Baptists

Any and all mistakes, typos and errors are my fault and mine alone. If you would like to get in touch with me, go to my web site at http://jimrileyweb.wix.com/jimrileybooks.

I thank you for reading ***The Girl in the Woods*** and hope you will also enjoy the rest my books.

Lightning Source UK Ltd.
Milton Keynes UK
UKHW020318270221
379474UK00010B/560/J

9 781034 470816